# Dale Wilson. The man was hot. He was smart and funny, observant and kind. He was alive.

She watched as he moved closer. And when Dale reached her, lifting her chin with one finger until her gaze met his, he asked, "You want to?"

She looked him straight in the eye and nodded.

Dale meant to take it slow. To savor every second of the experience. To make sure it was good for her, first and foremost.

The second he pulled Millie to him, and their mouths opened for their second kiss, he was lost. Caught up in a maelstrom of emotion and sensation that consumed him.

By the time they made it to the living room, his clothes were off. He picked her up and carried her back to his bedroom, kissing her the entire time.

He couldn't remember a more perfect moment.

Dear Reader,

Happy Thanksgiving and Merry Christmas from Ocean Breeze! This is a very special story written to help you find hope and joy—a deep, real kind—during the holidays. No matter who you are, where you are or what's going on in your life, there can be moments of happiness. This is that book. Those hours.

I started out writing *Christmas Cottage Getaway* with a bit of a grieving heart. This story showed me, as WG teaches Dale, and Millie and Dale show each other, the way out.

And if you're in a super great place already, you're still in for a treat. The beach filled with holiday lights. The holidays. Dogs. A very special Christmas present. Love that won't be denied. A sexy marine. And even a bit about how to make beer at home!

Families come in all shapes and sizes. My own has been larger. And smaller. Sometimes biological, sometimes not. They say home is where the heart is. Well, family is, too. And today, I'm wishing every one of you a family of your own to love.

*Tara*

# CHRISTMAS COTTAGE GETAWAY

**TARA TAYLOR QUINN**

**SPECIAL EDITION**

If you purchased this book without a cover you should be aware that this book is stolen property. It was reported as "unsold and destroyed" to the publisher, and neither the author nor the publisher has received any payment for this "stripped book."

# Harlequin
## SPECIAL EDITION

ISBN-13: 978-1-335-18019-3

Christmas Cottage Getaway

Copyright © 2025 by TTQ Books LLC

All rights reserved. No part of this book may be used or reproduced in any manner whatsoever without written permission.

Without limiting the author's and publisher's exclusive rights, any unauthorized use of this publication to train generative artificial intelligence (AI) technologies is expressly prohibited.

This is a work of fiction. Names, characters, places and incidents are either the product of the author's imagination or are used fictitiously. Any resemblance to actual persons, living or dead, businesses, companies, events or locales is entirely coincidental.

For questions and comments about the quality of this book, please contact us at CustomerService@Harlequin.com.

TM and ® are trademarks of Harlequin Enterprises ULC.

 Harlequin Enterprises ULC
22 Adelaide St. West, 41st Floor
Toronto, Ontario M5H 4E3, Canada
www.Harlequin.com

HarperCollins Publishers
Macken House, 39/40 Mayor Street Upper,
Dublin 1, D01 C9W8, Ireland
www.HarperCollins.com

**Printed in Lithuania**

A *USA TODAY* bestselling author of over one hundred novels in twenty languages, **Tara Taylor Quinn** has sold more than seven million copies. Known for her intense emotional fiction, Ms. Quinn's novels have received critical acclaim in the UK and most recently from Harvard. She is the recipient of the Readers' Choice Award and has appeared often on local and national TV, including *CBS Sunday Morning*.

For TTQ offers, news and contests, visit www.tarataylorquinn.com!

### Books by Tara Taylor Quinn

### Harlequin Special Edition

#### *The Cottages on Ocean Breeze*

*Her Christmas Wish*
*Beach Cottage Kisses*
*Christmas Cottage Getaway*

#### *Furever Yours*

*Love Off the Leash*

Visit the Author Profile page
at Harlequin.com for more titles.

To Aerin Dennis. May you always feel the arms of your family around you. Including mine.

## *Chapter One*

The cottage was perfect. Magic, her very large, very temporary live-in companion, was equally so. Millie wasn't at all sure about the next-door neighbors, though. More than a football field's length away from her, they waved from their back porch the second she stepped outside.

The man and woman did, anyway. Their two dogs just stared.

With a short nod, Millie stepped back inside without exploring the gorgeous back deck, built-in fireplace included. Wouldn't do her much good if she couldn't have privacy out there.

She was leasing the place to heal.

Not to be picked at and prodded.

Or stared down and judged.

She'd spent her whole life with small-town neighbors. Everyone in everyone else's business was fine when you were the one helping out. Not so much when everyone was barreling down on you to ease a pain that wasn't going to go away.

If Ocean Breeze—the heavenly sounding mile or two stretch of private beach lined with full-acre plots bearing cottages—turned out to be its own small town, she might have to rethink her plan for the next several months.

Chelsea had said that everyone minded their own business. Sure didn't appear that way to Millie.

"So, what do you think?" Chelsea stood, with Magic at her side, facing Millie as she came back inside that second Friday in September.

She was happier in that cottage, with the private beach right outside the door, than she'd been in a long, long time. But the people...she just couldn't be a joiner. Or the recipient of empathy, sympathy, curiosity or neighborly kindness of the kind that included physical visits.

"Tell me some about the people," she said, as though just curious about those who'd be sharing that very private neighborhood with her. One road in, which was the same road out, down a steep mountain way, with a gated access at the top. Perfect for keeping the world at bay.

Unless the beach was going to end up being a microcosm of the small-town environment in which she'd thrived growing up.

"Scott and Iris are next door to the right, facing the beach. They're home today, but that's a rarity. He's a lead prosecutor, she's a highly sought-after photographer, animals mostly. They work long hours and spend a lot of time further up the beach with Scott's sister when they're around. People here respect everyone's privacy. We meet up on the beach. Whoever isn't out on the beach, doesn't meet up. Take Dale, about halfway down the row. When Scott, next door, got hurt surfing, Dale was right there, helping with the heavy stuff, and he's the beach dog sitter whenever anyone is out of town or working late. We know he's some kind of writer. And has a service dog named Juice." Chelsea pursed her chin and shrugged, and then said, "But no one even knows what kind of service dog Juice is. And Dale is almost never out on the beach, at least not when anyone else is around to see him. Stays on his deck. He doesn't say much. We don't ask. All the way down at the far end of Ocean Breeze are Sage and Gray Bartholomew. He's a veterinarian. Sage is a corporate attorney and the twin sister of Scott, next door. Sage and Gray have an adorable five-year-old and a new baby. If you want to get to know them, though, you have to spend time on the beach. And on the other side of me, down at the end, is a doctor and her husband. They don't ever come down to this part of the beach, other than to introduce themselves to newcomers and offer assistance to anyone who ever needs it…"

Magic had been staring at Millie during her owner's entire preamble. If the dog blinked, Millie didn't see it. But just when Millie was thinking that Magic didn't approve of her, the hundred-pound dog walked over, put her head under Millie's hand and sat.

Chelsea chuckled. "Well, I hope you're about to tell me that you love the place, because Magic has decided you being here is a done deal."

Millie smiled, the feeling attached to the expression, bland at best. And said, "I love the place." As much as she loved anything. The head under her hand pushed up against her and her fingers started to move of their own accord. Lightly rubbing the double-palm–sized head of fur.

Millie's smile grew so much the unused muscles in her face hurt a little. "I've got my bags in the car," she admitted. "And a small truck ready to deliver the rest."

Doing a hands above her head, on tiptoe stretch, Chelsea was smiling as she nodded. "I had a feeling this place would help. Unless things change with my sister's pregnancy, I could be gone as much as six months. Until after the baby's born. I can't tell you how much I appreciate you keeping Magic for me while when I'm away. My sister's husband's allergic. And when you need to be away, Dale's set to keep Magic. He's the one I told you about mid-beach."

Keeping her landlord's dog was the least she could do. Chelsea—an illustrator of children's books and adult fiction covers—could very well be saving Millie's life. She'd hit a wall. Had been looking for over a month for a place where she could find her next steps. Until Chelsea had offered her place after conditioning class one night. Millie had stayed after to do some more stretches, thinking herself alone in the room. And ended up saying more than she usually did.

"And if you like living down here, there are a few more cottages scattered along the beach that haven't yet been renovated that are for sale," Chelsea added.

Millie smiled again. Thanked the woman.

But couldn't imagine herself deciding to stay anywhere long enough to invest in housing.

That part of her life—along with her deepest heart and all of the dreams she'd harbored since childhood—was dead and buried.

Dale Wilson was sitting on his back deck with Juice Friday midmorning when the email came in from his editor, congratulating him on another dream come true.

He hadn't only hit the *New York Times* Best Sellers list with his new release. He'd hit the #1 spot.

Reading the news on his phone he sat with the sense of

satisfaction of a job well done. Not the "dream come true" his editor had deemed it. Still, it was nice. Nodding, he put a hand on Juice's head, scratching the big boy behind his left ear just as he liked it best. For a service dog, Juice had certainly learned how to train Dale to service him.

He didn't tell the apricot-colored standard poodle about the book doing well. Juice didn't understand such worldly accomplishments. Neither did Dale. A spot on the prestigious list brought him more money—of which he had plenty—but that was it. It had no power over life, death and empty hearts.

It wasn't likely that someone's life would be saved by reading his fiction thriller, either. Or rather, that of WG Gunder. A man no one had met, knew about or would find no matter how hard they looked. Because WG Gunder didn't exist. He was just a name on a contract, and on the LLC to which royalties were sent.

Not even Juice was aware that Dale Wilson—the retired marine who spent his days mostly alone on his back deck—and WG Gunder were the same man. Which was wholly by Dale's design.

Gunder was merely a rendition of the pain that lived inside him. He spoke in the dark of the night and Dale had learned that allowing him to do so helped. Giving him a voice on the page had been his way of clearing his mind of the devil so he could sleep.

The fact that it now served two purposes did not detract, at all, from the main goal. Writing until he was numb was better than getting hooked on sleeping pills. Which was the reason Gunder was still churning out four books a year.

Still, the *NYT* nod was nice. Lifting his pre-lunch lemonade in a toast to the ocean in front of him, Dale cocked his head as a woman he didn't know waved back at him.

She'd just come into view. Walking along the shore. Far enough away that he couldn't make out her features clearly. Or hear her voice. But close enough that he knew he'd never seen her before.

Attractive women were nothing new on Ocean Breeze. One he didn't know, most definitely was. Their neighborhood was private, with a security gate blocking the steep road down. And Dale knew every resident on the more than a mile stretch of beach. By sight, at least. He was a marine. Retired far earlier from the corps than he'd intended, but still one who scanned the world around him for potential danger, with a willingness to go into battle and give up his life for the citizens in his world.

Instead of serving his country, he served on Ocean Breeze. A self-appointed task that only he knew about. And that suited him.

What didn't suit was a newcomer to the beach about whom he knew nothing. Just because she was a looker with the slender form, and a ponytail of long dark hair bouncing against her back as she jogged, didn't mean she wasn't an interloper. A trespasser.

Dale didn't jump up and get his gun. Didn't even think about the weapon tucked away in a locked box on his closet shelf. He didn't get up at all.

But he watched the woman even when she was just a dot of movement on the sand, and then waited to see if she headed back up the way she'd come.

Her only other choice, if she didn't enter a cottage, would be to head behind one of the residences to the road that ran along the backs of them, the way by which residents drove home and accessed their garages. Part of what kept their beach so private were the two treacherously steep and slippery mountainsides that bordered them on both sides.

She could then possibly climb the gate and head up the steep but paved blacktop to the world above them. There were standard surveillance cameras at the gate that would catch any such activity. And more at the fine dining establishment at the top of the mountain, too. All Dale had to watch was the beach.

And so, every day, that was what he did.

She'd waved at the man. Millie was still fretting over the totally uncharacteristic, completely reactive lift of her hand as she reached the far end of the beach. So much so that she couldn't bear to run back by that deck a second time—even with the acre of beach between the cottage and the shoreline where she'd been jogging.

What if he'd thought she'd been flirting with him? Or even open to being approached? She'd never in her life sent a come-on signal to a member of the opposite sex. Why would she? She'd known since junior high who she was going to marry. It had been their secret until they were old enough for their parents and others to understand that they'd recognized their bond even before they'd understood about romantic love and sex.

The entire small town of Embry, Alabama, had come out for their wedding...

*Nope. Done.*

Walking along the sand at the end of the beach, parallel to the jutting side of mountain that bordered the beach, Millie made it up to the road she'd driven in on.

Walked along it past the fronts of the cottages spaced an acre or more apart. The nearly two-mile trek ahead of her wouldn't be nearly as esthetically pleasing as the trip down had been. Her fault for responding to the man's lift of a cup.

What the hell?

The fact that it was a gut reaction ate at her. Like she'd been unable, or unwilling to control the response. Every thought she had, every move she made, was by design. No more trusting in the heart and soul of life.

She'd been robbed of both.

What she had left...she was on Ocean Breeze to figure out. Working herself to death hadn't done the trick.

The man. The raised glass.

It had to have been the Dale guy Chelsea had mentioned. The guy who was there for the heavy lifting. For assisting his neighbors with dog sitting. But who rarely joined in socialization on the beach. And apparently shared nothing about himself during those times he did have contact with others. To the point that no one even knew what kind of service dog the man had.

The nurse in Millie—the only part of her that lived and breathed at full capacity—wanted to know.

And...she felt a kinship with his withdrawal from the party, too.

As though they had something in common that those around them didn't have.

Shaking her head against the fanciful thought, Millie evened her breathing and upped her pace to a jog again. She wasn't in training. Had never been in training. But for most of her life, she'd run with someone who had been.

And knew of no other way to keep herself grounded.

Healthy. Able to face every day with a smile and compassion for those she was on earth to help.

What kind of service dog was Juice?

Was there a man on the beach with physical limitations? Had she been meant to catch his attention, to respond to the brief lift of the glass, in case he had need of her nursing skills?

Feeling better once the conclusion hit her, she upped her pace a little more. Until another thought occurred. What in the hell was she doing sliding back into meant-to-bes?

The whole concept was misleading, at best. Opening one up to potentially life-threatening devastation in a worse outcome.

A reminder that set her instantly straight. The residents on Ocean Breeze would know soon enough that she was there. If anyone needed emergency nursing care—which would be doubtful with a doctor also living on the beach—they'd know where to find her.

Beyond that…she wasn't moving in to socialize.

She was there to rest—preferably without nightmares. To heal.

And to figure out what to do with the rest of her life.

## *Chapter Two*

The woman was bugging the hell out of him. Taking up Dale's time alone on the beach. Robbing Juice of his midmorning run. There was a set pattern on Ocean Breeze. Everyone went to work. Either at home or elsewhere. And Dale got a run in while the beach was deserted.

On weekends, he either went out before dawn—a way for WG to unwind before lying down for a few hours—or, on occasion, after dark.

He was fond of the people with whom he shared the beach. Their mutual respect for privacy suited him. As did their friendly smiles. Most of all, he enjoyed their trust in him to help out when needed.

But the newcomer...she bothered him. No one but Chelsea knew anything but the most basics about her. Scott Martin, the attorney who occasionally stopped by to share an evening beer on Dale's deck, had said his temporary next-door neighbor was a nurse. Named Millie. On a six-month lease that included dog-sitting. Information Chelsea had shared with Scott's wife, Iris.

How an illustrator knew a nurse, he didn't know. Hadn't asked. Scott probably wouldn't have had the answer if he *had* queried.

And really, Dale knew as much about the newest resident as he did about most of the others living around him.

Except why in the hell she was stealing his alone time on the beach.

An obvious answer presented itself: because she worked second or third shift. Skilled nurses were needed around the clock.

The wave she'd sent in his direction was what was really stopping him. If she was one of those women who couldn't help but be friendly—or worse, a woman who'd come on to him—his whole world would be mucked up with a tension he didn't need.

More than five years on Ocean Breeze and he'd never once had a blip on his radar. Which was why the place had become home to him.

He couldn't risk running into her alone out there. Couldn't give her the opportunity to catch his eye, to call out to him.

Requiring him to respond or appear rude and unfriendly. Neither of which he'd ever been. He managed his life by strategically planning his activities to avoid just such situations.

But how in the hell did a marine stay in combat shape if he didn't get in his daily workout?

For the entire week she'd been there, he'd had to run predawn or at night. But, dammit, he yearned for the view during his exertion. The scent and sound of the waves that seemed to carry vestiges of the spirits he'd lost. He missed communing with them.

Which was why, on Monday, the start of the second week of the new move-in's arrival on Ocean Breeze, Dale donned his running shorts and shoes and headed down to the water during the hour he knew would be pre-lunch for those working from home. He'd purposely held off beginning his trek until after the nurse had passed. Timing his start so that even with his faster pace, they'd only cross paths on her way back up the beach. He'd be early enough in his run that he could be forgiven for the speed with which he zoomed past her—so quickly that eyes wouldn't have time to focus, or gazes a chance to meet.

The maneuver was well planned and perfectly executed. To the point that Dale almost did a double take behind him. The woman hadn't seemed to even notice his feet shooting up sand beside her. Or hear his breathing.

He'd caught both of those coming from her.

But the glimpse he'd had of her head…it hadn't turned at all from its straightforward course. Almost as though she hadn't known he was there.

Which was exactly what he'd wanted.

Good.

The mission was a success. Disaster had been averted.

And he could resume his normal life.

Was the man deliberately trying to get her attention? Yeah, so she'd waved at him. Once. From a distance. Over a week ago.

She'd just been starting to feel as though she'd made the right move, renting on Ocean Breeze for a few months, had been getting into a routine of sorts, when all of a sudden after a week of peace and tranquility, the guy with the service dog who did some kind of writing was invading her run.

A time that had always been sacred.

The first day, figuring he'd just had a change of schedule, she'd made sure not to give him any hint of wanting to make something out of the wave the week before. It had taken a lot of strength, though, not to turn around and watch him down the beach.

There was the bare chest and shoulders—yeah—but nothing she hadn't seen before. Well, maybe a little more perfectly hewn out of the muscles and flesh he'd been given than she was used to, but still. A chest. Shoulders.

The huge poodle running beside him—Juice, she knew—had been worth a second look. A third, too.

But mostly it was her need to study the big muscled, two-legged man's movement, rhythm, the lightness in the step that had tempted her to look back. He ran like a... runner. The professional kind.

Something she knew almost as well as she knew herself.

So whatever service Juice provided didn't reflect an inability to be physically active. On a purely professional level, she was happy for him.

Beyond that...not at all. All she needed was an hour on the beach a day. And there he was, for the third morning in a row, coming right at her as she made her way back down to the cottage she was renting from Chelsea.

She was so intent on trying to figure out his motive, that she failed to prevent herself from looking over at the man as he passed. Just a brief glance. More like a twitch of the eye than any kind of formal head turn. But enough to realize that he was not paying attention to her. If she had to guess, she'd say he hadn't even noticed her. Which, if he was a professional runner, wasn't all that surprising. He'd be in his zone. Doing whatever he did in his head to build the physical endurance to make it for the long haul.

A 26.2 mile marathon?

Competition of some kind?

Was he in it for the money? The endorsements he could get if he managed to get good enough?

All questions she shook off almost as soon as they hit her. Not her life anymore. No. Done.

Ones she refused to consider when, the next day—Thursday of her second week on the beach—the man again acted as though he didn't know she was there as their paths crossed in the sand. She barely glanced his way but saw the sand flying from his shoes. Heard the heavy, evenness of his breathing.

And spent the rest of the way back trying to figure out why on earth the man was invading her daily activity. A possible answer hit just as she was walking barefoot up the beach, shoes in hand, toward her back deck.

What if he wasn't invading her private time in the sand?

What if she'd invaded his?

Chelsea had said the man kept to himself. That he didn't socialize on the beach. And the whole reason Millie had chosen the running time she had was because she'd ascertained, from a conversation with Chelsea, that, with the various work hours everyone kept, there was likely only a small window of time when there was no chance that anyone else would be out.

Her landlady obviously hadn't known that Dale ran every day. Not a big stretch to imagine since Chelsea, as much a workaholic as Millie was, wouldn't have been aware enough to actually witness the daily outside activity. Nor did Dale run down to her place. His was only three or four cottages up from Chelsea's. He ran the mile and a half or so distance between his place and the far end of the beach.

Furthermore, based on Millie's own actions, if Chelsea had had a day off at home, Dale might have skipped the run. As Millie had done one day last week when Iris, the photographer from next door, had been home and photographing her and Scott's two dogs on the beach.

She could be wrong about all of it, of course. Dale's motives for running when he did. Him trying to make something of the wave they'd shared the week before could all just be coincidence and an overactive imagination on her part. A malady that occurred when one wasn't challenging her thinking enough. Occupying her time with worthwhile concerns.

But how did one recover from workaholism and stay occupied with worthwhile concerns at the same time? How was she supposed to relax, take it easy, rest and remain active enough to keep her mind on track all at once?

Millie was still working on that one. But didn't let her lack of answers keep her from her jogging routine the next day. She just headed out better prepared. The few seconds in which she and Dale would pass were to contain sacred privacy bubbles for each of them. It was how they both got what they wanted and needed while living on the same beach.

And no more glances, not even millisecond ones at that bare chest. Or the shoulders above it.

She was not in the market for either. Ever again.

After a couple of weeks of morning jogs with the new renter on the beach, Dale was fine with having her there. She'd become part of the landscape. A sea urchin of sorts. Like a starfish. Or dolphin. Something he knew was there, that had a right to share the space but had no direct bearing on him or his life. And would never have contact with him.

Other than that time of day, he never saw the woman. Never heard anyone mention her.

With Juice's help, running beside him and ignoring the woman other than to watch her as she approached, as Juice did with everyone, Dale had relaxed with the daily intrusion. Had begun to accept it as normal. Was even to the point of being perfectly fine with it. Watching for it.

The service dog hadn't been purchased for him, but Juice was good for him, just the same.

Right up until he wasn't. On Wednesday of the following week, Dale was just a hundred yards away from the jogging nurse when Juice suddenly stiffened and then, without warning, took off up the beach toward her.

"Juice!" He called out urgently, sternly, order in his tone. The woman had a right to her privacy. The dog, who was better behaved than most humans Dale knew, ignored Dale's missive to halt his forward motion. But stopped a few feet before he reached her and moved toward the water instead.

Upping his own pace to a full-out run, Dale reached the dog before the woman did. Grabbing Juice's collar, he held on, his back to the path the nurse was taking while she passed.

Except that she didn't. "Look," she said, out of breath from her physical exertion. Acting as though they conversed on a regular basis, or had ever spoken before.

The tone of her voice drew his immediate response,

though. His gaze went straight in the direction her finger was pointing.

"What is that?" she asked then, coming in closer to study the shadow in the shallow water that had Juice at a full point.

The dog was telling him that something was wrong. He got that much. Would make it up to the boy later for having yelled at him. But... "It's a green sea turtle," Dale said, awed, and concerned at the same time. "If it's female, she could be coming up to nest, but she doesn't look old enough, big enough. And look at how she's holding her front legs." He'd seen a mother nesting during training in nearby San Diego. Had read about them and all other types of ocean life since his time on Ocean Breeze.

Millie, in tight sky-blue leggings and matching crop top, leaned down to the water. "She's not swimming, she's crawling with her back legs," she said, reaching toward the creature.

"Careful," he warned, his tone authoritative enough to stop her forward movement. "Normally, green sea turtles are passive, gentle creatures, but if she's hurt, she might bite. And she's definitely female. Males have longer, thicker tails." For mating. He didn't share that piece of information.

"I can't just leave her here suffering," Millie said, moving forward again, slowly. "That left front leg, see the gash, it's bleeding badly..." Pulling a sweat band from her arm, Millie glanced at Juice, who'd approached the turtle and stood at attention.

Dale moved in as Millie did, prepared to grab the creature by the neck if the turtle moved its head at all, and watched as the woman—with soothing tones that might or might not have been recognized—reached for the injured leg, and gently, but efficiently got the cut wrapped.

"That should provide enough pressure to at least slow the bleeding," she said.

Dale reached into the pocket of his shorts for the cell phone that was never out of reach. Dialing a number he'd put in his contacts when he'd moved to Ocean Breeze, he quickly reported his location and the situation. Listened to the instructions he was given and hung up.

"That was the local branch of the National Oceanic Atmospheric Administration," he said, keeping his gaze strictly on the suffering turtle's mouth as he continued with, "NOAA Fisheries. Used to be the National Marine Fisheries Service. They said to stay with her if we can. Try to keep her from swimming back out to sea until they can get here and check her over. And, of course, to be careful." His attention hadn't left the head he was guarding. And wouldn't.

Not until help arrived.

No way a woman was going to be hurt on his watch.

Period.

Tending to a medical situation, Millie was in her element. The place where she was comfortable. Where she'd lived almost exclusively for the past couple of years. Other than conditioning class. And jogging. They were the two things she'd done for herself.

"You're Millie, right?" Dale's deep voice came from above her. Noncommittal. Not unfriendly, but not inviting more, either.

She nodded. "And I know you're Dale. Chelsea filled me in on names and beach basics."

She'd checked the young female's other front leg and found swelling, but nothing that felt like a break. Her patient didn't pull the limb back as would be natural, but didn't seem to be in much pain to the touch. Something muscular then?

Juice stepped forward, and Millie said, "Chelsea left for up north, and I've got Magic for the time I'm here. I was thinking about bringing her jogging with me. Would that be a problem for Juice?" She didn't look up as she asked the question. Continuing to check the turtle over, instead.

"Other than that they'll want to run together." Dale's reply wasn't encouraging. Unless...surely he wasn't intimating that *they* run together?

Nodding, she said, "I'll leave her at home just to be safe."

And was a little...disappointed when the man didn't jump in with an assurance that they'd be fine. Make it work.

Or a more direct invitation for them to run together?

What would she have said if he did? No. Of course. But...for a brief second there, the idea had been tempting.

She'd spent most of her life running with a partner.

One in particular.

And she wasn't one of two anymore. That part of her was dead. Just a fact. Something she'd accepted.

Still, it would have been nice to have Magic there with her. The Newfoundland was as big as a person. And at one hundred pounds, weighed more than Millie, too.

Scott, the lawyer next door, ran with his little corgi, Morgan, and Iris's little collie, Angel. She knew because Morgan and Angel had come to say hello to Magic the night before. Millie hadn't joined the foursome on the beach. She'd smiled, nodded, and remained in her seat on the deck. With a brief nod in her direction, Scott had left her alone there.

Chelsea had told her the dogs were friendly. Millie had no desire to curtail their relationships. She just wasn't open to socializing with human participants. She was no longer whole. Didn't have as much to contribute.

Dale didn't say much else as they waited for help to arrive. Squatting down, he helped her secure the turtle when the youngish girl started to move. He told her a bit about the breed of sea turtle—the second largest in the US—and how the female adults returned to the beaches where they were born to nest and lay eggs. "It takes twenty to thirty years for these turtles to reach maturity." His information continued to fill the void between them, and she welcomed the kindness.

"I'm guessing she's roughly around fifty pounds now," she said, judging by the body mass she'd helped move, comparing it to the children she'd been lifting her entire career.

Dale nodded, whether agreeing with her or not, she didn't know. She saw the movement of his head peripherally. She didn't actually look at him.

"She'll be three to five feet long and somewhere around three hundred pounds by the time she reaches adulthood," he told her, also focused on the animal they were rescuing, while Juice continued to look on, standing guard.

That close to Dale, Millie could smell his sweat-activated deodorant, mixed with maleness. A scent that triggered memories she wouldn't let herself resurrect.

She'd become a master at avoiding their sting. Had

grown so skilled that it generally happened without her having to put forth any effort. A muscle memory.

But that morning, the struggle was back, real, in her face, and as soon as the representative from the fisheries place arrived and she gave her report, Millie took her leave.

She was on Ocean Breeze to rest, to heal, not to fall back into the abyss.

## *Chapter Three*

Dale looked forward to his run more than usual every morning over the next week. He waited as usual for Millie to pass and to get far enough of ahead of him, and then started out, per the routine he'd set. But there'd been a major change in his plan.

When he passed her, he looked at her. From the time she came into view until she was behind him. And she looked his way, too.

They'd smile. Nod. She rolled her eyes once. He shrugged.

And throughout those days, more and more, he'd find himself thinking about her. Nothing serious, of course. Just little awarenesses that she was there. On Ocean Breeze. Chelsea had mentioned that her temporary renter was on some kind of sabbatical. Home full-time. She'd made the mention when she'd stopped by his back deck to let him know that she'd be up north for an extended stay with her sister, but that Magic would still be on the beach. He'd offered to keep the big girl while Millie was at work.

Only to find out that his usual services weren't needed.

He'd been fine with the Magic part. And the rest, too. Just felt…odd…having someone else on the beach full-time. Which prompted an awareness or two throughout his day.

He couldn't say the same for WG. The guy was always asking why about everything. Dale understood that was how his writer persona did his job. He had to look at all sides to tell the whole story.

But WG wrote thrillers. The dude was always looking for danger lurking around every corner. Or tragedy in every past. A nurse living alone on a secluded beach did not mean anything other than she was a woman on sabbatical.

Except Millie couldn't be more than twenty-eight. Thirty, tops. Why would a woman that young be taking an extended time off from work? Unless she was independently wealthy. Came from wealth, maybe. But then, wouldn't she be off in some plush resort where she'd have staff to tend to things like making the bed, doing the dishes and laundry…

She could be hiring it all in. It's not like he actually kept watch on the road behind their cottages. There were cameras and all. But he didn't access them. There'd been no need.

And the sabbatical could have been forced. But she could still afford to rent on Ocean Breeze.

Or…it was something else. A health situation? WG came up with all kinds of possibilities on that one. Dale ended the onslaught of speculation with a single vision of Millie jogging on the beach. Followed up by the stop to help the turtle the previous week. She'd been jogging over half an hour based on the distance she'd traveled and hadn't even been out of breath.

More likely, she had enough financial security from

some source that was allowing her to take a break from work. Another career. Another path.

This explanation rang true for Dale. WG was Dale's own second path. Found right there on Ocean Breeze.

He worked it all out the last Saturday in September, running in the dark as he did on weekends. Told Juice all about it. And figured, as he stood in the shower later that morning, that he'd put the woman to rest. No more need for her to pop up in his thoughts throughout the day.

The reassurance gave him peace of mind. Right up until his weekend houseguests opted to play a game of tag that morphed into a chase and a race to the finish line. Which apparently, to Angel and Morgan, was the beach in front of their own back deck as they were heading in that direction at Mach speed.

Dale knew because when the dogs had run off, with Juice quickly keeping pace with Angel, the leader, Dale had jumped the rail on his deck to sprint off after them. Barefooted. And in nothing but the beige cotton shorts he'd pulled on after his shower. Throwing billows of sand up behind him.

Ten yards behind the dogs, he slowed his pace to a walk when he saw what the hubbub was all about. Angel and Morgan hadn't been heading home. They'd heard Magic, their next-door neighbor barking.

Down by the water in front of Chelsea's place.

The Newfoundland had found a sea lion that had swum up onto the beach and was cornered against a boulder. The poor guy was squatting there, tail flapping, unable to get back to the water that was his home. Magic was only a foot or so from the trapped creature, and Millie was heading quickly down to the dog.

Dale caught the scene in one glance. "Stop!" His tone was loud, and clearly an order.

With Angel and Morgan dancing around her, Millie froze in place, and Dale walked up to her. Picking up the miniature collie, he handed Angel to the nurse who was squatting and already securing Morgan. "Sea lions are pretty friendly in the water, due to their ability to swim so fast. But on land, most particularly when cornered, they get tense and attack," he said quickly, before emitting one short, sharp whistle.

Juice's head popped up, his ears at attention as he looked at Dale. With one short hand gesture, he commanded the dog to work. And the standard poodle approached Magic, nudging the bigger dog in the hind thigh. Motioning Millie to stay put by putting one hand behind him, Dale approached Magic and Juice slowly, speaking softly. "Good boy, Juice. Magic, stay." He repeated the words over and over, patting Juice on the head as he reached the twosome. And then, with one swift movement, had a hold of the one-hundred-pound dog's collar.

He didn't pull back immediately. Didn't want to risk setting off Magic's natural instinct to fight to protect. He just kept the sea lion from being attacked. And hopefully from attacking. While he continued to speak softly to his canine companions, Dale kept his gaze on the sea lion and slowly pulled Magic backward a step at a time, knowing that Juice would follow suit. Keeping his head close to Magic's thigh.

A couple of minutes, and it was all over. The sea lion, seeing his path to the water opening, made his way home and swam out of sight.

He turned to see Millie, wearing calf-length skintight

jeans and a short-sleeved shirt, still crouching barefoot in the sand, containing the two smaller dogs. "Wow!" she said. "I was just sitting on the deck and heard Magic bark, but she was behind the boulder, and I couldn't see... I had no idea...do sea lions visit often?"

Keeping his hold on Magic by petting the dog's head, Dale rubbed Juice, on his other side, behind the ears—letting the boy know he'd done a good job and work was done. "Only very occasionally," he told her. "There's a cove not far from here, up in La Jolla, where they breed, and every now and then one will swim ashore here."

With a last glance to make certain that the sea lion was far enough out to sea that the dogs wouldn't go after him, Dale let go of Magic. And Millie stood, leaving both Angel and Morgan free to play in the sand.

"I'm sorry for not keeping a tighter hold on her," Millie said, nodding toward Magic. "I've had her weeks and she's never even given a hint of running off." Cocking her head, she looked toward the other dogs. "But she does like to play with those two. I didn't see them out this morning. And since they're with you, I'm guessing my neighbors are gone."

He nodded. "Just overnight," he told her, not as anxious as he'd have expected to be to get back up to his deck. "Iris is a professional photographer. Scott's twin sister lives down at the end of the beach. The very last cottage, which you'll have seen if you jog to the end of the beach..."

He paused, catching her gaze. Blue. Her eyes were blue.

She was nodding. And Dale looked for Juice. Saw his

boy gallivanting like a kid in the sand with Magic while Morgan and Angel ran circles around them.

"Sage, Scott's sister, and her husband, Gray, just had a baby in July. Scott's nephew. They all went north for the night, to Lake Arrowhead, to do a family photo shoot with the fall foliage. According to Iris the colors are breathtaking." Oh-he-of-few-words was rambling on like he hadn't done since—ever.

"I'm guessing Iris and Scott hung out with Chelsea some, too, since Iris and Chelsea are both in the visual arts field."

He nodded. Purposely kept his mouth closed until he'd determined the source of his wordiness. And put it to permanent rest.

"Magic must be missing her friends," Millie noted then. "Especially since she lives next door to them. I never let her out when the others are around."

The words brought his attention back down to earth—and the dogs in his care. "You could bring her up for a while this afternoon if you'd like. I generally sit on the deck from four until six or so." He glanced over at her as he finished the sentence. Wondering who on earth he'd become in the past five minutes. He'd never, not even once, invited anyone to his place.

Folks walked up to talk to him sometimes while they were out on the beach. Scott came up for beer now and then, but the lawyer always invited himself.

And Dale enjoyed the man's company.

"Okay," she said, nodding. "I might do that."

A blow off. Thank God. "You like beer?" The words were out. He'd said them. And immediately regretted them, too.

"I do. But you don't have to put yourself out on my account. I have my own beer. And can carry a bottle down." The abrupt way she'd finished the sentence made the pause awkward.

Dale turned toward Juice. And Millie said, "If I decide to take a walk this afternoon."

Which drew his gaze back to her. "I make beer." The statement was bald. Attached to nothing.

She turned, looked at him and continued to watch him as she said, "You do?"

He nodded. Slid his hands in the pockets of his shorts. And saw her gaze lower at the movement. Landing on his chest.

The one he'd failed to cover with a shirt before bolting down the beach at the sound of trouble.

"I've been working on perfecting the recipe for the past four years," he told her quickly, to get her attention off his lapse. "Scott critiques for me occasionally. I could use another opinion."

"You've piqued my curiosity," Millie said then, seeming to relax, as she glanced toward the dogs and smiled at their antics, as though the sight of his naked chest had had no effect on her whatsoever.

Relieved, Dale grinned, too, whistling for Juice, which brought all four dogs to his side. "I'll have bottles on ice," he said as she took Magic's collar and he clicked his fingers and said, "Come."

He didn't turn around as his three companions trotted up the beach with him. Didn't look back to see if Millie was watching.

But he was smiling.

His lack of having anything substantial to give in the

human interaction department didn't seem to faze Nurse Millie any more than his impressive physique had done.

And that was nice.

She wasn't going to go. There was no point. Millie hadn't had an appointment to see anyone socially—let alone a man—since…well, since she'd been alone. Two years.

Chelsea had asked her if she wanted to head to the juice bar after class once. When she'd declined, the fellow classmate and conditioning coach had initiated a conversation right there in her studio. A strange meeting of minds that had ended with Millie agreeing to take a look at the beach cottage Chelsea had to sublet—inexpensively due to the fact that dog care came with the lease.

Hard to believe one conversation had changed her life.

And yet…why not? One second had changed her life. From one step to the next. Life had been spectacular. The other foot had come down and it was all over.

Which was not what she was on Ocean Breeze to think about. She was there to crochet. To paint. To pick up her guitar.

To invite something besides illness and death into her life.

To get some sleep. Take deep breaths.

Not to make friends. She'd never be enough.

But to have a beer? With a man who appeared to be as much of a loner as she was? Who was there to help but then retreated to his own space immediately afterward.

A human being who seemed to be more like her than anyone else she'd met during the past twenty-four godawful months.

Someone who, for the first time, gave her hope that there was enough of her left to have a life. A diminished one, to be sure. She wasn't looking for joy. Or anything akin to happiness. But a sense of peace—like that which seemed to surround Dale—and the blooming of an occasional heartfelt smile would be nice.

Stopping suddenly, on her way from a Magic potty stop to the back deck, Millie checked herself. Reassessed the thought she'd just had. And then again, taking it on for a third time.

The new insight withstood the scrutiny. And she smiled.

Almost a month into her self-imposed sabbatical and she finally had something solid to put on the blank sheet that was awaiting her list. She had a goal.

An attainable positive objective toward which to strive.

Or rather, two of them. To tap into the essence she felt emanating from a near stranger on the beach. And the ability to feel a smile with more than just her facial muscles.

Relief rushed through her. A sense of, not quite hope, but of purpose. And later, when it was beer time, grabbing her phone, she walked to the back door. Waited, as usual, while Magic went out before her. But instead of heading to the chair she'd placed to allow her a full view of the waves gliding onto the beach, she followed the Newfoundland down the few wooden steps to the beach. And kept walking.

Watching Magic. The girl had stopped to smell the sand, but kept Millie in sight, too, and as soon as she seemed to get that Millie was heading out, the girl was at her side. Keeping pace. Glancing over continuously as if to ask, "Where are we going?"

The question didn't matter much. The happy look she was certain she saw glowing from Magic's eyes, the way the dog's tongue lolled out of a mouth that had widened and the way her paws almost seemed to be prancing kept Millie moving forward.

Not looking back.

Or thinking about what she was leaving behind.

Luckily, surely just by chance, no one else was out on the beach between her place and Dale's that fall Saturday afternoon. About a hundred yards out, she glanced up at his deck. Just in time to see him walking out with what looked to be a bucket in his hands. He didn't glance in her direction. Rather, he seemed to be fully focused on whatever activity was occupying him.

Which meant that he wasn't waiting on her. Expecting her. If she got there she did, if she didn't, she didn't. Nothing more than that.

Just to be sure, she kept an eye on him the rest of the way to his place. Even when Magic pushed her head beneath Millie's palm. She petted the girl, but didn't look away from the deck she was approaching. She had to know that her presence wasn't watched for.

That she wasn't getting into anything that she couldn't follow through on. Or sending messages she couldn't sign.

She was just heading up from the shore to Dale's place when he seemed to notice her. He didn't stand up. Just sat there on his deck, watching her—or rather, watching Angel, Morgan, and Juice come down to greet Magic.

Millie hadn't planned to stall the next minutes—before the point when she climbed a man's steps to his deck to sit with him and drink a beer. But with the three girls and boy wiggling around her, she had to stop. To squat down and give all of them attention. They were like her children at work. Just looking for kindness, for gentle touches, safety and attention that didn't hurt.

Giving it to them filled her with strength.

Which she carried with her as she eventually made her way to the steps separating the deck from the sand. And climbed them. Making it to the top without a sweat. Or cramps of fire shooting through her midsection.

She opened her mouth to say she couldn't stay, but was distracted when Dale reached down to the bucket he'd carried out and pulled up a bottle, uncapping it and handing it to her.

She was still standing there, thinking she'd head on back down the beach, but took the bottle. Looked at it, and the cap in his hand, and had to ask, "You make this beer?"

Sitting back with his own bottle, he looked out to the beach and said, "Yeah. But if you can't tolerate it, it won't hurt my feelings."

Good to know. That she couldn't hurt his feelings. Let her take a breath.

She held the bottle with both hands. Looked at it. "I was just wondering…how do you get the cap on it? It's like store-bought, not some plastic at-home thing you can just press on." She sounded juvenile to herself. Didn't much care. Nor did it matter what he thought of her. She'd be leaving as soon as she had her answer. Question was whether or not she'd be taking the beer with her.

She didn't want to be rude. But she really wanted to try a sip. He'd made her curious. She'd never known anyone who brewed their beer. She'd heard of it happening, of course. Just hadn't ever been exposed to the process.

"I have an apparatus that has a screw-on clasp to go over the edge of the counter. From there, I place the metal cap on the top of the bottle, put the bottle under the tool, and simply pull down on the lever. It does the rest."

Looking at the bottle, her brows rose. Made sense. She'd learned something new. A fact she found interesting. And something else occurred to her.

"How do you get the beer in the bottle without it foaming a head all over the place?" It could take hours to fill a six pack.

"There's another tool," he said, his gaze still turned toward the beach. Watching the dogs in his care, most likely. "It's kind of like a straw, the same width as one. It attaches to the vat that holds the beer that's ready to be bottled. I slide an empty bottle up the tube, making certain that the tube touches the bottom of the bottle, and then turn on the dispenser. Then watch the beer climbing up the sides of the bottle until it's as full as I want it. And turn off the dispenser."

He had her attention. Millie sat in the only other chair on the deck—a much smaller and less elegant deck than hers—while a slew of questions started hitting her. How often did he brew? How long did it ferment? How many bottles at a time?

Before she could ask any of them, Dale asked, "Are you going to try it, or just sit there staring at it? It might not taste great to you, but you can trust that it's perfectly healthy and safe for you to take one sip."

As though to prove his point, he put his own bottle to his mouth, took a long sip, and swallowed. She knew because the movement had drawn her eyes to look in his direction.

He was wearing the same shorts he'd had on earlier. But had put on a dark green T-shirt that was tight against his chest as he lifted his bottle to his mouth.

"Brent didn't like tight T-shirts," she said. Heard herself. And sat there, unmoving, waiting for the world to crash around her.

"Good to know," her companion said as though she hadn't just done the unthinkable. She had to get out of there. To leave the state and...

Go where?

To do what?

"Did he say why?"

The question reached through the hazy red panic taking hold of her, and she looked toward the sound. Saw Dale. Sitting right where he'd been. Looking out toward the waves in the distance in front of them. Then Juice was there, climbing the steps, but not heading toward Dale. He stopped right in front of Millie. Pushing his curly head under her hand. Her fingers moved of their own accord. Gently. Recognizing the springy soft hair. The warmth.

And she said, "He liked to feel the air moving around his skin when he ran. It's why I always wear crop tops. So I can feel the air on my skin." When she ran.

With Juice right there, moving his head, calling her back, anytime she started to see red again, Millie chanced a glance at her companion. Just to make sure he wasn't staring at her, analyzing her, assessing her. And felt the muscles in her stomach relax a notch as she recognized the side of his face, as his gaze focused in front of him. Not toward her.

As it had so many mornings on the beach.

"You want to take a sip of that beer?" he asked then. "If not, I'll put it back on ice."

Millie no longer had any idea how to want. Other than to want to escape the pain. But she had a sudden flash of what she didn't want.

She didn't want to hand back that bottle of beer.

And so she sipped.

## *Chapter Four*

The woman was having an anxious moment. Juice told Dale that much. The rest... Brent...the way she'd said the name. The half-dead tone of voice.

Dale recognized those, too. And understood.

As she took a second sip of the beer he'd brewed, Dale watched the waves. Letting them take his thoughts and then hand them back to him. Sometimes with more clarity. Sometimes not. And he watched the dogs on the beach, too. Always.

They were his helpmates. The keepers of innocence. Unconditional, unwavering support. The givers of joy. And the warning of all troubles. Natural and human-born, too.

Juice let out a small whine. More of a love note. But Dale knew the sound. Glancing at the dog, not the woman, he noted the way the poodle's head was tapping gently upward. Every time the fingers on top of it stilled.

Dale's helpmate was working. Hard.

Warning of anxiety in the human he was attending.

It was his canine companion, not the waves that cleared Dale's mind of all doubt as he said, "What happened to him?"

"He died."

Jutting his chin, he took a quick glance at Millie. Recognized the blank expression as she turned her head out toward the beach. And he said, "Her name was Lyla."

If she looked at him, Dale didn't catch the movement. His gaze was seeking the peace his soul had learned how to access. Through the steady movement of waves.

"How long ago?" he asked then.

"Two years."

Ahhh. She was just coming out of what he'd deemed his shock mode. Counselors had different terms. Specifically named stages. Even those changed from doctor to doctor. He'd talked to a number of them during those first two years.

"It's been five for me," he told her. And had to glance over. To connect with the living.

Millie's head was turning slowly, just as his was. Her gaze met his. Seemed to be clutching in an effort to hold on. "Trust Juice." The words weren't of Dale's calling. But when they came to him, he uttered them immediately.

Millie blinked. Was still looking at him. She nodded. And he could almost physically feel the deep breath she took. Could sense as well as see when her shoulders relaxed.

Another couple of minutes, and Juice was bounding down the steps to join his friends.

While Dale sat with the first person he'd been totally real with, raw with, in five long years.

He'd lost his love.

The information was like some kind of gentle waterfall, washing over her with comfort. With warmth. Not because of his loss. But because she understood the past weeks.

And her choice to walk down to Dale's place for beer.

They were twin souls. Only half alive, with less to give others than most had.

Knowing that set her free in a way she hadn't been since her one disastrous grief counseling group meeting. Being in that room, with all that suffering, had nearly buried her alive. She'd barely been able to cope with her own broken heart, let alone take on others.

And yet sitting there with Dale made her feel oddly more whole.

Which was the point of grief counseling.

Maybe she hadn't been ready. Had tried too soon to make herself better. The idea held merit. Was one she would visit again. Right then, watching the dogs on the beach, she had to ask, "Were you married to her?"

"Yeah."

She didn't glance over, but knew he was staring out to sea. There'd been no peripheral movement from his direction. "Me, too."

People lost spouses. Some young, some not. And some moved on better than others. She'd lost the love of her life. Her soul mate.

And sensed that Dale had, too. His solitary life was testament to that fact as much as her killing herself with work was.

Because life was only going to be half lived from that point forward. It wouldn't be fair to ask someone else to fill the void, because you could never give to them what they deserved to have. Millie had given Brent her whole heart. Her soul. It was his not just until death parted them, but forever.

She no longer had it to give.

And had never thought she'd meet someone else who had the same lack of ability. Who didn't need what she couldn't give.

The moment was freeing. She didn't want it to end just yet. So said, "I like the beer." And then spent ten minutes asking questions about the different grain choices used in production, fermentation and the yeast and the sugar that fed the yeast. Content just to hear Dale's voice. A human living in her same world.

Comfortable to just sit and learn something new.

She finished her bottle of beer. He offered a second, and she took it.

Sipped slowly from it. Petting the dogs as they came up to lie down around them on the deck. And still wasn't ready when Dale asked, "How?"

She'd told the story countless times. In the beginning. But not for a while. Chelsea knew. She'd recognized Millie's name from something she'd heard in the news. Because she followed sports and conditioning stories.

And it had happened right there in San Diego, not far from Chelsea's studio.

"He was a professional runner. Competing at an event here in San Diego. Crossed the finish line first. And..."

"...Brent Monroe," Dale said as her voice fell off. "From one step to the next."

It was as though he read her nightmare straight out of her mind. She was a registered nurse. A trained medical professional. A healthy twenty-six-year-old man did not just stop breathing in the space of picking up a foot and putting it back down.

"He had a heart defect that no one knew about," she said prosaically. Just as she'd been told. More than once.

She'd been hysterical at the time. Yelling at the doctor. Or any medical personnel who tried to give her the information. It hadn't been what she'd been equipped to hear.

"I remember," Dale said. Just that. Nothing more. No condolences. But then he'd know...they were so hard to take. More so after time went on. At least for her.

And, she suspected, for him, too.

There were some things others would just never feel, relate to, or even comprehend. Not if they hadn't been in that particular heart space.

Minutes passed. A lot of them. A couple strolled down by the water, hand in hand. She didn't know them. Figured Dale did, but didn't ask who they were.

He didn't say.

Her second beer was almost gone, and she was still glued to her seat. Not ready to take the next step. Unable to leave until she did.

"How?" she finally asked, her throat stinging as though the word had been yanked up out of her. And held her breath while she awaited his response.

"Caught in the crossfire of a bullet aimed at someone else. There one second, gone the next. Wrong place, wrong time."

The next question had to be given voice. He hadn't put the same burden on her. But, staring out at the ocean, she asked, "Were you with her?"

"No." The one word had a tone all its own. A very clear "no trespassing" message attached. And, nodding, Millie sipped her beer.

\* \* \*

There were some things Dale would not talk about. Over the years, he'd managed to make that information clearly known. He cared about his neighbors, more than most of them probably knew. But only to a point.

Until it reached that place where all he had left was burned, scarred remains.

But he wasn't ready for Millie to leave.

It was nice. Sitting with someone he didn't feel like he had to hide from. Even as he entertained the ridiculous notion, he felt a familiarity with it, too.

Opening his third beer—the batch they were drinking from was his three percent alcohol attempt—he shared that piece of news with her as he uncapped another bottle for her, as well.

And relaxed some when she took it from him. As though she was finding in him some of the same sense of common ground he was discovering in her. A freedom to be who and what he was.

"Did you always want to be a nurse?" he asked, glancing at her and then back out to sea. Life at a distance. That was how he rolled.

"Yeah. When I was growing up, my dolls were always sporting boo-boos that needed fixing." He heard humor in her voice and felt a hint of a smile coming on.

Just a hint and then it was gone. But still...the second of more than just placidity was nice.

He wanted to know why she'd quit. Even temporarily. But didn't ask. He wasn't up for a quid pro quo interrogation, which meant she probably wasn't up for that conversation, either.

"Can I ask you something?" Her query came too closely on top of his own ruminations, and he stiffened.

And answered honestly, "Depends on what it is. You can ask. I might not answer."

He braced for her to stand, call Magic and leave. Even had a thought as to whether or not she'd take the nearly full bottle with her. And hoped she did.

He wanted them to part on good terms.

"In the beginning, did you bury yourself in work?"

Not anything as invasive as he'd been expecting. A quid pro quo, after all, actually. He'd asked about her job. "Nope. I quit and moved here." That wasn't quite right. And would break trust with her. "I was offered an honorable discharge, and I took it," he reworded his response. "Then I moved here."

He glanced over at her, just as she turned to look at him. "You were in the service?" she asked, curiosity, interest shining from her gaze, but nothing more.

He looked back out to the water. "The Marines."

"Chelsea said you're some kind of writer now."

He nodded. And gave his standard answer. An honest one. "I sell enough articles to keep Juice in dog food."

"What do you write about?"

"Anything that interests me. From homebrew to physical training." He controlled his world by learning everything there was to know about it. And once he knew what there was to know, he wrote articles.

"Let me guess," Millie said then, with a light note to her voice. "If I looked you up, I'd find some pieces on marine life, the sea animal variety. As in fisheries."

With a grin, he nodded.

And didn't want the night to end.

\* \* \*

She had to go. Three percent alcohol or not, Millie hadn't eaten. She needed food before she consumed any more beer.

And didn't want to outstay her welcome.

Mostly because she hoped her little sojourn with Dale wouldn't be the last. It was nice, having someone to just sit with, and not feel like you were sprouting horns, and everyone saw them but were afraid to tell you.

Or to sit in a pool of their empathy, with unasked questions floating around in it.

When Dale stood and said he'd be right back, then disappeared inside, with all four dogs, including Magic, following right behind him, Millie knew that as soon as he came back out, she had to take Magic and head home.

She wasn't ready. But she wasn't not ready, either. Life was what it had become. Doing. Not becoming attached to the doing.

She heard the door open beside her, picked up the half-full bottle she'd set down by her chair, and sat up, intending to stand, was just waiting for Dale and his crew to give her room, when she saw the tray he'd brought out with him. One he set on a table he pulled over between them as he sat back down.

The thing was loaded with meats and cheeses. Crackers. Even sliced celery and cucumbers. With…grape jelly? She had to be seeing that one wrong.

"I had this ready in the refrigerator for tonight's dinner," he told her. Then handed her a paper plate and kept the second for himself.

When she sat there, assimilating, he said, "Don't feel

like you have to stay, if you'd rather not. I just needed something to eat with the beer."

As she did. And there was nothing prepared in her refrigerator waiting for her. Before she dug in though, she eyed the whole array, and had to ask, "Grape jelly?"

"I had it in Italy," he told her. "Don't look askance until you try it. Save yourself a bit of backtracking. I did not do so."

With a shrug, and a sense of curiosity that was welcome, she watched him load a cracker, meat first, then jelly, then cheese, cucumber on top, then followed suit. Took a bite. And nodded. "This is really good."

"I know," he reached for another helping. "I never would have tried it, but Ly..." His words ended right there. Midstream. But he didn't stall in his cracker building.

And neither did Millie. She built cracker after cracker. Ate them. Wondering if Italy had been their honeymoon.

Hoped so. It felt good that he'd be open to eating a meal he'd shared with his Lyla, to share it even. It felt healthy.

And getting to that point was her greatest dream.

Appetite satisfied, Dale took the nearly empty plate away, so the few straggler crackers didn't tempt the dogs. Then, asking permission to feed Magic, which felt a little odd since it was something he'd done many many times in the past, he fed all four dogs before returning outside.

Millie had her beer bottle in hand, and her head back, her face turned toward the setting sun. The day was ending.

He wasn't ready for their visit to do so. And knew there was nowhere else for it to go.

As he took his seat, stretching out as though he meant

to stay awhile, he thought of an earlier question she'd asked. And figured, with replete stomachs, and the beer still flowing, with dusk bringing on a curtain against the brightness of day, the time might be right to help if he could.

If she'd been looking for help.

"I take it that's what you've done," he started in, then quickly added the tagline which would make sense of his long way in. "Buried yourself in work?"

He knew the question could be a night ender. Waited to see what would happen next.

And felt gratified when Millie said, "Almost literally. Buried myself. Worked myself to death. Not physically. But..."

She stopped. He sat there. If she wanted to share more she would. He wasn't going to make her feel as though she had to.

"Other than the time off I took to be a part of...something else... I've been working with sick kids since I volunteered as an aide at eighteen. It's what I do."

Chin jutting, he nodded. Kept his gaze forward.

"Last month, we lost one. A two-year-old boy who'd never spent one day out of the hospital. He'd been sick all his life. Was no longer suffering..." Her voice trailed off, and Dale was regretting, hugely, having pushed the conversation.

Until she shuddered and said, "I worked in the Neonatal Department for a couple of years. In the children's surgical unit after that. My gift is being able to make them smile, even in the midst of their suffering. I don't know how I do it. I just do. This time it was different... like that little boy was mine..."

Her voice faded away, and Dale drifted some, too. A bit further out to sea.

Long minutes later, Millie said softly, "I'd worked myself to the point of emotional exhaustion. Which made me no good for those children."

And he asked, "So now what?"

Standing, drawing his gaze from the water to her, Millie said, "That's what I'm on Ocean Breeze to figure out." Then clicked her fingers for Magic, who was at her side, at the top of his steps, ready to go down, instantly.

"You could learn to make beer." He said the words to her back as she headed down the steps.

Turning, she glanced back at him, and he was pretty sure he saw a grin on her face. A sad one maybe. A hint of something.

"You offering to teach me?" she asked what should have been a flirty question, given that they were healthy, good-looking, unattached man and woman who'd just enjoyed each other's company.

It hadn't been, though. He heard honesty. And interest.

As though she was open to spending time with him. And to finding anything that might spark the next step forward for herself. Even it if was just a desire to learn how to brew.

"I am," he told her.

And was gratified when she said, "You're on," in lieu of good-night.

Dale kept an eye on her as she made her way down the beach with the huge dog at her side. He noticed how her hand lay on Magic's head a good bit of the time.

He noted everyone on the beach. Watched out for all of them. Because it was his job to do so.

But with Millie, the watching felt a bit more personal. And he didn't know what to make of that.

## *Chapter Five*

Millie debated taking Magic running with her that next week. It wasn't like she had to worry about the dogs wanting to run together. If they did, they did. The beach was wide enough to take all four of them at once. Or she could fall behind Dale.

And while the idea held merit—a lot of it at various times during the days and nights—in the end, she held off for Magic's sake. Chelsea had never taken the girl running, and as big as she was, Millie wasn't certain a two-mile sprint would be good for her.

So she set out alone, as usual on Monday—a day and a half after she'd last seen Dale—but had only made it a few hundred yards before she saw him—Juice in tow—jogging in place down by the water in front of his cottage.

Waiting for her. He didn't say so. Didn't even say hello as he fell into step beside her, with Juice in between them. And she didn't ask or say a word as the two joined her. She kept pace. And other than a glance or two, held her gaze facing forward, watching her path.

She'd been training more than half her life. Had been clued-up long ago.

On the return route, Dale veered off at his place, and she kept running. She didn't wave, or smile. Or look to see if he did. She didn't miss a beat in her workout. But she felt better inside than she had in a while. As though he and Juice could somehow suck angst out through her pores just by existing in her sphere.

She wasn't averse to that. And if she could somehow offer Dale the same service, she wanted to do so.

Which was why, when, the next day, the man and dog joined her again, she nodded at them. Waited for his nod back and found something besides habit in the run. Not joy. But…a hint at inner peace, maybe.

For the rest of that week, the three of them ran together every morning. And Millie spent the rest of the time getting things settled at Chelsea's place. She'd given up her apartment, had boxed everything and had the movers stack the boxes floor to ceiling along one side of the two-car garage on Ocean Breeze. Had planned to leave them there during her stay on the beach. But, had been unpacking some things.

Moving in, temporarily.

The cottage had twice the square footage of her apartment and while all of Chelsea's furniture was there, and her kitchen things in the cupboards, she'd packed up most of her personal items for the sublet. Which meant Millie was finding herself being called to the process of filling the space. Finding a sense of beginning, as opposed to just enduring, as she occupied herself with the tasks involved. She made several trips to the hardware store for various storage and hanging items.

Stocked up on the essentials she'd always just purchased in small amounts as needed.

And, in a fluke moment, stopped at a craft store and bought a couple pieces of wood, too. She'd unearthed her burning tools and paints. Supplies she hadn't used since college. And still might not get to it, but she'd have the wood there, just in case.

While there, she walked by the yarn section. Saw a sale on baby yarn and had to get out of the store. Had there been a line at the check-out, she'd have left her pieces of wood behind. As it was, she paid and was out in less than a minute.

Drawing cool fall air into her lungs. Her shopping spree over, she drove straight home. Left the wood in the back of her small blue SUV and spent an hour sitting with Magic on the beach. Letting the sand warm her butt through the capri jeans she had on. Soaking up serotonin. Taking deep breaths.

And refusing to cry.

She was fine by dinner time. Stable. Her usual self. But took the experience to heart. She could reach forth, but only so far. At least the reminder had come while she'd been alone.

It also made her pause the next morning, Friday, when, at the end of their run, Dale didn't veer off at his place. He kept pace beside her all the way down to hers. Pushing their limit. Something she was afraid to do.

And yet, she wasn't upset with him.

He slowed, when she did, walking beside her, and she continued past Chelsea's place rather than walking Dale up to it. "I'm going to be starting a new batch of brew tomorrow," he told her.

Saturday, one of the two days a week she didn't see him on her run. Sunday, the other day, she didn't see him because she didn't run. A day of rest. Letting her muscles heal. Strengthen.

"Ale or lager?" she asked. Ale was a lighter beer. The kind she liked.

"Ale."

Had he made the choice for her? She didn't ask. Didn't want to know. Just nodded.

"You're welcome to help."

Help. Not watch. Funny how one word made such a huge difference. "I'd like that," she told him. Because she really did want to learn. "Can we put a touch of peach in the recipe?" She'd always loved peaches.

He shrugged. "I'll look into it."

And she had to tell him. "I already did." Then, "And... um...ordered the extract, just in case. You can add it to secondary fermentation or during the bottling process even, but since, practically speaking, I know nothing about the actual process, I'd leave that call strictly up to you."

His brow rose. She didn't blame him. Over the past couple of years, she'd noticed that she'd developed a tendency to appear to take over situations she was involved in. But in reality, she just needed to keep tight control on her own world. Not try to manipulate what others did.

She was discovering that the line between the two might not exist.

Her muscles were tightening in her back, her shoulders and neck until she saw the grin start to spread on Dale's face. "Your interest was piqued," he said. "Nice. A touch of peach it will be."

He'd turned and with Juice at his side, was gearing up from walk to run. She didn't want to be controlling. "Do you like peach?" she called out after him.

Jogging in a circle, he turned back, said, "I like

peaches. Never had it in beer," and completing his circle, headed back up the beach toward his home.

It wasn't until he was almost out of sight, and Magic was whining at the door, that she realized she was just standing there feeling…good.

Better than she had in a very long time.

Dale didn't have a lot to do to prepare for the upcoming brewing session. His cottage was as neat as always—a throwback to the barracks training he'd had. And living with a woman who'd been a bit of a cleaning enthusiast.

The brewing itself had become like everything else in his life. He had a system and completed the task.

What had him seriously rethinking his invitation to Millie was the fact that he brewed beer in his kitchen. And hadn't had a single person in the place since he'd moved in. Period.

His cottage was his sanctuary.

The situation was made worse by the fact that he hadn't even considered the resulting invasion when he'd issued the offer—not the week before, the day before, or that morning, either. He'd simply been tending to a like-minded soul.

Or his own spirit. He didn't give a lot of thought to such things.

He helped others. She needed help. He knew how he could give it to her. End of story.

Except that he either had to figure out how to brew beer on a deck that barely had enough room for his table and two chairs, or prepare for another body in his haven.

The third choice presented when neither of other two were fitting the bill. He could cancel.

He *could* cancel. That was what he'd do. He pulled out his phone, getting to the "how" of the matter, and realized he didn't have Millie's number. Or any way to contact her other than walking down to her place. Hoping she was out on that fabulous deck of hers—maybe enjoying a fire in the fireplace. Or he'd have to knock on her door.

He wasn't big on the door-knocking thing. The year before, when he'd helped Iris lift Scott after his surfing accident, he'd merely set times that he'd be there and had let himself in.

He could knock. He just didn't want the directness. Standing there, looking at each other, eyes meeting, having to make conversation. Giving others the chance to see how dead he was inside.

He didn't feel quite as dead in Millie's presence. She didn't need things he didn't have to give. Or try to make eye contact during conversation. With her, for the first time in five years, he felt…a kinship. Not good. Not bad. Just there. If he couldn't help his kin, what good was he?

Of course, he'd put up with someone in his kitchen. What the hell kind of odd man out had he become?

One who'd grown lazy if he couldn't buck up and open his door to another.

He had his supplies out, sanitized, and ready to go when he heard Magic's paws climbing up the back steps of his deck. He'd left the back door open, with only the screen door between the deck and his kitchen. Juice, who'd been standing watching him, heard Magic just before he did, as she'd headed to the door, mouth open with tongue lolling, tail wagging.

"Come in," he called, before Millie had a chance to knock, keeping his back to the door as he rearranged his supplies to two inches apart instead of an inch and a half—not because the measurement mattered, or he'd ever done so before—in order to keep himself occupied.

"Since we don't know how this is going to taste, I've pulled the five-gallon kettle for today's batch," he told her as soon as he heard the door close. Magic sauntered up to the counter, her head able to reach there while she perused his activity. Dale petted her before guiding her out of the galley part of the kitchen and, with a wave of his hand for Millie to enter, pulled the gate across.

"I usually let Juice observe while I cook, but sanitization is extremely important in the brewing process. We have to cool the wort before we transfer it to the fermenter—" he nodded toward the apparatus on the far end of the counter "—and any small particle could ruin the batch."

He glanced over enough to see that she was focused on the supplies on the counter, not him—and to notice that she was wearing a pair of skintight black jeans and a silverish button-down blouse that ended at the top of her jeans—and then didn't look again.

Rather than showing her the process, Dale, mostly directed. Having her fill the kettle halfway with water. Turning up the heat. Filling the grain bag and steeping it for the twenty minutes it took the water to reach the appropriate temperature. He told her to be sure not to squeeze the grain bag because anything that fell through could affect the taste of the beer.

And while the water was heating, he either told her more about next steps, or remained silent. Other than asking pertinent questions about their process, Millie didn't speak, either. Yet their lack of conversation didn't feel awkward. He had another person in his kitchen, and he was fine.

Comfortable. Maybe even enjoying himself a little. As much as he was able. The peace that he'd spent years coveting and had finally accessed was present.

"Now you have wort," he told her when she'd removed the grain bag successfully. "Basically, sugar water." It was time to cool the liquid. "It's imperative that we do this as quickly as possible," he continued, having her insert the chiller into the pan, and then running cold tap water through it.

From there, he told her how to use the valve to transfer the liquid into the fermenter, then add the other two and a half gallons of distilled water, aerate it and then add the yeast. And the peach extract. He was there if she needed help, ready to jump in and catch any stumbles, but the woman followed instructions explicitly, accurately, never missing a beat.

When the process was done, and the kitchen cleaned, he handed her a beer from his previous batch and lead the way out to his deck. Holding the door for the dogs to go first.

Taking his usual seat, he didn't invite her stay, or even sit. She could take her beer and go. Their plans for the day were complete. Magic and Angel were on the beach, romping around.

If Scott or Iris walked by on their way down to Sage and Gray's place—as they often did on Saturday evenings—the two big dogs would go with them partway. Nudging at Angel and Morgan. But they'd turn back before Dale's cottage was out of sight.

Scott and Iris would see Millie on his deck, though.

He was fairly certain she wouldn't want that. Because he was pretty sure he didn't.

The choice was hers. And he wasn't entirely disappointed when she sat. He couldn't stop his neighbors from drawing erroneous conclusions, but he could rely on the fact that whatever they thought about him wouldn't reach his ears.

He just hoped that Millie received the same respect. And felt the need to warn her. "Scott and Iris were out of town last week when you were here, but most Saturdays they head down to Sage's place."

She stood. "You want me to go. I'm so sorry..."

"No." Dale was standing, too, before he'd had the conscious thought to rise up. "I don't." The words weren't easy. Nor was looking her in the eyes as he said them. "I'm fine either way. I just want you to know in case... you aren't...fine. Being seen here. With me."

Wow. One of the most difficult speeches he'd made in a while. Feeling deluged with awkwardness, he sat back down, took a sip of beer, and focused on the waves. He could always count on them. To be there. Anytime of the day or night. And to calm him.

She didn't respond. He didn't blame her. Waited to hear her sandals on the deck steps, but heard the chair next to him creak, instead, as she sat down. And he cheered for her.

She'd made the choice to be seen. To be viewed as living life. For most, the moment would have gone unnoticed. But he knew.

And said, "You were impressive in there, never missing a beat. I was beginning to think you'd actually made beer before, but then it hit me. You were a nurse in a pediatric surgical ward. Where following instructions immediately and perfectly was an everyday requirement." Too long. Too much. But bringing it back to the beer.

There couldn't be any more than that. Not for him.

He suspected not for either of them.

There were just some things that couldn't be fixed.

Millie didn't have to worry about what others thought. On the beach or anywhere. She didn't open herself up to conversation that would invite them to speak that kind of opinion.

She couldn't. There was too much of her that she couldn't share. Some by choice. Most by fate.

And just as she was welcome to the privacy of her thoughts, and to form the ones that were appropriate for her, that fit her, so was everyone else.

Including Dale.

But for some reason, as she sat there next to him, sipping beer again—more slowly than she had the week before—she wanted to know his thoughts.

Like learning how to brew beer...it was almost as if he had something critical to teach her. Or the ability to show her a piece of herself she hadn't yet discovered. His life was so...peaceful.

She wanted that. Above all else.

And, after a conversation with Chelsea that afternoon, and then glancing into one of the boxes in her garage, she found a topic that was stealing her calm. And was the reason she'd sat back down.

"You decorate for the holidays?" she asked him. She'd heard the whole beach was a light fest. Starting around Thanksgiving. That while the beach couldn't be accessed, other than by their private road, that it had become something of a tourist attraction from the ocean side. With all of the reefs around them, boats couldn't get close enough to disturb their privacy, but apparently they floated out there by the hundreds to enjoy the view.

Chelsea had offered to provide the decorations if Millie didn't have any.

"I do a lighted military and patriotic display, with a Christmas tree someone gifted me thrown into the middle of it."

She nodded. Felt a bit of tension slide out of her. Their viewers wouldn't just want to see the same display of lights at every cottage. Different expressions, through light, would do. She just had to pick a theme.

Which meant going back to the craft store... Refocus. "Who gave you the tree?" she asked him.

Dale's shrug as he took a sip of beer brought a bit of a smile to her face. And she watched him as she waited for his answer. When the silence grew to more than a few seconds, she glanced back out at the beach.

Keeping an eye out for her next-door neighbors as they headed down the beach. With Morgan and Angel prancing in the sand, they wouldn't be hard to spot. She just wanted to be aware for exactly when she had to start bracing herself.

Not having to worry, and not worrying were two different things. A distinction she was trying to meld into extinction. Not having to worry, and not worrying.

"I honestly don't know who provided the tree." Dale's words pulled her back to him. To her beer. The deck. A lighter feeling in her chest. "My first year on the beach, I didn't decorate. One morning, I came out to run and down by the water, but not so close that it risked meeting up with the tide, was this Christmas tree, all lit up. When all the decorations were taken down that year, that tree stood there until I went and got it. I've put it out every year since."

She loved the story. Truly just found goodness in it. "Maybe everyone chipped in," she offered.

He didn't respond, but she latched onto the idea. Preferring it to be true. For no reason other than that it sounded nice.

"Do you have any decorations from the past?" The question came of its own accord. She'd been debating asking him about it since Chelsea had called.

"No idea."

The response grabbed her attention so strongly, she turned to look at him. Wasn't sure what to say. And ended up with, "I had everything boxed up and stored it floor to ceiling. I've been slowly going through a bit of it this past week."

Until she got to the holiday decorations. "I've spent the past two Thanksgivings and Christmases at work. Hospitals don't close down for holidays. And not many people want to take those shifts." She had no idea what she was going to do with herself that year. She couldn't very well come back from sabbatical for just two days. Didn't work that way.

She didn't take offense when he didn't respond. It wasn't like there was a lot to say about facts. They just were. She took a couple of sips of beer. And a deep breath.

Watched the dogs on the beach.

"We were living in base housing and when two other couples we knew in the neighborhood offered to pack things up, I accepted their generosity. I rented a storage unit, and while I dealt with police and the funeral, they'd loaded it up, and there it is."

She wanted to be appalled. But wasn't. At all. And told him, "I'm not sure it helps, going through it. Except that the albatross around my neck feels a tiny bit lighter."

"How much did you get rid of?"

She gave a dry chuckle. "The boxes are still out there. No point in opening boxes of household goods, dishes, pans, blankets. Chelsea's are all still there. And I haven't tackled holiday decorations and Brent's personal things. I donated his clothes right after it happened. Along with his healthy organs. He'd already opted to be an organ donor."

She glanced over at him. Was surprised to see him looking at her. "We could…maybe do it together?" she asked. And then added, "Start with my three boxes of Brent's things and holiday decor, since they're right here on the beach, and then hit your storage unit. Just look inside, maybe. To see."

He didn't respond. But he didn't look away, either.

And Millie was glad she was there.

## *Chapter Six*

Scott and Iris passed, down by the water. They appeared to be in conversation, and didn't look up at Dale's deck. Whether by accident or design, he couldn't say. But he could guess. Juice and Magic had gone down to greet Angel and Morgan. His neighbors knew he was out. That he had company. And were respecting his right to privacy.

The conscious consideration and respect of his boundaries lightened the weight that had fallen on his spirits at the thought of hitting up his storage unit. Millie wasn't wrong. The unit was weighing him down. But had always been the brick wall he hit when he considered himself cured of the grief that had crippled him for a while. The unit was his point of "not ready."

It had been five years. Millie was finding the strength, the determination after just two.

Five years and he hadn't even driven by the place.

Had he just gotten lazy? Quit trying? Had he fallen into a place of accepting his half-alive existence? Passing his days with no forward-moving goals?

Letting life pass him by one wave at a time?

Was he wasting his life?

The barrage of questions disturbed him. He couldn't shrug them off. Block them.

And he had no answers for them, either.

Except one. He was not going to be less than his best self. He would not waste the breath, the mind, the awareness he'd been given. WG was testament to that.

Maybe he'd settled. Let WG do the work for him. And the rest...had he gotten lazy?

Complacent?

Millie hadn't said a word in too many minutes. She had to have seen Scott and Iris pass with their dogs. But, like him, she'd just sat there, sipping beer occasionally. Gaze turned toward the waves. He glanced over at her. Really looking at her. Beyond the beauty, the long dark hair that was loose around her shoulders, the perfectly toned body with all the right female curves. She was like him. Content to just sit on a Saturday night while others gathered and socialized.

But she was sitting with him. As he was with her. He wasn't a fanciful guy, but WG gave him insights now and then. The guy was knocking at his brain with an incessant message. One that Dale wasn't ready to examine. And yet, there it was.

Millie had been sent to him. For his sake, and for her own. Their meeting wasn't a mistake. They needed each other in their current space and time. They were facing the same roadblock to life. He needed her. But she needed him, too, and that's what hit him hardest. And what took his focus.

How did he help her? Had to be more to it than jogging silently and making beer.

He had to know more.

"How long did you know him?" He'd known Lyla a couple of years before they married.

"My whole life. We grew up in the same neighborhood."

The answer shocked him, though he wasn't sure why it should have. "Where?" he asked, intrigued at the picture she was painting for WG. Two kids from the same neighborhood...making it? Until tragedy struck of course. But...what were the odds of that? WG looked for more. Putting twists like witness protection, or criminals on the run to what should have been a sunshiney tale.

"Alabama." She named a town he'd never heard of. Followed it with, "Population, 2201." He was watching her, not the waves. Her face was still facing beachward. But her tone seemed easy enough as she answered his questions. There didn't seem to be tension tightening her face or shoulders.

So he asked, "Do you still have family there?"

And if so, why in the hell was she in Southern California, sitting on a deck with him?

Her nod was slow and deep.

"Why are you here?" He didn't get it. And needed to. How could he hold up his part of the bargain—them helping each other—if he didn't know what he was lifting?

He wasn't prepared when she turned those blue eyes on him, showing him a shimmer of pain he wasn't ever going to forget.

"Everyone knows me as Brent and Millie. Or Millie and Brent, depending on which family member or friend you might be talking to. I'm not that person anymore."

That shut him up. He had nothing. Was second-guessing his purpose in her life, figuring WG for having gotten it wrong. Or himself for imposing his own thoughts on his muse.

"We'd moved away, temporarily," Millie said then, softly, facing forward again. Dale listened, but didn't respond. It was almost as though she was talking to herself. Reminiscing privately, and yet he wanted to hear every word. "Brent's success...he'd been offered some lucrative sponsorships...our lives had changed so much. We came out here because the weather is balmier all year, and found a whole new life outside the world where everyone knew everything about us. We intended to go back..."

The words just stopped. As though she'd hit that wall that was so much a part of him. The one that saved him, kept him separated from a pain that wasn't bearable. A wall that seemed to be growing thinner, though he hadn't really noticed that fact until Millie had appeared on the beach.

He wasn't entirely resistant to the idea of finding more in the years ahead. Had no idea what that more could be, but if it was there, it was his duty to reach for it. Or, at the very least, be open to the possibility.

His bottle was almost empty. He got up, went inside, grabbed two more. If she didn't want a second, he'd drink a third. It was Saturday night. And it was the three percent stuff.

Setting the newly uncapped bottle down by Millie's chair, he settled back. Dusk was falling—time for WG to kick it into gear. Dale didn't feel like working. The book wasn't due for several months. He was relaxed.

And it felt good.

Millie was still sitting there. Sipping from a second bottle of beer. She'd talked about home. About who she'd been. And she hadn't exploded into little pieces. Or fallen into despair. The pain was there. She'd accepted that it would always be a part of her. But for the first time in two years, it didn't define her. Or propel her every movement.

"What about your family?" she asked, a good ten minutes after Dale had delivered the second beer. "And Lyla's?"

He shook his head. She thought in denial of her question. Refusing to answer. And understood that, too. Not even Chelsea knew that she was from Alabama. Or that she and Brent had been together since they were toddlers.

"There isn't any to speak of."

A nice way of saying he didn't want to talk about it. Had he been concerned that she was going to push the issue? He didn't know her very well yet.

Yet? Where in the hell had that come from? As though she was expecting him to get to know her better?

Yeah. The answer settled on her softly. She was expecting that. And didn't know what to do with the realization. Her expectations had died with Brent. Or so she'd thought.

"I grew up in foster care," he told her. "Decent homes, kind people, just not in any one place for more than a year or two. Lyla's parents raised her, but her father was abusive. Not to her. But to her mother. Yet she stayed with him. Lyla couldn't. She left home at eighteen and never looked back."

Wow. Such a completely different world than the one she'd known. And probably explained why Dale was such a loner. In addition to his grief. She didn't have close relationships, but she'd been in the world interacting with others all day every day since Brent's death. She'd been isolated from the people around her, and yet, they'd provided the purpose that had supported her, emotionally and mentally, too.

"Do they know?" She asked the question quietly. Letting it fall softly into the stillness. Putting it out there in case he wanted to be a part of it. But not requiring that he do so.

"They were at the funeral."

She waited for more. And let his silence fill in the blanks.

"I'm assuming you went home for Brent's?" he asked a few minutes later.

"Yeah, but I didn't stay more than a few days. I couldn't. I'd have succumbed to the grief completely." And she wasn't doing that.

At least, she hoped she wasn't. Not anymore. Staying in Alabama hadn't been the answer, but burying herself in work, taking on double shifts, volunteering in a local free clinic when she wasn't on duty, had most definitely been succumbing.

But, she had to believe, saving herself, too. What she had left of her.

"Hey." Dale's tone drew her gaze to his, and he said, "You want to get dinner sometime? Out?"

She blinked. Drew a blank. And then had only one word presenting. "Yes."

Dale didn't see Millie on Sunday. He and Juice were outside a good part of the day, while he sat on the deck working on an article he was writing about the sea turtle that had washed up on shore in front of him and Millie. He'd been following the creature's progress and had photos the fishery department had sent him of the girl swimming back out to sea.

But as the day wore on, he found himself screening the beach down her way a lot. Over and over. He'd see her Monday morning, for their jog.

Unless their conversation the night before had gotten too personal for her. Bitten too deeply into the skin that was newly growing around her ripped-apart heart.

He'd asked her to dinner. She'd accepted. But neither had mentioned the fact that they hadn't set a time for that to happen.

Maybe she wasn't ready. He wouldn't have thought he was.

But off and on all day, he'd thought about that accepted invitation hanging out there.

Scott stopped by on his way down to Sage's for dinner. Iris was on an overnight whale photo shoot several miles out in the ocean. The lawyer sat in Millie's chair—the mental moniker a statement in itself as Scott had occupied the seat countless more times than their new beach resident had—and talked about the changing tide. An upcoming case he was handling. And the dogs'—Juice, Angel and Morgan—antics on the beach.

As usual he asked no questions.

And he made no mention of having seen Millie Monroe on Dale's deck the night before. He didn't bring up the woman at all. Not even to share that his new neighbor seemed to be fitting in on Ocean Breeze. Or not.

All of which pleased Dale, but had him thinking about the woman even more. What if she'd gone home the night before and had a breakdown? Was in emotional trouble?

Who would know?

Not his business. Except that...there was Juice. And the way the service dog had tended to Millie the night she'd told Dale about Brent's death. Staying right by her side, rather than running down to the beach to play with the other dogs. Nudging her hand over and over.

Juice had told him something that night. Millie was dealing with panic attacks. Anxiety. On a high enough level to alert a dog trained to notice such things.

A dog who, by some miracle, had been spared the bullet that had killed his owner. But had stayed with her until police arrived.

Dale had heard the details by telephone.

He also knew, from his own experience, how important it was to be able to deal with the aftermath in peace. In his own way. And time.

He had no business inserting himself in Millie's process.

She'd accepted his dinner invitation. Had thrown herself fully into the process of making beer in his kitchen. He might be suffering from five years of emotional density, but maybe he'd been right the night before, after all. Maybe they'd been brought together by design, as much by the coincidence of her knowing Chelsea and needing a place to stay right when the artist had been wanting someone to move in and care for her dog during the months she'd be with her sister.

Nights were the hardest. He had WG to spend them with. But the evenings that Millie had spent with him—he'd slept through the night.

Dale was sitting alone on his deck when Scott passed back by on his way home with Morgan and Angel. Dale watched Juice run down to greet his friends, and then return to the deck. But instead of turning his attention back to the moon shining silver rays along the waves, his gaze followed Scott's back down the beach.

When he realized that he wanted to be the guy walking down toward Millie's cottage, he got up, clicked his fingers for Juice, and headed out in the darkness.

He had no idea what he was going to do when he got there. If he'd approach her place, or just see lights on and satisfy himself that she was there and having an okay Sunday night.

He just couldn't accept the idea of allowing himself to grow lazy.

Millie had had a decent day. She'd rearranged some of her belongings in the closet. Finished putting things in drawers and the cubbies she'd bought—finding freedom in making choices by herself.

And sad, too.

She got through most of the day without feeling as though half of her was missing. Without conscious thoughts of Brent.

She did some wood burning. Then added color to the crudely inscribed vase of sunflowers. And left the unfinished piece in the room that held Chelsea's desk and Millie's computer—one that also now contained the eight-foot-long craft table she hadn't had out in years.

Making herself a chef salad and homemade bread for dinner, she'd washed it down with tea livened up with a drop of peach extract. Was pleased with the result. Ate on the back deck. Sharing bits and pieces with Magic. The dog liked cucumbers.

And she wondered about Dale's storage unit. Wishing

she knew how to help him get there. To find whatever was waiting, and deal with everything he was avoiding.

Because...that was her...the one who saw others suffering and had to jump in and save the day. Or, maybe, she was good at helping people because she had a talent for it. Like Brent's had been running.

Running. She felt like she'd been doing nothing else for the past two years. Running away. Filling every conscious hour with work so she didn't have to deal with broken dreams.

Or do the real work—finding her new place in the world. Forging a life very different from the one she'd envisioned. Reframing her sense of self.

The past many weeks on the beach seemed to have brought some clarity. Meeting Dale had certainly done so.

Feeling more than just a hint of the peace she'd sensed and witnessed in her beach mate, Millie went out to start a fire in the stone fireplace on the back deck. But didn't ignite the flame. She wasn't ready for fire.

Just more calm quietude. Sitting on the top step of the deck, she felt Magic settle down on the treated board just behind her. The dog's warm weight pressing up against her back felt good. And she thought of Dale with Juice. Of how much he tended to his companion. And how the service dog never let him out of his sight.

She didn't have a whole heart to give to another partnership in life, but what about a human-canine relationship? Magic was testimony to the fact that she could be good at that. Having the big girl around had brought no hardship in terms of her healing. And some measurable progress, once she thought about it. Sharing life with another living being was still possible. A being who counted on her.

She needed a dog.

One of her own that she wouldn't have to give back.

It was up to her. If she wanted a dog, she could have one. And so she would. The decision was made. With a certainty that confounded her. When Chelsea returned, Millie was going to get a dog.

A rescue. She had to save a dog's life. And let the creature save her. The idea fit her perfectly.

So there. She had a concrete goal. The start of her new life...

And...wait...was that movement down there? Juice? With Dale? Heart pounding, she stood, wondering what was wrong. Before she could form another thought, Magic had brushed past her down to the sand and was galloping toward man and dog.

She didn't join them. Didn't want to push. But didn't resume sitting, either. She was there, waiting, if Dale wanted to chat. No pressure if he didn't.

At least, she wanted there to be none. Truth was, she wanted to see him. To know, first and foremost that he was okay. And then just to hear his voice.

To not be so alone.

The thought was alarming. But the second she saw Dale head up toward her, she started taking steps in his direction. Encased in the night's darkness, her desire to be with him right then was allowed to win out over everything else she knew.

The things she'd never have, or be, again, didn't shine so brightly under the moon's glow.

## *Chapter Seven*

She was outside. She'd seen him. He had to go up. Couldn't be that he was checking on her. People like them...just felt more set apart when others looked on them with sympathy. Felt they needed looking after her.

What business could he have to discuss that couldn't wait until their morning jog?

He had no plan. And he always had a plan. For everything. Plans were the way to maintain control of one's life.

His world careening out of control again was not acceptable.

She was six feet away. Looking at him. Time for him to state his business. He opened his mouth and said, "I was thinking about you."

She nodded. "I've been thinking about you, too. It's nice, isn't it, to have someone who sails in the same make of boat? You know, so there's a sounding board for challenges that come up."

With a tilt of his head, he studied her. Full on. Had she seen through him? Did it matter if she had?

Could it be that simple? He'd walked down. No big deal?

"I wrote an article today about the sea turtle," he told her. "Already sent it to my agent." He wasn't speaking to report on his his work life, but to give an update about an incident she'd been involved in. Seemed like she should know he'd taken it further.

"Let me know if it sells," she said, with a small smile forming. "I'll buy a copy."

Hands in the pockets of his shorts, he nodded. Wanted to tell her that he knew it would sell. Just wasn't sure to who. But he kept quiet. His success, such as it was, was his business. He didn't want it to change how others on the beach looked at him. Treated him.

He was the guy they called on to put their dogs out to pee for them while they were busy off living their lives. He liked it that way. The one who ran for food in times of ill health.

The one who'd been called on to help Scott change his pants—to basically do it for the guy—when he'd been fresh out of surgery. The lawyer had drawn the line at letting Iris—who'd been just a good friend to him at the time—get that intimate.

"I'm getting a dog." Millie's announcement came as she was watching Juice and Magic chase each other in the sand.

The announcement pulled Dale out of his trip of self-absorption. A negative by-product of living privately. He nodded again. Wanted to talk to her about her decision. Cocked his head toward the shore and said, "You want to walk a bit?"

When she fell into step beside him, he asked her, "Do you know what kind of dog?" Each breed had its own strengths and super abilities. And her wanting a dog… had just hit a chord in him. One that fell too much in line with his earlier thoughts regarding her and Juice to be just coincidental.

"A rescue," she said. "I heard about a shelter at work a couple of months ago. The parent of one of our patients had just started volunteering there. She told me about dogs who'd been purposely left behind when someone moved away. About those who were homeless due to the death or incapacitation of their owners. Some that were just dropped off because they were no longer wanted." She paused then said, "Who knows, I might get two."

He listened, appreciating her intent. Admiring it. And thinking beyond it, too.

"You thinking large or smaller?"

"Smaller than Magic," she said. "I'm super fond of her, would keep her if I could, but starting fresh, I'd rather have a dog I could pick up and put in the car if it was ever injured and I had to get it help quickly."

Dale's appreciation for his new neighbor rose a couple of more notches. The woman thought like he did. With her being a nurse, it made sense.

"Rescues are often mixed breeds," he told her. "But if you could get a poodle, or King Cavalier mix, they might be good for you." He had to speak up to be heard over the surf.

They'd reached the shore and were strolling slowly along in the sand. The breeze cooled his skin, and he welcomed the sensation. Mixing Millie with darkness, his waves and a stroll were making him a bit warm in a way that wasn't fitting the occasion.

He wanted to be around the woman. He wasn't interested in starting more than a like-soul connection with her. Been there. Done that. Over.

"Good for me, how?" She'd asked the question seconds before. He was too busy getting himself in order to choose his words as carefully as he might have done.

"They make good psychiatric service dogs."

She stopped. "Psychiatric? You think I need mental assistance?" He hardly recognized her tone. Authoritative with a hint of hurt weaving through it.

"No. Although, if you did, it wouldn't make me think any less of you or want to be around you any less."

Looking up at him, she said, "You want to be around me?"

*Danger, Will Robinson.* A quote from an ancient television show one of his foster father's had been fond of came back to him. Choosing his words slowly, he said, "Isn't that obvious? I'm here and I wouldn't be if I didn't want to be." Then added, "You're here, too."

She nodded, started walking again, and said, "Juice is a service dog."

The poodle had still been wearing his vest outside the house when Dale had first moved onto Ocean Breeze. He'd assumed that neighbors had noticed, though no one had ever spoken to him about Juice's abilities.

"He is," he told her. Ready to blurt out more, but not wanting to sabotage the conversation. He used to be so good at conversing with women. With men, too, but he'd never been so twisted up choosing words with a woman in his life.

Could be his chosen solitary way of life had had another negative effect. One he hadn't foreseen.

"Do you have PTSD?" Millie's question came as softly as the roar of the waves would allow. Sounding like the caring medical professional she was. One trained in how to ask personal health questions. And gifted with the ability to do so.

"No." And then, to forestall more awkwardness, said, "He was Lyla's dog. I bought him for her before I left for overseas duty."

He felt her swift intake of breath more than he heard it. Their arms had brushed as they'd moved to get away from an incoming wave larger than the rest.

"You said others cleaned out your house…were you on tour when…"

She let the words drop. He appreciated the gesture. And said, "Yes."

Dale felt almost strangely lightheaded for a second. Having told someone about the hell that raged inside him every single day…what happened next? With the deep truth set free. Those who'd known him, who'd known, were all out of his life. He hadn't kept in touch with any of them. Thinking it better to start afresh.

To bear his burden on his own.

"I'm sure you know this, but it wouldn't have been any…easier…if you'd been there. I was standing two feet from Brent when he collapsed. And I'm a nurse."

One who'd been with him before the race, living with him, training with him…facts she'd previously given him presented themselves to Dale with precision. And his "if I'd been there," suddenly lost a small bit of its power to hold him underground for the rest of his life.

"I might have been able…" He stopped midstream when Millie nudged him with her elbow and shook her head.

That was it. No words. And his burden was no longer just his. It was shared with someone else who knew.

And that made a difference.

\* \* \*

Millie had to say something. To pull him back from the vestiges of darkness that could consume a body if left untended. Dogs. They'd been talking about dogs. He'd had advice.

Because of Juice. He thought something was wrong with Millie. That she needed service. The same kind his wife had needed apparently.

"Why did Lyla need a service dog?" she asked the question in the way she could.

"Growing up in an abusive household like she did—one from which she couldn't escape because she was very well loved, cared for, never abused and because neither parent would admit to the abuse, or press charges—she developed what I suspect would have been...a lifelong battle with panic attacks. Until Juice." Shaking his head, he said, "It eats at me that her last moments on earth were violent ones. That she died at the hand of it."

Panic attacks. She'd think about that revelation later. "No, Dale," she said then. "If, as you described, she was caught in crossfire, she wouldn't have been conscious of the violence. If she was conscious at all, she'd have been in shock. Her last moments were spent with the dog who brought her comfort. And companionship."

She knew how to help others through grief-stricken moments. Parents who were blaming themselves for birthing sick children. Or who were wishing they could take their child's suffering upon themselves.

The nurse just couldn't heal herself.

Apparently.

Dale thought she needed help.

"Juice brought you comfort the other night." The words came at her out of the blue. After more than a minute of walking in silence. "He was working, Millie. I recognized his behavior. He's trained to sense when someone is suffering from anxiety. And he tends to it accordingly. I can tell you when you were over the attack, as well. It was when he trotted down the steps and went to play on the beach with his friends."

She listened intently. Had no response to give to him on the matter. Poodles and King Cavaliers. Not likely candidates for a rescue shelter. But there would be other breeds. Mostly mixed, from what she'd understood. She might do some research. See what training entailed. It wasn't like she'd been planning to run off the next day and bring home a new member of the household. She still had months with Magic.

"You've got an orange and gold splotch on your shirt." Dale's voice broke into her reverie a second time. Glancing down she saw his finger close to a spot on her shirt that was in direct line of the moon's glow. And drew in a long clear breath.

"I unpacked my art supplies," she said then. "I hadn't yet done so after the move from Alabama, with all the traveling around I did with Brent."

"And something had opened? Or had a leak?"

Good. Art supplies. She appreciated the conversation. "Nope," she told him, feeling better again, stronger. "I started a new project. I always was a messy creator."

Always was. Still was.

She'd lost parts of herself. But not all of them.

The realization, and so the moment, was a good one.

Dale was ready to get home. To be alone. Unchallenged. He acknowledged to himself that he could be running away. But allowed the need, anyway.

He'd asked Millie about the types of art she did because he'd been starting to suffocate under the intensity of the conversation, and suspected she could be, too. He'd also asked because he was truly interested. Being a creator himself, he enjoyed hearing about others' processes. Usually on the internet. Reading about them. From strangers to whom he'd never spoken.

Not in person.

The silence that had fallen between them as they headed back up the beach toward her place was a kinder one than had lain heavily in the midst of earlier conversation. As the end of their walk drew close, he was oddly loath to leave, after just needing just that.

He needed something more. If he walked away, they might lose some of what they'd had. Because if it was too hard...it stopped their individual processes.

Or maybe, he just stopped his own. And didn't want to anymore. Not with her.

"So that dinner," he blurted, as they passed Scott and Iris's cottage. "I was thinking seafood. I know of a place right on the ocean..." He stopped. Clarified. "I read about it. Saw some photos. Have never been there, but would like to give it a try. You up for it?"

Not a date. Just an excursion to check out a place that could be awful. And might be...nice.

"Yes." Pretty unequivocal. Just like her response when he'd suggested dinner in the first place. He still had something, apparently. Enough social awareness to be worthy of a chance.

"When?"

She chuckled then. A tired sound. "Doesn't much matter to me. I'm free all day every day," she told him. Then, more softly added, "Doing the hardest work of my life."

He understood. And wanted to be a part of it. Needed to be. Because he knew he had good to offer her on that particular journey. "How about Tuesday night?"

Monday had been on the tip of his tongue. But they'd been together Saturday night, and Sunday...the hermit in him changed the words on him at the last second.

"Tuesday's good," she said, then added, "See you in the morning," and headed catty-corner up the beach toward her house.

Without a backward glance.

Dale watched her, though. With his hand on Juice's head, he stood there until she and Magic were up on her deck and out of sight.

It was only as he glanced down at his boy, when he saw his own fingers, that he realized that they were moving. And that Juice wasn't. He was sitting still. His gaze, not on their departing friends, but on Dale.

The boy was working.

And probably had been for all the years they'd been alone together.

Dale had thought himself cured. Over the past as much as he'd ever be. Well-adjusted and content with his life. Satisfied with who he was and what he'd grown to be.

Seemingly pleased with the future he had stretching out in front of him. Right there on Ocean Breeze. Alone. But not really. He'd found family. As much of one as he'd ever known.

But as he scratched Juice behind the ears, and headed back up to his cottage, Dale felt as though the dog was talking to him. Man to man.

Asking him one question. Which lingered there.
Without answer.
Just question.
What if there was more?

She couldn't just go out to dinner with him. She'd responded affirmatively when he'd asked. Because she wanted to try out the restaurant with him. To be a friend and accompany him so that he'd go. And because trying different tastes was one of the pleasures she still was able to experience in full. But meeting up just to go out to eat…reeked too much of date behavior for Millie.

She told herself that people who were just friends ate out together all the time. But every time she pictured herself getting in a vehicle with Dale, just the two of them, sitting together at a table for two in a restaurant, she grew anxious. Nothing like an actual panic attack, as Dale had attributed to her the other night. She recognized the signs and got herself out of dangerous territory before it took over her ability to rationalize.

Everyone who could feel got scared now and then. Even the strongest and bravest people in the world.

Yet…wouldn't it be nice if she had a companion, like Juice, who could warn her before the insidious sense of lack of power, of fear, punched her in the gut?

And…she couldn't go on a date. But if they stopped for dinner on their way home from, say, completing a task?

She didn't put it to Dale quite that way. Didn't want him to think she was misconstruing his invitation to check out a restaurant with him into more than it was. She wasn't. She knew he wasn't any more open to having a relationship than she was. Went with the territory. How could you give what you no longer had?

The question she'd been up against anytime she'd tried to resume any semblance of a normal life since Brent's death. And the reason she'd accepted the response, too. You couldn't. There were many things she'd never do again.

And it still didn't diminish—if anything, it intensified—her need to make it clear to herself that she was not going on a date. Because...for a brief second there, out on the beach, she might have wanted it to be one.

So on Monday morning, as they came to the end of their run, she was panting a bit as she said, "How about tomorrow afternoon we hit up your storage unit? If you're open to it. I just know it's helped me to finally get through some stuff. Feels more like I'm accepting and moving to a new me."

He jogged in place, with Juice looking up between the two of them. "I've got three years on you," Dale told her. "I've long since accepted and made a new life..."

She caught the long glance Juice turned on him. And an instant replay flash of him telling her that the dog's reaction had let him know that she'd been struggling the other night. And, watching Juice, she said, "So why is the storage unit still sitting there full?"

She wasn't arguing that he was further along in the process of moving on. His three years gave him a huge head start. But if she could help him get even further... it was the least she could do after all the steps forward he'd already helped her take. Even if the assistance had been unknowingly on his part.

He'd stopped jogging. Was standing there eyeing her

intently. His brown gaze seeming to connect with her in a new way. Deeper. More personally. She didn't understand what was happening, but she couldn't look away.

When he finally spoke, his words were oddly unsettling as well. "I don't have an answer for that," he said.

The admission didn't sound like him. Throwing her off balance. She didn't know what to do with it. And slid back into nurse mode—as she always did when she needed to feel like she had control of her life. To get perspective. And feel...safe.

"So maybe we take a drive over, and see if there's one there," she suggested gently. "I won't push, Dale, but what if it's okay, and you just don't know it yet?"

She'd struggled going through memories left from her and Brent, but not as badly as she'd expected to do. She'd been slowly learning how to hang on to all those years in a separate place. And letting go of them in other parts of her.

His gaze narrowed. He stared at her for long seconds and then with a shrug said, "Whatever. If you want to, that's fine."

Something inside her settled. Visiting his storage unit wasn't about what she wanted, and she figured they both knew that. But Dale was trusting her enough to give her suggestion a shot.

Which, right then, meant...the world to her.

And dinner afterward would be a way to slide back into current reality, to the half lives they'd been left with. Which *was* what she wanted. Because a step-back dinner with a friend was the only kind of night out she could have.

## *Chapter Eight*

Dale did not want to go to his storage unit. At all. Not in the least. He'd just as soon pay someone to empty it, dispose of the contents and end the lease. And considered doing so on and off all day and night on Monday. He searched moving companies. Charity organizations that offered pickup of goods. Decided that was the way to go, and was narrowing down which organization Lyla would likely choose, were she able to give her opinion, when he saw a list of the items the charities needed, and the few things they could not accept.

Which then stopped him cold.

How did he know if any of those items were in the storage unit? Furthermore, some places needed things to be boxed for pickup. Others couldn't accept small loose items, but would gladly haul away other unboxed items.

They all wanted to know the size of the donation. Some had to know if there was any furniture, and if so, how many rooms' worth.

The questions made sense. Those who came to collect would need to know what size truck they needed, and how much manpower would be required to complete the job.

And therein lay his problem. Dale had no idea what was boxed. Or not. Or even what furniture was in storage and what had been given away to those who'd helped clean out his house. He'd told the marine families that had helped that they could have whatever furniture they could use.

He knew he'd never be wanting to use it again. He'd see Lyla, smell her, anytime he went near any of it. She was the one who'd occupied the home they'd moved into shortly before he'd shipped out. He'd wanted her on base while he was gone, where she'd have fellow marine wives with husbands deployed to talk to. Socialize with.

And where she'd be safer.

Right. She'd been off base for a doctor's appointment when she'd been shot. Because she hadn't wanted to switch from the doctor she'd been seeing from the time she'd been in high school.

Had she driven from their previous home, she wouldn't have been at the gas station where she'd stopped to fill up when a robbery had been taking place.

But there could have been another crime, someplace else. How could he possibly have been everywhere at once for the rest of their lives, preventing danger from happening to her?

Millie's words, "I was standing two feet from Brent when he collapsed. And I'm a nurse," rang through his mind. She hadn't been able to save her husband's life, and she'd been right there. With a medical degree.

What if he'd been with Lyla when the place was robbed? What would he have done—stopped a stray bullet he didn't know was coming with his bare hand?

Jump in front of something he had no idea was headed their way?

It wasn't like there'd been a barrage of shots. There'd

been one. It had missed its target and the shooter ran. Not even Juice had been aware of the danger before it was too late.

Sitting out on his deck Monday night with his computer, thoughts hit one after another. Lining up in a row for him to peruse as they presented themselves.

He accepted their legitimacy. Didn't much change anything else about him. He'd dared to love. He'd lost.

And he had a storage unit filled with he didn't know what, crated he didn't know how. But would be held fully responsible for the contents.

He had to go. Find out what was there. How it was packaged.

Then he could move forward with a charity choice. And give it all away.

Millie was expecting an eight foot by ten foot cement unit with some kind of garage door closure. Knowing Dale, even as little as she did, she knew the unit would have climate control. And be in a secure area with top-rate security.

Sitting in Dale's SUV, with Juice in the second row behind them, his head resting on the console, close enough for his nose to touch her elbow, she paid attention to the little things. How many black cars were on the road, as opposed to blue. How many red lights. The hem of her lightweight green cotton capris. A string was hanging down.

She didn't have her sewing machine unpacked yet. Had to be in one of the boxes in the garage. Along with the Christmas decorations.

Glancing at her sandals, she knew that, like him, she

should have worn running shoes. His shorts and polo shirt were like any of the others she'd seen him in on his deck.

She'd tied her hair back, at least, so it would be out of the way. And had purposely not made up her face. Why bother? They were going to be doing manual labor and then grabbing something to eat before heading back to the beach and their separate lives there.

The shadow on his chin was growing darker. She only noticed because Juice had nudged his shoulder, and she'd glanced over at the movement. He hadn't said a word since she'd climbed in beside him. The dog's nudge gave her a hint as to why.

He was struggling with their outing. She'd figured as much. Hadn't wanted to push herself into his process. But, thinking of what might help her, she blurted, "You ever think of growing a beard?" Distraction. It helped kids who were facing injections, stitches or worse.

Counting cars, focusing on colors was her own particular brand of it.

"I've had one on and off for years," he told her, sounding...pretty much like himself. "Just shaved it off over the summer..."

The question might have helped him. It hadn't been good for her. She was sitting there picturing the man with a full beard, getting a little tingly as she let a full body image of him form in her mind's eye. And before she could get her gaze to focus outward, on black cars, he'd signaled a turn and, stopping to type in some codes, entered through the huge iron gate that opened in front of him.

And took a couple of pretty quick turns as though he knew exactly where he was going.

"You've been here before?" He'd said he didn't know what was inside his unit.

He shrugged. Then said, "A few times."

But...

"I've just never unlocked the unit or looked inside."

He made the admission as though he'd been mentioning that he used liquid hand soap instead of solid. And the words, even the ease with which they came, stabbed at Millie's heart. In a way she'd never have predicted could happen.

Deep empathy, she knew. Strong because it was feeding off an answering pain inside her.

He pulled up to a garage-like door. Parked outside it. And without thought or even any consideration for him or the moment, she grabbed the unit key that he pulled out of a cubby in his vehicle and got out.

If he followed, he did. If not, she wouldn't blame him. He'd opened his door but hadn't yet joined her.

"I'm just going to open it." She raised her voice loud enough that he'd be able to hear. Made note that Juice was sitting in the vehicle right where she'd been.

The lock was caked with disuse. Millie wasn't sure she'd be able to get the key all the way in, but on the third try, shoved with all her might. She didn't want him to open himself up as much as he was doing and end on a fail. Not of her doing.

After a short tussle to get the key to move once inserted, Millie managed to unlock the door. Then, grabbing the handle, she yanked upward until the metal frame was over her head. Turning to put both hands on the bottom of the closure and push, she stopped instead, staring.

The place was larger than she'd expected. Three times

as large. And filled almost full. Meticulously. Furniture on one side, set up so that one could see every piece, get to every piece, in the event a single item was needed. And on the other, stacks of boxes of all sizes, every one of them bearing the same big labels, with typed and printed lists of items inside.

Wow. Just...

"Ask a group of marines and their wives to complete a task, and this is what you get," Dale said, too closely behind her. She hadn't been aware that he'd exited his SUV. Before she could respond, move away, he said, "I'm pretty sure I didn't thank them nearly enough."

Hearing the tone in his voice, seeing his life laid out before her, she felt tears prick her eyes.

He didn't enter the space. Just stood there with her. Staring. And Millie got out of her own world and into help mode. "I'm certain you'd have done the same for any one of them," she said, moving toward the furniture side of the room. Whether the big pieces would be less overwhelming to him than boxes with long lists of items, she didn't know. She just had to get a little distance between her and Dale. To breathe. And remember who she was. Who he was. Why they were there.

It was an exercise in moving forward. She was helping him to let go of what had been and bring what was left into what would be. Period.

The pieces before her were clean. In light grays and patterns with grays and whites, mostly. A faux leather couch and loveseat. Didn't appear that they reclined. End tables that looked newish, but not overly expensive. A high-top kitchen table with four backed stools turned legs up on top. A queen-size mattress and box springs in zippered plastic bags against the wall, with a bed frame, in pieces tied together, standing next to it. There was more. Her eyes blurred, and Millie had to turn away. She had no business taking in Dale's personal life to such an extent. She should vacate. Leave him alone in the space, as she'd been alone in her garage, going through some things over the past month.

And shouldn't press him to stay long. "It took me a week to get through the first box," she said aloud, turning toward the door, and noticing Juice standing outside, looking in, but not entering. "It got a little faster with the second one." She finished more slowly, heading toward the dog.

Not at all trained in service animal technique or protocol. Was Juice working? Could she touch the dog?

Dale was no help. He'd moved over to the boxes, stacked from floor to ceiling. Was moving slowly along them, his gaze seemingly focused on the lists they each contained.

A positive sign. A great sign!

Taking heart, she stepped outside the unit, and taking her cue from the dog who knew him so well, she just stood next to Juice. Prepared to wait for however many hours it took.

To be there if needed. But not in the way.

As she did so, she felt a change come over her, too. She might not ever be who she was, but she was still whole enough to tune in to another individual, on a personal basis. To be there for him.

And that was good.

Dale made mental notes of lists, as he'd done when sizing up the potential enemy on charts, in film clips and on radar during his time in the service. He took stock of supplies, cataloguing what he had and how it might be of use. He breathed in deeply trying to notice any scents that could be lingering.

He did not call Juice to his side.

But when, out of the corner of his eye, he noticed Millie standing with the seventy-five-pound poodle, he said, "I'm not sure about bringing him in here. He was Lyla's dog. If gets any whiff that reminds him of her…" He let the words trail off. He didn't want Juice to have to mourn a second time. Or to run around looking for someone he'd never find.

Dale should have left the service dog at home. Had thought it best to have Juice at the restaurant, for Millie's sake, just in case. She'd been skittish with him ever since he'd issued the dinner invitation. Not meeting his gaze at all on Monday except to issue what could only have been called a challenge to him about visiting his storage unit first.

As though, if he didn't agree, she'd back out of dinner. And issued in such a way that he was left with a sense that she'd expected him not to agree.

Which was why he had, of course. He was man enough to admit the truth to himself.

*Wedding Photos.* The words glared out at him from a box in the middle of a stack and halfway down the row.

He couldn't just callously leave them there to be picked up by some charity organization that would have little choice but to destroy them. It wasn't like they could be sold.

Grabbing the two boxes off the top of the one he needed—both marked pillows—Dale had the box out of the stack within a minute. Leaving it in the aisle, he moved on to the next stack.

There were other things listed along with the photos in the box he'd pulled. All personal items. Mostly Lyla's. Some he didn't recognize. The thought gave him pause. But didn't stop him. He was helping Millie get to dinner. And would be soon benefitting some people in need, too.

He should have thought of donating to a charity earlier.

Standing there, he knew exactly which organization he was going to call. A national hotline designated strictly to help victims of domestic violence. Lyla hadn't been one directly. But what no one had seen—except Dale and Juice—was that the girl who'd been loved, adored and well cared for by her parents, had suffered every day from the abuse going on behind closed doors in her home.

If the group didn't have a local donation center, he'd arrange to have someone conduct the sale on their behalf. And then gift any remaining items to a local women's shelter.

Millie and Juice hadn't moved much. He'd detected Millie's hand landing gently on top of Juice's head, but hadn't noticed, with his peripheral glances, any constant or nervous movement of her fingers. More like she was comforting the dog.

Because the demon Dale was facing, while trying to slay him, wasn't getting anywhere near her. She'd already won the battle. On her own. Over the past month.

At least somewhat. There were still a lot of boxes in her garage. Three, he recalled, that had her husband's things. And Christmas décor. She'd suggested maybe they do them together…

"When are we going to tackle boxes in your garage?" he called out.

Her response back was immediate. "Another day."

He almost smiled at the authoritative tone. It was like in the past couple of weeks Millie had begun to blossom right before his eyes.

It was a thought that reoccurred to Dale as he sat across from Millie on a patio overlooking the ocean later that night. He could swear that her blue eyes were shining brighter. Losing the dullness that had first attracted his attention as it mirrored what he saw in the mirror every morning.

A lack of anticipation for what lay ahead. More like an acceptance of whatever it would be.

But... "You were right," he told her, as they waited for the local crab they'd ordered to be prepared. "I should have gone through the storage unit a long time ago. It does feel better." It wasn't like there was any sadness lifted, or happiness added. But the sadness hadn't increased, either, and the load seemed a little less heavy.

"Wait until you open the boxes," she warned him. He had a total of three. Not purposely matching the number she had waiting. Just had had items listed that a charity couldn't use. All three were in the back of his SUV.

Juice, who'd been lying with his service vest on at the side of the table, between the two of them, rose, and nudged Dale's hand. He petted the boy, scratching him behind the ears as Juice liked, and took a sip of the wine their waiter had recommended to go with the dinner they'd chosen. One glass. He was driving. Never more than one.

"One of the boxes is going to be a pleasure," he told her. "I might need to update connections, or buy a new unit, but the entire box is the only collection I ever purposely cultivated." He was still shaking his head over the fact that he hadn't thought about it in years.

Millie leaned forward, a gleam of humor in her eyes. "Let me guess, fishing lures," she said. Then shook her head. "No, you wouldn't need a unit or connections for that. And all three of the boxes are pretty big..."

She wasn't ever going to guess. And he felt a bit sappy having even brought the matter up. Except that...she was Millie. A like soul. Not someone he was trying to impress or entertain. Not a date.

"It's DVDs of every season of old television shows. Some from before I was born." He was going to stop there, but figured, rather than have her draw her own conclusions at the admission, he'd just go ahead and put it out there. "Growing up as I did, the shows were like family to me. No matter what household I lived in, as long as I had a television, I could hook up with the family I knew. Or be able to genuinely laugh out loud even when I was living with people I didn't yet know."

He met her gaze; there was no reason not to. He wasn't ashamed of who he'd been, nor of who he was. The sheen of tears in Millie's eyes caught him. If she was feeling sorry for him...

Shaking her head, she gave him an odd smile and said, "It's getting weird, how you make me feel okay." Then said, "I'd love to take a look at your collection. Over the past two years, I've streamed every show I could find, looking for those that helped me escape enough to fall asleep, and would still be there if I woke up, to lull me back to sleep. I have the television on all night. With shows on autoplay. And... I didn't think I'd ever admit that to anyone. I didn't think anyone would get it."

Dale was the one having trouble with an unexpected stab of emotion, then. Swallowing with difficulty, he smiled at her and said, "I'll make a deal with you. We get through the pertinent boxes in your garage, and then have a watch-in."

She started to nod, then her gaze narrowed. "We get through both sets of our difficult boxes, leaving the shows for last, and *then* have a watch-in," she told him.

And with Juice nudging Dale's hand, he felt as though he had no choice but to nod. "You're on," he said afterward, and wasn't sure why he'd had to put the period on the end of the agreement.

But he didn't take it back.

## *Chapter Nine*

It stood to reason that they both had wedding photos in the boxes they'd left, all together, in Millie's garage. She'd suggested doing so when Dale had dropped her off. Figuring it might make the process easier for him to ease into. They'd still be in storage away from his residence, just closer. And easier to access.

They'd waited until Saturday to dig into them. A day when so many others were on the beach that she tended to stay inside anyway. She was only a temporary resident on the beach. Not one of them.

And, other than Chelsea, who wasn't there, and Scott and Iris, with whom she'd exchanged less than ten words—but quite a few neighborly nods—didn't know any of them.

She found the photos first. Didn't look at them. Just set them aside. Until, half an hour later, when Dale—who'd been busy in his own portion of the garage where she'd laid a tablecloth for him to set out and organize the items he'd pulled from boxes—grew completely still.

Juice, who'd been lying with Magic on the blanket she'd brought out for them, clued her in. The dog stood and quietly moved toward him. Standing beside him, but not seeming to be working.

She noticed the unopened photo book in his hand. The white embossed cover. And said, "I just found mine a little while ago. I didn't open it."

She'd found other photos, too. Catalogued in small photo boxes. Mostly, she knew, from when she and Brent were younger. Their parents had given them the boxes as a Christmas gift the first year after they were married.

As she stood there, watching him, wanting to know what she could do to help, Dale opened the album. His expression softened, and he turned the page. Then another. Standing there, motionless, Millie envied him.

If she thought she could look at her photos and pull out the good, rather than dying inside...

"We got married in a park, just the two of us, since I didn't have family, and she wasn't in touch with hers... the guy who married us, someone from the base, showed up in full military dress, shiny shoes and all, and Lyla and I were in shorts and sandals. We were heading to Disneyland..."

Disneyland. She'd never been. And of all people she'd have expected to never go there, Dale would have been top of the list.

"She'd been with her parents and there'd been some kind of altercation. She wanted to go back to start her new life, her new family, with gentleness, kindness and love," he said then, almost as though quoting his wife with complete accuracy.

And maybe he was. The look on his face, as though he was getting lost, caught in a void, drew Millie to him. Not to take from what was. Just to be there.

The first photo she saw was a much younger-looking

Dale, posing with the big mouse. And then there was Lyla. Blonde. Petite. Gazing adoringly up at her husband.

The look in the woman's eyes, gloriously happy, struck Millie. She understood the feeling that projected such a look. Hadn't known it in a long time. Chest tight, she almost couldn't breathe as she recognized that she'd never know that joy again.

A wet nose hit her palm. Jammed up inside it.

And Millie's fingers went to work on the fur.

The whole wedding day had been for Lyla. Done her way. Dale had very much wanted to marry her. He'd just envisioned a trip to the courthouse. Followed by an elegant dinner out.

But Lyla had been far more fragile than him, and he'd enjoyed making her smile. From the beginning of their relationship, he'd gone her way with most things. He'd been happy to do so. He'd loved her. And making her happy made him happy.

He was turning a page, not sure what was coming next, when he noticed Juice tending to Millie. Saw her staring at a big white photo album on the back edge of the table she'd had set up in her garage with various things lining it. The results of her month-long quest to get through certain boxes, he'd assumed.

The book hadn't been there when they'd come out. Wanting to retrieve it, to open it for her, he knew he couldn't do so. But said, "Let's do yours," and moved to the side of her that Juice wasn't already occupying.

With a nod, Millie jutted out her bottom lip and moved to her table. She pulled the massive volume forward, laying it in a clear spot on the front, and opened the front cover. After a couple of minutes of page turns, Juice returned to lie down with Magic, who'd been lying there watching them.

Dale stayed where he was until suddenly Millie turned to him, shaking her head. "It was a chaotic day," she said, holding the book up enough to show him a photo of her being held up by six strong-looking men. Wondering which one was Brent, he heard her say, "They were Brent's groomsmen. Pictures took *forever*. By this time, I wanted to get on with the festivities. Half the town was there, waiting for the reception to start. My face hurt from smiling and the expressions weren't genuine anymore. But our parents...and Brent, too...wanted the whole shebang."

"You didn't?" he asked, joining her at the table, looking over her shoulder at the photo of her with the smiling men. Surprised by the kinship he suddenly felt with her.

"I wanted the wedding, of course," she told him. "I'd been dreaming of it my whole life. But I'd envisioned something smaller, more intimate. I never was a big party girl, but Brent...he loved crowds of people cheering him on. Not in a stuck-up selfish way, he just loved being around people. Like the more people who were around, the more people he could make happy, the happier he was. And by the time we were married, he'd already won enough national championships to garner him some sponsorships. He was like the town hero."

And he'd been hers. Looking over her shoulder at the photos, as she slowly turned the pages, Dale picked out Brent almost right away. A bit shorter than Dale, smaller boned, cropped black hair, the man still reeked manhood all the way. And looked adoringly at his wife, too. Even in unposed photos.

"There were definitely moments when I yearned for some quiet time for us. And look what I got for wishing. More quiet time than I'd ever imagined there could be."

"No." Dale didn't stop her hands from turning the pages. He stood there and perused them with her. But said, "Yearning is natural. And healthy. It helps guide us through life. Brent's death was his journey. You have no idea why it happened. You'll never know. But it most definitively isn't because you needed something different now and then."

When she turned to look at him, her face was so close he could have just leaned and touched his lips to hers. The thought flew in and back out as soon as he saw the gratitude shining from her eyes. "Just like you told me the other night," he said, holding himself steady and in place. "We aren't to blame for what happened. It was fate."

With a curious head tilt, her expression changed, almost to one of question. She opened her mouth, as though to speak, but closed it again.

"What?" he prompted with some urgency. Feeling as though he had to hear her answer before she turned away and the moment was lost.

Shaking her head she turned back to the table. Closed the book.

"Millie?" Dale asked, maintaining his stance right behind her.

Uncomfortable seconds passed as Dale stood there, unmoving. He braced himself when she turned her head back toward him. "I was just wondering if fate brought us together, too," she said then.

And with a strong jolt to his gut, he stepped back.

But said, "Kind of seems that way, doesn't it?" Before he turned and walked back to the boxes he hadn't yet emptied.

The chore he had to get through.

Because that was how Dale dealt with life, apparently. He paid attention to what had to be done and did it.

End of story.

Was it possible that fate had a new story for her life? A brighter future than she'd ever envisioned? One that could include her loss, but also bring new opportunity?

Even the thought of some kind of future involving another committed relationship made her shudder. With fear. With denial.

And with an image of Dale in her head, with a bit of something more, too. She wanted him in her life.

Had wanted him to kiss her...

The thought stopped there. Midstream. But was on her mind Sunday evening while she sat in one of the two reclining chairs in Dale's study, watching back-to-back episodes of a show she'd grown up attached to for no reason she could ever understand. A spin-off of a show about a bar, the sitcom involved a psychiatrist who, though a screwup, ultimately gave his life to helping others find happiness. She'd gained an understanding of herself through that show. Figuring out what mattered most to her—tending to those around her. She'd found her life's purpose.

But what if she didn't have to spend the rest of her life completely alone as she fulfilled her destiny?

Or, what if she was at a crossroads that would define her? And was heading for a major mistake? Was it possible she was looking for forgetfulness, trying to pretend there was more, out of some selfish weakness that was a result of burnout from overwork? It had only been a little over six weeks since she'd quit her job. It was only mid-October, and she still had months to go on her self-imposed sabbatical.

The show turned dark while she was still contemplating the validity of her feelings. Halfway through the first season...a doctor unexpectedly dies. The man's death was played down. There was comedy. Reactionary comments and actions. But then, as an aside to let the main character get his lines in, there was a short scene with the widow. A comment.

Nothing to do with Millie's dilemma, but it shot her right back to it, anyway. Back to who she was. A widow.

At a loss with feelings that were seemingly emerging out of the ashes of who she'd been. Sensations that were growing stronger, every time saw Dale.

Ones that could prompt actions that would give him wrong ideas. And ultimately make him suffer. She couldn't do that to him.

Needed to go. To take Magic for a walk on the beach.

Sitting forward, she pushed to lower the footrest of her chair and both dogs were right there, watching her. Juice stepped forward. An intent look in his eyes she was beginning to recognize. And yes, she was anxious. Reaching forward, she ran her fingers through the curls on the top of the boy's head, taking comfort, and offering reassurance, too. She'd be fine. She just needed to get out...

"You don't have to run away." Dale's words weren't accusatory. More like an offer of comfort. One she couldn't afford to avail herself of.

"I've been sitting in one place too long," she said

inanely. "And Magic didn't potty on the way over. I'm guessing she probably has to go."

She knew *she* did.

Dale put his own footrest down at that. Lifted two remotes to click off the devices they'd been using to watch the DVDs. "I'll come with you," he said. "Juice should go out as well."

There were designated pee spots by all the cottages where pets lived. Chelsea had explained the protocol to Millie on her first day on the beach. Each owner chose, designed, built, and cleaned their own areas. The dogs would go on the beach, too, down by the shore, but the waves took care of that. And for the other business, there were little trash cans with bags hanging from them all up and down the sand.

Millie didn't just need to go. She needed to be away from Dale. But couldn't very well tell him he couldn't take his dog out. Most particularly not when a part of her felt wrong leaving him as she was doing. Like she was being unfaithful to who and what they were.

But that was the whole problem. Who were they? What could they ever be? What if she wanted more, but couldn't give it back?

Confused, she exited the cottage first, and didn't wait for him to follow her. She walked slowly, though, half waiting for him to catch up. And then headed off in the direction of her cottage. He could walk as far as he liked. Turn back when he was ready. And if, by the time they reached her cottage and he was still with her, she could go in. And just head back out when he was out of sight.

She needed air. Lots of it. And darkness, too. She needed to hide until she had herself in line enough to withstand the scrutiny of a bright sunny day shining down on her.

If by daylight she was still in a quandary, she'd skip her morning run and work in the garage. That was the beauty of living alone and being on sabbatical.

"It was the widow." Dale's words caught up to her from behind. His body followed right after them. Juice had beat him to her, his head just to the right of her hand. Magic, bless her, remained close to her other side. The sacred faithfulness of the animals almost brought tears to her eyes.

"It's okay, you know," he said. "To have moments when it all feels so new again. So raw. Like it just happened. Looking through the wedding books yesterday, it's probably to be expected."

She didn't look at him. But felt herself tuning in more than a stranger would have done. "You've had some bad moments today?" she asked him, so much better equipped to help him than herself.

The realization probably wasn't a healthy truth, but there was no denying it. How did she help anyone else when she couldn't heal herself?

"I've…had some…moments," he said. "Not so much raw ones, just…seeing her…reminded me what I had that I will never have again."

*Yes.* Oh, God, yes.

Slowing her step from couched determined escapism to a more relaxed casual pace, she said, "That moment at the funeral back there…she wasn't just saying goodbye to her husband, but to what she'd thought life was going to be."

"And even with that, goodbye doesn't end it."

"You can't let go of something that will always be a

part of you," she said, her tone filled with an emotion that would have embarrassed her with anyone else.

"I don't think we're supposed to let go," he said then. "But we are meant to move on. We'll always remember our time growing up, that person we were in grade school, in high school, will always be with us. And we become someone new at different stages of life, too."

His words brought comfort. A lot of it. But maybe not enough. Brent had been more than a stage of life. "But when you give someone else your everything, they take half of you with them when they go."

He was quiet for so long, she thought she'd lost him. Alienated him from the world that had seemed to be encapsulating them. Was thinking it was probably for the best, but feeling no lighter for having escaped the confusion that being with him had built within her.

"But if you find someone who is missing the same pieces, yet is still young, healthy and with a future in front of them, then maybe you find comfort in knowing that with them, you're understood, and that what you gave away won't be expected to show up."

Oh, god. He'd thrown the door wide open on the parts of her she'd just managed to kill off. Was giving them cardiopulmonary resuscitation, rejuvenating them, and she felt...better.

The tightness around her chest dissipated. The knots in her stomach loosened.

And Millie said, "Maybe you do," with a smile on her face.

## Chapter Ten

Dale's days, weeks and months had been blending into years filled with calm contentment. So much so that five years had passed with him barely taking note. The rest of the month of October and into the beginning of November, not so much. Weeks, days, sometimes even hours and minutes were of note.

He was no longer trapped in his own private world of loss. Millie had joined him. She not only understood what could and couldn't be for him. She could and couldn't, too.

They ran, they talked about their pasts, they watched old reruns. One Saturday, they bottled their peach beer, and two weeks later, made a production on his deck, complete with trays of snacks and veggies, to have their first tastes. Both gave it a thumbs-up, and the next day, they started another batch with a dash of mint some alcoholic, some not. Dale wasn't as hopeful for that batch, but the mischievous smile on Millie's face as she'd suggested it had convinced him to go along with the idea.

They did not touch. Talk about their own relationship. Or go out to eat together again. They didn't see each other at all except for on Ocean Breeze. And never with others around.

Dale had seen Scott several times. Had joined him and

Iris and Sage and Gray and a few others on the beach for a bonfire over Halloween. Something he'd done occasionally in the past. Sitting a bit apart. But there. He'd figured a few years before that he stood out more sitting alone on his deck watching them, than he did out among them.

Besides, he liked bonfires. And certainly wasn't going to have one of his own.

Millie had been invited. She hadn't shown up.

No one had asked him about her. Then, or any other time.

But most of note over the most recent passing days was Dale's first seconds of consciousness in the morning. The calm nothingness that had been greeting him for years had been displaced by thoughts of Millie. Almost as if he dreamed of her at night. He never remembered his dreams upon waking, but figured he had them.

And in those moments, with him lying nearly naked in bed, he couldn't as easily deny that he was physically responding to the woman. During the times he was with her, fully conscious, he could control himself—distract himself—so that nothing actually transpired within his pants. And then put the stirrings down to those of a normal, healthy male who'd done without for a very long time. Telling himself he'd respond to any woman he spent one-on-one time with in the sometimes-close quarters he and Millie shared. His kitchen was small.

As was his television room. He didn't generally spend a lot of time there.

But his bedroom? She'd never even seen the space. And yet, every morning for the past week, with Millie on his mind, he'd been waking up so hard and ready he had to get under a cold shower just to give himself relief.

He'd never, ever, not even as a pubescent kid, wanted a woman so fiercely.

And he had no idea what in the hell he did about that.

Turning his back on Millie wasn't the answer. Wasn't even an option. The woman was starting to sparkle before his eyes. Her eyes. Her smile. Even when discussing the tough stuff, as they both did now and then, she didn't lose her new glow.

If physical discomfort was the price he had to pay, he'd do so every time.

A fact of which he reminded himself, profusely, when, on the first Friday in November, Millie stopped at the end of their jog and said, "Can I talk to you for a second?"

The look in her eye, like she was maybe a little excited about something, had instant fire raging inside him. Standing there as she was in her skintight leggings with no panty lines, and the long-sleeved crop top, that also showed him her shape to perfection, she seemed to be ready to take a step forward. With him.

Was it possible that she was experiencing the same resurgence of sexual desire that he was? And on steroids, too? Was that how it happened when parts of you came back to life after so long dead? His preoccupation with desire for her was just part of the process they shared?

Like going through boxes in storage, and trying out new beer flavors?

Realizing he hadn't answered her when some of the glow in her expression started to segue into confusion, he said, "Yes, of course. Always." That had become a given with them. They were each other's sounding boards. Confidants. Unofficial co-counselors with Juice there to step in when necessary.

The thought occurred to him because the poodle had just moved subtly to Millie's side. And her fingers were at work in the curly fur on the top of the boy's head.

"I was offered a part-time paid position with Young Runners, here in San Diego."

Dale floundered for a second as his wavelength faltered. He was the only one on it. She wasn't about to ask him to have sex with her.

Or even discuss a minute possibility of such in the future.

She'd been offered a job. And while she'd seemed somewhat excited, telling him about the opportunity was making her anxious. Or the offer itself was doing so.

"Young Runners is a national organization that trains teenagers for competitive sport. Like the Olympics. The Boston Marathon..."

She stopped talking when he waved his hand and nodded. "I know who they are," he told her. Then said, "And they know you through Brent."

She shrugged. "I actually trained with them, too, for a few years in junior high and the beginning of high school. But yes, they know of my skill level, which qualifies me for the open position, through my association with Brent on tour."

He was impressed. Found the fact that she'd received the offer kind of sexy. Until he stopped himself. And focused on her. Something wasn't right.

She was exuding apprehension as much as any eagerness he'd thought he detected. Could have been there all along and he'd just been too much in his own business to notice.

Narrowing his gaze, he said, "So...you just wanted to

let me know you were going back to work?" he asked. Were her hours going to interfere with jog time? Was that it?

She seemed to freeze in place. Her fingers on Juice's head quit moving. Her feet remained solid in the sand. "That's just it, I'm not sure I'm going to accept." And with a slap to his mental slowness, Dale quickly moved up to speed. Put himself in the current situation, not some imagined future one, and listened for what she wasn't saying as much as she was, watched her expressions, as she continued.

"It would be three days a week, three hours a day, after school, Tuesdays and Thursdays and then Saturday. It's kids, and I've definitely got the skills to work with them. I'm pretty much an expert on running..."

She let the words trail off before Dale had ascertained what she needed from him. Looked inward then, for her sake. To see if he could find any angst he'd gone through when he'd started to sell articles. Or had the offer on his first novel. Found nothing except that he was glad he'd done both. And maybe that was what she needed.

"If you want to take the job, you should," he said.

She nodded, but was also biting her bottom lip. And more to keep the conversation going until he could figure out where he was failing her, he asked, "How's the pay?" Was it insulting to her level of experience and education?

"More than generous," she told him. "But I don't need it. Brent invested a lot of his sponsorship money, and had a life insurance policy that has given me enough to live off for a couple of years, at least."

He'd wondered how, at twenty-eight, she was affording to take so much time off. And rent on Ocean Breeze.

Had half figured her parents for providing the opportunity for her to heal.

"Plus, I have my own savings from nursing."

She was most definitely not living off Mom and Dad. He got that one quite clear. Not that it made a difference to him. He wouldn't have thought any less of her had she been. If anything, he'd have been thankful that she had parents who would be there for her.

"So what's making you hesitate?" he asked what he should have clued in on all along.

Millie glanced at him, adjusted the elastic in the ponytail hanging down her back. And then returned her hand to Juice's head. Rubbing gently. Petting the boy. "Am I going backward?" she asked him. "I avoided facing the future by burying myself in my work with kids. I let the fact that I was needed, that I was helping children, distract me from facing my own needs."

Dale knew the answer to that one. And while he felt a bit like he was being left behind, he said, "The fact that you're even questioning the matter should be proof to you that you aren't going to let that happen," he told her.

She didn't look convinced. He hadn't expected her to. She had more traveling to do on her journey before she learned to have confidence in her ability to manage the long haul successfully.

He very definitely remembered that one. Had struggled with who he was becoming when he'd hit the *NYT* Best Sellers list and had signed an unbelievably, to him, lucrative three-book contract afterward. He'd had his uneasy moments, but he'd signed. And had never regretted that decision.

Not something he could share with her, since WG was

just a secret product of his imagination. Dale could sign the contracts, write the books, have large amounts of money deposited into an LLC. He couldn't play the part of famous writer.

Which he had to make clear to his publisher and agent each time WG had a new release and they wanted to send him on tour. Hoping he'd change his mind.

Just wasn't him.

"When do they need an answer?" he asked when Millie stood there, transferring her weight from one running shoe to the other in the sand.

"Today. First session is tomorrow."

Frowning he blurted, "And they waited this long to make the offer?" No wonder she was floundering. And was maybe wondering if she wasn't a first or second choice, but rather, a last resort after someone else reneged on a done deal.

"No," she told him, her fingers working on Juice again. Dale stared, not at her, but at those fingers as she said, "They made the offer a couple of weeks ago. I've just put off giving them an answer. And they refused to ask anyone else until I did."

No third or fourth choice there. She *was* the first choice. He'd bet last resort, or a couple of them, were waiting in the wings.

She'd had two weeks. Was at the last minute. And had come to him. The facts finally lined up and Dale said, "Do you want to do it, Millie?"

Meeting his gaze, she held on unusually long for them. Too long for him. But he didn't let go. He let her drain whatever lifeblood she needed from him, until she said, "I think I really do."

"Then...don't you have your answer?" he asked slowly, tenderly.

And felt like he'd hit a homerun with the bases loaded when her face broke into a large, genuine-looking smile. "Yes, I believe I have," she told him.

Thanked him.

And trotted off.

Leaving Dale strangely calm. Happy for her. And like she'd just left him behind, too.

Life took a new turn for Millie that week. She had purpose. None of the crafts she'd been working on had panned out. Mostly because her heart hadn't been in them. She hadn't cared about the creation at all. She'd only been doing them because she'd thought it was how she reconnected with her inner self.

Turned out, Dale was helping her to do that. Including by encouraging her to take the position with Young Runners. She was on a team of trainers who each took small portions of their larger group of kids, trading off with each other, to work on specific skills. Hers was breathing, physical stamina and physical health—which incorporated ways to avoid shin splints and to protect against long-term joint damage among other things.

Dale was also helping by offering a friendship in which she was enough, even with her missing pieces. In such a short time, he'd become a closer friend to her than any she could ever remember having. Other than Brent. And in some ways, she felt a deeper bond with Dale than she had even with her husband, because when Brent had been alive, she hadn't known deep sorrow. Hadn't experienced debilitating grief. There were just places she and Brent had never gone. Either apart, or together.

Places Dale had not only gone, but where he still dwelled. Right alongside her.

She didn't kid herself into thinking that either of them was capable of giving a whole heart to another, as they'd done in their separate marriage vows. But knowing that life wasn't completely empty on a close companionship scale put a bit of renewed energy in her step.

More and more every day, it seemed. With a clarity that she would have fought, if having an ability to feel more fully alive again, even for a second, hadn't been such a welcomed discovery.

She wanted the man. Physically. Not whole heart, one for life, as her joining with Brent had been. Just…an experience that happened and ended. For however many times it might happen. Not that she actually allowed herself to delve too deeply into exactly how that would go. Or even to spend more than fleeting seconds on thoughts of her lips, her hands, her body, comingling with his.

But the awareness was there, floating around in the background of their interactions. And had been steadily growing since the first week she'd connected with him. Her secret little pleasure.

One she had absolutely no intention of sharing with him. Ever. No way she was going to risk ruining the invaluable friendship that had grown between them. Nothing, not even the most mind-blowing sex in the world, would be worth that to her.

Orgasms happened. The sensations faded into the ether.

Friendship was forever—as long as they were both alive.

The thought held her steadfast on Saturday night when Dale showed up at her place with mint beer, in a shirt with the top couple of buttons undone, giving her ample view of his chest hair. And skintight jeans detailing his other parts. But it was the grin coming through the shadow of growth he was allowing to accumulate on his face that gave her stomach a jolt.

She quickly trumped the feeling with a gladness to see him. To have him just show up unannounced, like a friend on the beach might, rather than making some formal plan that could be emotionally misconstrued by some parts of her as a date.

"I'm not here to stay," he told her, stepping up onto her deck where she'd been sitting in front of the fireplace with Magic—watching flames jump and dance. And thinking about...well...all of the above. Juice's step up behind him gave a small bit of lie to the statement. And he said, "Or, rather, I don't have to be. The mint beer is done. I need to know whether we're keeping or dumping it so I can sanitize the bottles and ready them for the next batch. And since this delightful idea was yours, I feel it's only fair that you be the one to take the first sip. If you gag, I'll take that as a no on this trial and head home to clean out the cooler."

Mention of the large wine cooler he had in his pantry, one that was filled with various bottles of homemade beer, brought to mind the first time she'd seen the appliance. He'd been showing her where to put the freshly capped beer bottles when she took them from him. Not realizing that he was just going to open the door and point, she'd followed right behind him and bumped her nose on his chin when he'd turned suddenly.

Struck with a sudden desire to kiss him, she'd jumped back as though she'd been stung. And had felt like a fool for having done so. Had worried that he'd noticed her over-the-top behavior, but if he had, he'd never let on. That had been more than a month ago. During the peach beer phase.

"Then bring it on over," she said, a little more loudly than necessary. A cover-up for the tremor she'd feared would be evident in her tone.

He did. Handed her one of the two capped bottles he held. Stood there watching her. Which made the whole tremor thing a bit harder to ignore. "It's not fair for you to stand in judgment," she told him. "Sit."

When he did, she realized the error of that suggestion. She could smell the sea soap he used in the shower. Which made it a lot harder to distract herself from the body that was alighting her nerve endings. With a quick twist of the cap, she figured a good swig of mint beer ought to clear her senses of any unwanted residue.

And took a long sip. Uncaring if the brew tasted like sawdust. She was hiding within it and that was that. She'd swallowed before the taste really registered. And took a second sip, just to be sure.

Swallowing, she held up the bottle to him. And nodded toward the one he held. "You need to taste it," she told him. "It's surprisingly good. Dangerously so, maybe. So fresh and bright that you don't feel like you're drinking alcohol."

Who'd have thought? She'd just pulled the flavor out of the ether one night when he'd asked her what kind of beer they should do next. She'd been trying to think of bad breath, to get her mind off the possibility of their lips touching. Bad breath had led to breath mints, which then would have allowed the kissing, but had segued into an answer for beer flavor instead of said touching of lips.

She watched as Dale took a swig. Looked for his expression to give her his first reaction. And saw his nod as he also went for an immediate second taste. "Not bad," he said, as he lowered the bottle.

And she heard herself say, more than deciding to say, "Well, since you've been relieved of bottle sanitizing duty, you might as well sit for a few." She knew, from the little he'd said the night of the Halloween bonfire, that he enjoyed sitting by the flames.

Made sense to her. The man took on danger. And spent his life with an eye to protecting against it as well.

Magic had flopped back down by the back door, and Juice lay down between the big girl and Dale's chair. Other than Magic, Millie was going to be alone for the holiday. Her first one spent that way. Every other one since Brent's death had been spent on the floor at the hospital, tending to sick kids without visitors and trying to ease the worry and discomfort of family members of others who were having to spend the holiday in the confines of a sick room.

The thought effectively cooled her libido. And, staring at the flames, she asked, "You ever try a turkey? Or taste one that had been?" Him with all his vats...the man could have a turkey fryer. And before he could answer, fearing that he'd think she'd been veering toward an invitation for them to spend the holiday together, she said, "One of my favorite holiday movies...this woman hires a guy to be her fake fiancé for Thanksgiving, after her fiancé breaks up with her at the last minute. She's the oldest of three girls, and her mother is obsessed with her becoming an old maid..."

She was rambling. Staring into the fire, sipping beer, he didn't seem to mind, and she said, "Everything got really awkward for many reasons, but in the midst of it all, the father, who's going to be in trouble for fraud, insists on frying the turkey for the huge small-town feast being held at their home. The bird blasts out of the fryer and into the tree above it. Ever since I saw that movie, I haven't understood why someone would want to fry a turkey."

"Because of the explosion? That would have been the fault of the temperature of the cooking substance in relationship to the temperature of the bird when it was immersed..."

She knew that, of course. She'd seen the movie. But, "No, just because it doesn't sound good. I like my turkey baked, and juicy. With lots of leftover juices in the roaster to make gravy." It's how her mother had done. And her grandmother before her. She'd learned before puberty how to prepare a holiday feast.

And hadn't had one in years. During their time in the apartment in San Diego, she and Brent had gone out to eat for the holiday.

"I spent so much of my youth moving from home to home, I can't really bring up any particular holiday memories," Dale said then, not sounding the least bit sorry about his situation. "Lyla wasn't feeling good our first Thanksgiving together. We were on the road from Texas to the new base lodging here for the second and I was deployed for the third."

They'd only been married three years, was what that math told her. And she said, "Brent and I were only married for two holiday seasons. Our parents wanted us to finish college first, and then it took a year to plan the wedding."

They'd been living together since high school graduation and their eighteenth birthdays. In an apartment an hour from home, near the university where they'd both opted to study. The place had been hers. He'd been on the track team. Had had a room in a house designated for some of the top college athletes. He just hadn't stayed there.

Unless one or the other of their mothers had come to visit and had stayed with Millie. At the time she'd felt so grown up. Looking back, it all felt…juvenile.

"I'm guessing then that you don't want to try to fry a turkey together?" Dale's suggestion floated through the air like a whiff of smoked barbecue. Hitting her hard and lingering.

If it meant having an excuse not to spend the holiday all alone? "I'm game if you are. Just like the beer, we don't have to like the results, but at least we'll have tried it."

And they'd be making a new memory for a very traditional day, rather than sitting in the midst of the ashes of old ones. Or, in Dale's case, a lack of them.

Even better, she wasn't thinking about sex.

"Let's use my deck," he said then, as though they were discussing something as mundane and unimportant as cleaning their running shoes. "That way if the thing explodes, there's less worry about the damage." His basic old deck was nothing compared to Chelsea's, she'd give him that.

And yet, if she had a choice between spending the holiday sitting alone in the luxurious cottage she was renting and hanging out at Dale's older, less fancy one, she'd choose his every time.

But didn't share that fact.

## *Chapter Eleven*

Dale wasn't so sure about spending the upcoming holiday alone with Millie. Holidays were hard for a lot of people, not just ones whose lives had been emptied by tragedy. They came steeped in expectation of family, love and good times and not everyone had those. Every holiday he could remember from his entire life growing up had been spent with him on the outside looking in. Whether he was a newcomer, or would be going soon, he was treated well. Included in the festivities. And yet...the families that had opened their homes to him had been family to each other long before he'd come to them, and long after he'd left, too.

Lyla hadn't had any problem at all just blowing off the holidays. Most of hers had been spent tense, waiting for her mother to do something that would irritate her father. While her parents would get through the day with smiles and gentle love for her, she'd known that as soon as she went to bed, her mother would be in tears. That tension had become an integral part of her. Something that not even being with Dale had been able to assuage.

But Millie...she had wonderful holiday memories. And her first one not spent running away, burying herself in others' suffering to avoid her own... Dale didn't like what he was seeing there. Her tears. Him reaching out to comfort her. Or Juice comforting her, and when she was better, him just reaching out.

He'd seen the way she'd been looking at him. At first, he'd told himself he was projecting his own desires onto her, but lately, there'd been moments when he'd look up to find her staring at him in *that* way. No matter how many years passed, or how old a guy got, that was one look his body translated automatically.

Each time it happened, either he, or she would find a reason to end their time together. But on a holiday, when they were already emotionally charged, and her first without running away, her first after having faced her past with Brent by going through all her boxes… Millie was going to be extra vulnerable. Looking for anything that felt good. He couldn't let her spend it alone. And there'd be no walking out if things got overheated.

All through the next week, thoughts of a similar nature kept repeating to him. They even got through to WG, who ended up with a pretty heated sex scene in a book that hadn't had a love interest, but now did. An unforeseen challenge that WG was now going to have to deal with.

Just as Dale would have to deal with anything that could happen between him and Millie on an emotionally overcharged day.

The following Saturday, just five days before Thanksgiving, Millie came over to take a look at the new turkey fryer he'd ordered. He'd texted her that it had arrived. Hadn't expected her to walk up the beach with Magic after track practice. Though he should have done. They'd managed to happen upon each other every Saturday since she'd started with Young Runners. She'd give him a rundown of the week, and they usually ended up sharing a beer.

The light in her eyes, the technicalities of the sport that she shared with him, pleased him for her sake. She was finding a way to bring a part of who she'd been to the present. And to help others. It also had served as a bit of a barrier between them as her past was not a part of his future. But it could be a part of hers. An answer outside of nursing that allowed her to use all the skills with which she was endowed.

Before Millie had shown up for turkey fryer tutelage, he'd already had a beer with Scott, who'd been on his way down to his sister's for a cookout. Iris was on another overnight photo shoot and Dale had almost invited the man back for another beer after dinner if he didn't feel like heading home alone.

That inclination had been enough to stop Dale mentally in his tracks. He'd never made such an invitation in the past. Period. If Dale was out, Scott might stop. That's how it worked. He'd been about to make the offer to avoid time alone with Millie in the dark. A situation made more dire by the fact that Thanksgiving, and their intimate turkey frying day together was only five days off.

And all for one reason. He knew he could control his own sexual urges, but if she was in need, and came to him—he didn't trust himself to say no.

Ignoring the situation wasn't helping. It was making things worse.

Which left him one of two options. Either he let the sexual desire brewing between him and Millie ruin their friendship. Or he let her know that it had become an issue.

The necessity was pushing so strongly from within him

that he almost blurted out that he wanted her the second she stepped up to his deck that evening. Juice, thankfully, rescued him from his own near fatality. The big poodle stood up, tail wagging to greet Magic, and just a glance at the boy reminded Dale to take a deep breath.

Pulling the large box containing the turkey fryer toward him, he unclipped his utility knife from his belt and cut through the bindings, pulling the flaps up just as Millie came over to peer inside. She reached, he reached, and they both pulled back as their hands collided. Maybe with a slight hesitation—he didn't trust himself to be sure that's what it was—she pulled out the foam frame at the top of the box. He watched. Waited for her to take out the various pieces and parts. A lid. A basket. Electrical supply. And then, when there was nothing left but the heavy vat and base, he stood to grab those. Reached down as she was heading back to the box from setting another piece of foam on the ground, and their faces met. An inch apart.

Dale stared. Throat tight, he stood there, half bent, and then fell back into his chair. Pushing the box away from the two of them with one foot, he said, "We've got a situation here."

If she left, she did. The attraction between them would win—stealing away a friendship that had grown to be almost invaluable to him. He'd get over her. He knew that. Lyla's death had taught him that much.

But he didn't want to have to. And it wasn't just his choice. He didn't eye her. Wouldn't be fair to put her on the spot that way. Instead, he turned his gaze outward, to the waves that sustained him. The givers and takers of life. But always there. Receding with things in their grasp, and returning with new, every minute, every hour, of every day.

He wasn't sure if he heard or felt her sit in the chair Scott had vacated. Her chair, he'd thought of it when the lawyer had taken the seat, as Scott had been doing for the past four and a half years.

"So, it's not just me." Her voice slid into him. Not gently. But not harshly, either. He kept his gaze steady on the ocean. Trying to control the hot need filling him at her words.

"Oh my God..." Millie's horror hit him hard, and he glanced over as she said, "It *is* just me and you wanted to let me down gently, and... I have to go." She jumped up so fast, both dogs stood. Juice blocking her way.

His boy was working, Dale noted in the back of his mind, as his mouth opened and spilled out, "I'd hardly say so," as he moved his arms and nodded toward the bulge in the thin jogging pants he was wearing.

He looked back out to sea as Millie turned her head. Couldn't bear to watch her looking at him...there. Heard her, "Oh." And then her chair scrape the deck as she retook her seat. Hard.

He had to man up. To fight for what mattered. The thoughts drove his mind away from his penis. "The way I see it, we have two options," he started in with the conclusions he'd drawn.

"We either deal with it, or we stop hanging out." Millie's voice completed the thought for him. As though reading his mind.

Telling him two things. She'd been aware, and contemplating the situation just as he had. And, once again, they shared understanding. To a point.

"I'm for dealing with it," he said. If she wasn't, he wouldn't blame her. Or think any less of her. He'd just change his running schedule. It wasn't like she was going to be on the beach forever. She wasn't an owner like the rest of them. She only had a six-month lease.

"That's good to know." Her tone of voice, while predominantly filled with nervousness, had a lighter note that gave him some hope. "I don't want to lose Juice."

The words yanked his gaze to her. And to the apricot boy who was standing right beside her. At attention.

Millie was staring toward the floor, but lifted her gaze to him slowly. And just...wordlessly held on to his. As hard as he tried, staring intently into those warm blue eyes, he couldn't decipher their message.

Other than that the next minutes mattered to her. A lot.

Did he reach for her? Kiss her, then pick her up and carry her inside? Get the sex out of the way so they could get back to being buddies?

Giving himself a mental shake, he put the thought, not the two of them, to bed. No way it would be that easy. Being naked together would change them. Irrevocably.

And he couldn't speak for her, but no way was one time going to be enough for him.

Beyond that, he had nothing. Except, "I'm willing to walk around with a hard-on all day long if that's what it takes to continue our friendship." He needed that known. He wasn't asking her to relieve him of his discomfort.

She, on the other hand, had only mentioned a need for his dog to remain in her life. "I'm willing to set up times for Juice to visit with you—every day—if that would work." He could give her as much time alone with Juice as she'd had with the poodle over the past two and a half months. He looked back out to the ocean. Took a couple of slow, deep, calming breaths.

"Seriously?" The disdain in Millie's voice sounded more nurse-like than anxious friend, and he glanced back over at her. "I thought when you started this conversation that you wanted to meet it head-on."

*He had a head that wanted to meet her.* The thought was base. Him at his lowest. Happened to a guy when he was hard with desire and drowning in a pool of unknowns.

Holding his gaze steady on her, he said, "I have no idea what I'm doing. I know there's an issue that, if not contained somehow, is going to get in the way. I know I don't want you out of my life. Beyond that, I'm out of my league. Sex is…messy. It's not just brewing beer. But the desire for it can make you drunker than any alcohol in terms of giving in to the choice to have it."

"You've got it that bad, huh?" There was not the slightest hint of a grin on her face, but there might have been a note of one in her voice.

Dale was beyond caring. "And getting worse by the second with this conversation," he told her.

"Good to know," she said. For the second time. Which was one time too many for him.

"Yeah, well, it might be good for me to know where you are in all of this." His tone had no hint of humor. At all.

Brows raised, she frowned, and said, "I thought that was obvious. My whole, 'it's not just me' back there… pretty much says that it *is* me. Hell, I've been afraid for weeks that I was sending out inappropriate signals, putting you in a position of having to let me down gently…"

Wait, what? Dale sat up. "Are you saying you want our relationship to become sexual?" He was ready.

The shake of her head, had him sitting back again. Right. He should have known. What? What should he have known? What was he missing?

"At least...not without some understanding between us..."

Her words had him. Hook, line and sinker. "That's what I'm missing," he told her honestly. "What kind of understanding keeps this from eventually breaking us up? You have sex, emotions get involved, feelings stand to get hurt along the way..."

"Except that, neither of us is capable of getting in that deep," she said softly. "I know that you don't have it all to give anymore. And you know I don't. Expectations are dead before going in. Just because we aren't looking for all in, or forever, for true love or lifetime commitment, doesn't mean we aren't live, healthy human beings with natural needs. Maybe this is a gift to us. A chance to have more than either of us thought, because we both understand, going in, what it is. And what it isn't. More importantly, we both *feel* the same way. It isn't just a cognitive understanding that we share, it's an emotional one."

He wasn't ready for the silence when her voice stopped spreading over him. Through him. When he could swallow again, he said, "You're saying you want to take our relationship to the bedroom." The words sent another surge to his entire groin area.

"No."

She was killing him. And death might be sweeter at that point.

"I'm saying that *if* it happens, it doesn't have to mean

the end of our relationship. That maybe it's a natural step that we shouldn't fear."

"You're afraid of having sex with me?"

Her long sigh was Dale's clue to get off his ass and get them both a beer. Mint flavored. So they'd have fresh breath. Just in case.

And then, taking a sip as he sat back down, he got his head out of said ass. "What you're saying is that while parts of us died with the loves of our lives, maybe the two of us sharing that circumstance is allowing the parts of us that are left to find more out of life than either of has since the funerals." It was one hell of a long sentence for him.

He sat still, calm as he awaited her response.

And when it came, he almost did.

*Yes.* She'd said yes. Millie fiddled with her beer bottle. Or rather, tried to. It had no label for her to pick at. And Juice was lying feet away, with Magic. She didn't need the animal's services. She wasn't anxious.

She was nervous. Wanting. Needing.

And... "I just...need a little time, though," she told him. "To get used to allowing myself to look at us...that way. And..." The practical part of her swooped in, a bit late, to hold her up. "...to get protection."

More than a condom, which was only effective ninety-eight percent of the time.

There could be no chances, zero, that...

No.

They were talking sex. Period. Or the topic was off the table. Permanently.

"Or I can get it," Dale offered. And she nodded.

"Okay," she said. They'd be double protected. She liked

that. Felt better already. No worries that she'd find herself with a situation that could unravel her. Another man's child in her womb...when...

Shaking her head, Millie gave herself a mental shakedown. Sure, she'd just figured out how to kill the desire raging through her. When for weeks...

But as she sat with Dale, with darkness falling around them, knowing that they were going to have sex at some point, the idea of being pregnant with his child didn't carry the sharp stab she'd expected it to. She wasn't going to let it happen, of course. They were friends and that's all they were ever going to be.

There was no future for them. She'd be leaving. He'd be staying. And neither of them had more than that to offer.

Just, in another lifetime, one where she hadn't given her whole heart away as a kid, she could see herself falling for Dale. And being excited about carrying his baby.

In another lifetime.

"If you get the protection, how long you think it's going to take to get what you need?" His voice, thick and yet somewhat playful, too, pulled her from a reverie that served no purpose but to send her backward.

Astute of him to realize that if she'd just wanted to use condoms, she could have had them within the hour. Or asked him if he had some.

For her, some things took longer than others. Luckily, she was fine with one that took no time at all, and had connections to get it. "A day," she told him.

"Guess I'll be going shopping tomorrow, too." He lifted his bottle as if in toast, and then took a long sip. And in the dusk, with the hint of moonglow, his chin looked... sexy to her. Strong. Capable.

Trustworthy.

A chin? Trustworthy?

"You're growing a beard," she said, wondering what the shadow of growth would feel like against her skin. Brent had shaved every single day. Always.

He shrugged. "I've had one ever since...for years," he said.

"Since Lyla died," she translated.

"Yeah." He sipped. She did, too. Comfortable with the conversation. What was, had been. And was a part of them.

"I shaved it this summer," he said then, almost ruminatively. "A step in moving forward, I thought."

"What made you change your mind?"

He turned to her in the near darkness. "You," he said.

And her heart lurched. A big no, resounding inside her, even as she glowed, too. "Me?"

"The beard is my new life. The new me. I didn't want to lose sight of that."

She frowned. That was kind of like her thinking that a workaholic nurse was the new her. Or was it? Life was a lot more complicated than growing a beard or being a nurse. The only way a person really knew was...

"Do you like having a beard?" she put the test to him. "Do you prefer it?"

"Not really," he told her. "It's a lot of work. Gets in the way when I eat corn on the cob. And it itches sometimes."

"You going to shave in the morning?" she asked him, then. Softly, but with a definite point.

"Yeah."

With a smile, Millie tipped her bottle to his, and when

his clinked against it, she looked toward the ocean and sipped. Certain that he did, too.

They were two peas in a pod that had been suffocating them. A pod they were slowly opening up to the light of day. Sometimes he was the one moving one or the other of them toward emergence. Sometimes she was.

Maybe they'd been meant to find each other, had been guided to Ocean Breeze for the right time to meet up, maybe not. Didn't really matter. They were there, helping each other to reach for whatever life was left to them.

And for that, she would always be thankful to have known him.

## *Chapter Twelve*

Dale bought condoms. A lot of them. Different kinds. Some colored. Some not. Even some ribbed for her pleasure, though he didn't ever intend to open that particular box. Just, if it was what she was used to, if she wanted them, he needed to be prepared.

If she was even half as on fire as he was, after such a long bout of abstention, their wait time before having sex was going to be short. Very short. He'd never, ever been so fiercely turned on by a woman. The thought had been occurring to him a lot lately. For good reason.

His overcharged desire was understandable, considering how long it had been since he'd had sex. And he knew the cure, too.

On Sunday afternoon, with a couple of plain condoms in the pocket of his shorts, he walked down to Millie's just to let her know he had them.

She had company. Chelsea was back to pick up some of her own holiday décor stored with the other stuff she'd cleared out for Millie, in a shed beside the cottage. He'd known she was due at some point. Her brother and sister-in-law didn't have much, and she was hoping to pick up her sister's spirits with a light show outside her sister's bedroom window every night. And when he heard voices through the back screen door as he approached, he clicked his tongue to signal Juice to stop, and headed back down to his place.

Knowing that he'd just been saved from making a mistake. He knew better than to rush things. Doing so would be giving sex the control, and that was the very beast they had to avoid. Stripping off his shirt, he left Juice on the shore, watching him, and took a dive into the frigid cold ocean instead. Swam for twenty minutes, and then, dry shirt in hand and dripping all the way up to his deck, went in to shower off.

Millie needed time. Not just to get contraceptives. To adjust to the door they'd just opened. And when he slowed down and thought about it from her perspective, he stopped himself cold. Lyla had been the one for him. The love of his life. But she hadn't been his first. Or even his second or third or fourth.

But Millie…based on the fact that she'd been in love with her Brent since they were in grade school…had likely had only the one lover. Maybe not. Didn't matter to him if there'd been more. But if, as facts strongly suggested, there'd just been the one, Dale had a huge responsibility in front of him.

He wasn't just going to be sharing mutual desire with her, giving each other shared pleasures leading to release. He had to be sensitive to that fact that he'd likely be going where only the love of her life had ever been.

While the thoughts didn't cool his desire for the woman at all, his compassion for her under the circumstances did bring forth the ability to calm the sexual arousal when it arose.

Millie mattered far more than his penis ever would.

A fact of which he reminded himself when Millie showed up to jog Monday morning in orange skintight leggings and matching, long-sleeved crop top. That sliver of tanned belly in between the waistband of the pants and the bottom hem on the shirt gave him a run for his money. In that first second, the idea of her only having had one lover just made him want to show her how phenomenal sex could still be. To prove to her that she hadn't lost one of life's particularly heady pleasures.

Luckily for him, they never chatted at the beginning of the run. He just fell into step beside her, and went into his zone, with Juice keeping pace between them.

Dale had an online meeting with his agent that morning, but when Millie hesitated at the end of the two-mile jog, he stopped, too.

"Chelsea told me I was invited to a Thanksgiving gathering down at the end of the beach on Thursday," she said, and while his gut sank a little, he nodded. "It's at the Bartholomew place," she continued. "And everyone on the beach is welcome. Iris and Scott, next door to me, are going, too, and maybe the couple that bought Sage's cottage."

Standing there thinking about frying his turkey alone, he said, "Sounds like fun." And meant the words. For the rest of them. He just didn't see the personal gain in getting together with a group of happy couples, but if it worked for Millie, he wanted that for her.

She glanced over at him, squinting against the sun as she said, "You want to go?"

He couldn't tell, in the sunlight, if she was frowning from the brightness, or at him. Nor did her tone of voice give him much. "You asking me to go?" He didn't want to turn her down. And didn't think it was a good idea, either, for the two of them to show up as a couple, in the midst of nothing but couples. With two little ones thrown in to liven up the party a bit.

On the other hand, being with the others, dealing with the fallout of that, would put a damper on any desire for physical intimacy that might have attacked him had they been alone at his place all day. Together. On a sacred day when the world was generally quieter as shops closed and people gathered with their families.

"I thought maybe Scott had said something to you."

"He probably will. He's pretty much last-minute." Dale always got the invites. And as far as he was aware, no one took offense when he rarely accepted them. The occasional bonfire on the beach, and generally in front of his place, was about it.

She seemed to be assessing him, and Dale finally had to ask, "What?"

"I don't want to go," she told him. "But if you do, we can fry the turkey another time. It's just…with this being my first time celebrating the holiday since…well anyway…"

"Relax," he interrupted her. "I get the invites, but I almost never accept them. No one is going to take offense. That's how it is on Ocean Breeze. Everyone is welcome. Everyone is here for each other. And respecting others' privacy is what makes it all work."

She frowned again. He was pretty sure the expression was aimed at him that time. "So you don't want to go?"

"Even if I didn't have a turkey to fry, you mean?" He had to egg her on for a second. Just seemed, in that moment, like the thing to do. But he quickly relented with,

"No, I have no desire to go sit among happy couples planning their families, on a holiday designed specifically for families. I'm happy for them all. I most certainly don't begrudge them their time. Or their life's joys. I don't even envy them. I just have no need to be a fish out of water." He'd said way more than he might have a few months before. Glanced at the water where millions of fish lived, instead of holding Millie's gaze.

"I should have known," she said, a noticeable lightness to her tone that drew his gaze back to her. "Chelsea's been good to me, and I didn't want to seem unsociable, but, like you, I saw either myself shriveling up in their midst, or, if you were there, us being scrutinized like two people in one hot seat. I could even hear someone talking about us having become friends."

He liked most of what she'd said. Figured he probably should have subliminally known that she'd share his lack of desire to be a part of such a situation. But that last part…sounding as though Millie found the idea of anyone asking about their association displeasing…he wasn't so sure about.

"You don't want others to know we're friends?" he asked her. Because he could pretty much guarantee that that ship had already sailed. The beach didn't gossip. But her residents kept track of each other. Out of sense of caring, not nosiness.

Millie's shrug eased his tension a bit. "I'm assuming they do know." She waved a hand around them. "Enough folks have walked past down by the shore on nights we've been out. I just prefer not to be interrogated about it."

He was with her there. But needed a bit more clarity on the other. "But...if they start to pair us up, is that going to bother you?"

Her brow drew together again, not so much in a frown, as a look of deep consideration. Except that she was looking right at him. Wondering what to tell him?

What he wanted to hear?

What he *didn't* want to hear?

Good luck with any of it. She'd have a hard time figuring any of that out when he wasn't sure for himself where he stood.

Except that he didn't want to stop whatever it was they had going on. Not until they'd arrived wherever they were heading. Until they'd grown however much they were going to grow. Until she'd healed enough to get on with her life. Until they were done.

Because that would come. The time when it was over. Logic had made that one clear from the very start.

"The only thing that would bother me is if they start thinking we're going to do like they all did," she said slowly.

He knew, instinctively, where she was going with that one. "Fall in love, get married, start a family," he filled in the three been-there-done-thats.

"Those are the ones," she said, not sounding all that weighed down by the future she was describing for the two of them. And ultimately, for herself.

He wasn't feeling as...cast apart...as usual, either. "As long as you and I understand, what anyone else thinks doesn't matter," he told her. "And if they ask, we can just smile and say nothing."

She smiled then, saying, "Smiling's good. I like that. Smiles hide fun secrets."

Not depressing ones. He smiled back at her and said, "So we're frying turkey on my deck on Thursday."

"And preparing the rest of the feast together while the bird is cooking?" she asked him.

Preparing it together. He liked the sound of that. Preparing the feast together. Something he and Lyla had never done.

"Did you and Brent ever do that?" he asked her. Wouldn't change the affirmative answer he was about to deliver, but he'd like to know if he had to be more sensitively aware of her while they were cooking.

"Nope," she told him. "We always went home for the holidays. And I cooked with our moms while he watched the games with our dads. It was all boringly traditional."

Her words didn't quite break on the words, but they seemed to catch as they passed her throat, deepening their tone. And he said, "I don't think it sounds boring at all."

But what would he know? He'd never had the chance to find out. Nor would he, so dwelling on that aspect of their plans served no purpose. "So...we'll cook together, and need to plan the menu, but right now, I've got an online meeting with my agent, so need to get going." His agent. But not really. He had no plans to speak with the woman who represented his articles for him. WG had a meeting to discuss another upcoming book tour. Which wasn't going to happen. And to discuss terms on a nice movie offer that had just come up for his first novel. Dale was moderately a bit excited about that development. Enough to have already done some research into the process on his own.

He'd barely seen Millie's wave as she'd run off toward her place. But he had her, and not any movie deal, on his mind the entire time he stood under the stingingly cold water of his shower.

Whatever it took to control his reaction to the woman.

He needed to be sharp for the meeting. WG would never let him hear the end of it if he wasn't.

Millie trained with her kids, ages nine to fourteen, on Tuesday and Wednesday that week, due to the holiday. And she shopped. Since she was already going to be out, she'd told Dale it made sense that she pick up the things they were going to need for dinner. And with him being busy with his writing after his video meeting with his agent—she figured he must have gotten a request for some article he had to research—he hadn't demurred a bit.

Other than running in the mornings, she hadn't seen him all week. Hadn't yet had a chance to tell him that she'd visited a couple of shelters and was thinking about bringing home an abandoned sheltie mix even while she was still at Chelsea's with Magic. She just needed to talk to Chelsea about Magic sharing her space with a three-year-old girl who was still regaining her strength and ability to trust humans to be kind to her.

But with Magic around all of the other dogs on the beach, and having spent time overnight with Dale more than once when he'd been housing other four-legged residents of the beach, she figured the Newfoundland would be fine. And maybe having Magic around would help the frightened girl acclimate easier, too.

She and Dale had made out their grocery list together, via text. They were going traditional all the way and making enough of each dish to accompany the nineteen-pound turkey she'd picked up. She'd figured that way they'd each have ample leftovers for the weekend, and to put in their freezers, too. He'd given her a thumbs-up on that one.

Because they were doing all the preparation together, at his place, she was headed to his cottage Wednesday just after six, to unload the bags of groceries, stopping by her place first to pick up the turkey she'd had thawing since she'd purchased it on Monday.

It felt good, being busy with preparations. Familiar. But in an all-new way. There'd be none of the people, the tables, the dishes upon which she ate to remind her of what she'd lost. They'd all become voices of the past. Dale was the present. And she'd yet to find her future. But making Thanksgiving dinner, with all the trimmings, felt like she was heading there. Coming back to life, one small step at a time.

She'd call her parents, of course, at some point during the day. And hear about everyone in the small-town Alabama she'd left. Maybe she'd even go back someday. For the first time since she'd bugged out of town after Brent's funeral, she felt like the possibility of a return might actually be on the table for the future. She'd issue, once again, an invitation for her parents to visit her in San Diego—with the added allure of Ocean Breeze to share with them if they'd come out before the end of February, when her lease was up.

And was fully prepared to hear them say how busy they were with her younger sister and brother and their spouses and children. It had taken Millie a while to realize that she'd lifted right out, and even longer to figure out why. Seeing her hurting, hurt them, too. She didn't fit anymore. Not with their way of life. They loved her every bit as much. She got that, too.

Gained strength from having them on call anytime of the day or night. At some point they'd all meet up again. When she was ready. Maybe sooner than any of them had expected, based on the energy pumping through her as she texted Dale from her house to tell him she was on her way down.

For the first time since Brent's collapse, she felt...a normal moment. Not like she was whole, completely, but like she could find enough left of herself to experience some true enjoyment in life again.

Baking the pies Wednesday night had been a Thanksgiving tradition her entire life. Just made good sense to have them baked to free up the oven for all the dishes, and then rolls, that would be needing it on Thursday. She'd bagged the pie supplies separately, planning to take care of that activity on her own. Right up until Dale, who was helping her unload, asked about the canned pumpkin that was not among the groceries he'd unbagged and set against the back wall of what would be their main work counter.

The same spot that had also served as their brewery.

He hadn't noticed the missing apples, was her first thought. Guessing, from there, that pumpkin was his favorite. She liked knowing that. And told him about her pie plan, the reasoning behind it.

"I thought the idea was a full Thanksgiving experience," he said to her, meeting her gaze head-on.

"You want to help make the pies?"

"Wasn't that the plan? To do it all together?" He met her gaze with a raised brow and added, "What, you don't think I'm capable of baking a decent pie?" He was teasing her. The tone of his voice, the challenge in his gaze made that clear.

"Are you?"

"I've never made a pie in my life. Or have even seen one being made, that I can recall. But I said I'd share the load equally. I've already conceded to you doing the shopping, since you were already out, but I feel that I must draw the line at the pies. If mine sucks, I'll eat it."

Millie had no idea why he was pushing things. Maybe just to have her say she really didn't mind, she liked making pies. To let him off the hook. Or, the other more likely possibility, that he was rescuing her from what could quickly have become a painful trip down memory lane. Either way, she went out to the front seat of her car, grabbed the pie ingredients, and carried them inside.

Dale had no pie pans, or plates as Millie called them. At her command, he started peeling apples while she drove down to her place to collect the requisite baking dishes. And mentally hit himself upside the head, too. What in the hell was he doing...making a big deal out of preparing a damned meal.

As if traditional Thanksgiving celebrations had ever been anywhere on any of his list of experiences he'd like to have someday. And yet, there he was, wanting to ease Millie's pain as she slowly found her way back into something that had meant a lot to her for her entire life—and yet would be living differently for the rest of her years. But wanting more, too.

When Millie had talked about her holiday traditions, the warmth in her voice, the light in her eyes before reality had hit and the glow had dimmed, had intrigued him.

As though, if he shared the experience with her, in particular, he could get some kind of inkling what the fuss was all about.

Seemed like one hell of a lot of work to him all to just sit down for fifteen minutes, eat, and then have another whole set of chores getting it all cleaned up and put away afterward. And yet, that glow on Millie's face when she'd talked about the sameness of it every year...he'd been seeing replays of it in his mind's eye ever since.

He'd never had cause to peel an apple before. Would have opted out of the apple pie for two pumpkin ones, but since apple was part of what had put that bit of radiance in Millie's eyes, he was all for the apple. Forgoing the potato peeler she'd suggested he use, Dale grabbed his freshly sharpened peeling knife from the block holding the set of knives he'd purchased five years before when he'd first started cooking for himself. He'd paid a mint for them. But they'd paid him back many times since.

Turning the blade of the knife on an angle against the apple, he experimented a time or two and then, holding the edge of a peel against his thumb, slowly turned the apple round and around until the entire peel was off. In one long strip.

Chin jutting, nodding, he picked up number two of the six apples Millie had placed before and repeated the effort. And was quite proud of himself when he heard her let herself back in his front door, and all six apples were lying on the counter, with six long strips lined up next to them.

Adding his own flavor to the new memories they were creating out of her old one.

He might not have any Thanksgiving know-how to

contribute, but he was there to assist in her fight to find moments of happiness for her future. Anything that put a smile on her face was a step in the right direction.

## *Chapter Thirteen*

Millie didn't want to throw away the perfect strips of apple peels. They'd not only made her smile, in their perfect symmetry by their apples on the counter, but Dale's creativity touched her, too. The man quietly gave so much to the world around him. To the people in it.

Pulling out her phone, she searched how to preserve apple peels, pulled out the baking sheet she'd brought to set the apple pie plate on while it was baking in case of spillover and carefully laid all six peels out on the sheet. Setting the oven to the required temperature, she slid the sheet in the oven. And turned to see Dale frowning between the very used handwritten recipes on notecards she'd also brought in with her.

"There's nothing here that says anything about cooking apple peels," he told her. Then shook his head, "I'm not thinking they'd be any good in a pie."

Good point. One she hadn't thought of in time. "They aren't for the pie, they're for me," she told him, and immediately broke into a litany of what he should do next—slicing the apples into precise identical pieces, while she did what she was going to do. In that second, she had no idea what that was, but she kept talking. Telling him why they were doing the apple pie first—had to do with oven temps as the pumpkin pie required two different ones—and then determined that when he was done slicing, he could mix the sugar and cinnamon and make the entire apple pie, while she worked on the pumpkin. Just made more sense to her.

And…it was how she and her mother had always done it. They'd switch up who did which one, but they always each took one and did it all.

They hadn't ever had long slices of peel to put in the oven to dry out, though. Which slowed the whole baking process by half an hour.

With both pies ready to bake, she turned from putting them in the refrigerator to await their separate oven times, to run straight into Dale, who'd been heading to the sink with dirty mixing bowls filled with measuring cups, spatulas and the blade from his professional kitchen mixer.

He didn't drop anything. She no longer had anything in hand to drop. It might have been better if she had. Instead of bending down to clean up a mess, she stood there, her face inches from his, staring into warm brown eyes.

Feeling as though he was reaching out to her with that gaze, telling her things she so badly wanted to hear, Millie opened her mouth to speak, but had nothing to say. If she allowed herself to believe what she was seeing, he was attracted to her. Was fond of her. Cared about her, even. She wanted all of it.

But…

He leaned in. Gave her a quick kiss on the lips, and then turned to the sink with his handful of work yet to be done. Hearing the water running, Millie stood there, her entire body seeming to tingle from that brief touch of his lips, not even sure for a second that it had happened.

That she hadn't just imagined it. Or had a flash from one of the many dreams she'd had of the man over the past couple of months.

Maybe she should go. He was consuming her.

She didn't want to go. Didn't want to leave him standing there alone with a sink full of dirty dishes. That wasn't the way holiday memories worked. Holidays were standout times, when everyone was at their best, kind of a moniker by which to live during the rest of the days of the year. From what Dale had told her, every holiday celebration he'd ever been a part of—because he and Lyla blew off such things due to the anxiety they brought her from her youth—had been him feeling alone. On the outside looking in.

Reaching for the drawer she'd pulled out earlier looking for a spoon, only to find dish towels, she pulled the handle, grabbed the top brown terry cloth and moved over to stand next to Dale, drying every piece he washed.

"I'd have put them in the dishwasher," she said, just to be talking about something that had nothing to do with a kiss. Not because she had a problem with his dish cleaning choice.

"I didn't want to run it with just these few things, but figured we're going to need every inch of available space in there tomorrow."

She nodded. Agreeing with his assessment.

Glancing at her as he put a big wooden-handled mixing spoon in the drainboard, he said, "I can get the pies in and out of the oven if you're tired and would like to head home."

She'd had a longer than usual session with her kids.

Plus shopping. But she stuck to the plan. "We're doing this together," she told him.

And moved away from him every chance she got as they completed the cleaning task. Putting away each dish, as soon as it was dry. Stopping to remove her apple peels from the oven and put the apple pie in.

Distancing herself from what had just happened between his lips and hers. Trying not to think about how badly she wanted it to happen again.

And finding it nearly impossible to think of anything else.

He wasn't sorry he'd kissed her. That particular ice had needed to be broken. He wasn't even totally sorry that he'd put Millie in such an apparent tizzy. Like she didn't know what to do with herself so close to him in the kitchen.

She hadn't left. He'd given her the out. She could have gone home.

He was taking that to mean that the kiss had interested her. At the very least, it hadn't scared her off.

He hadn't planned the turn the evening had taken. The quick peck had just happened. A natural reaction to the near crash they'd had in the kitchen. A healthy man. A healthy woman. Both unattached. Spending the holiday alone together. Purposely making a memory to look back on.

Clearly fond of each other. Sharing their deepest pains.

Having already had a conversation about contraceptives...

He wasn't going to push the moment. The next move was up to her. Dale didn't waver on that point, even when, after Millie hung her towel over the oven door to dry,

Juice went to her, nudging her hand. And her fingers started to move on the dog's head.

But she wasn't grabbing her keys and heading for the door.

"You want to watch some reruns?" he asked her. They were on the last season of the first of his many sets of full sitcom collections. And they watched from two different reclining chairs with a table in between them.

He hadn't intended to buy the set. He'd only needed the one chair. Had figured that was all he'd ever need, but the grouping had been on sale the weekend he'd gone shopping. He'd purchased all three pieces for the price of the one chair, plus a little change.

"Sure," Millie said, sounding cheerful enough. If he didn't factor in the more than thirty seconds it had taken her to respond to the invitation.

She wasn't leaving. They'd had a first kiss, and she was hanging around. His penis kept repeating the fact to his brain over the next hour, during shows. Between shows. When the show was paused for pie-in-and-out-of-the-oven duty. Egging him on to the point of needing Millie to go just so he could get some peace.

And a cold shower.

He wasn't kicking her out. If he ached until dawn, he'd do so, right there in that chair with the television running. The woman was facing her first holiday after grief, rather than running from it, and he was there to hold her up. No matter what it took.

The pies were out of the oven. Cooled. Covered. Her work there was done. Millie moved slowly in the galley kitchen, putting the foil back in the drawer where she'd found it. Rearranging the towel she'd hung but had messed up with her opening and closing of the oven door.

It was time to go. There were no more excuses not to do so. But it felt like there was more yet to come.

More that she wanted to happen?

Who was she kidding? She'd put her diaphragm in when she'd had to pee an hour before. That, with its ninety-four percent pregnancy prevention rating, and a condom with its ninety-eight percent, would be ample.

She'd made Thanksgiving pies with the man. Was covering old memories with a brand-new one. And she'd been dripping with desire for Dale for weeks.

Talking about sex, buying contraceptives, were all foreplay. But the final step, once taken, was irreversible.

There'd be no going back to just Brent.

There was no going back. Ever. Brent was no longer there. She wasn't being unfaithful moving forward. He'd gone to heaven. She'd been left behind on earth to live a different life. Without him.

God help her, she wanted to have sex with Dale Wilson. The man was hot. He was smart and funny, observant and kind. He was alive.

So was she.

He was also, she observed as she turned in the kitchen to see him watching her, carrying around a bulge in the cotton pants he'd had on all night. Once her gaze dropped there, she couldn't look away.

She watched as the bulge of zipper-covered fabric moved closer. Felt herself grow damp between the legs. And when Dale reached her, lifting her chin with one finger until her gaze met his, and he asked, "You want to?"

She looked him straight in the eye and nodded.

\* \* \*

He meant to take it slow. To savor every second of the experience. To make sure it was good for her, first and foremost.

He hadn't factored on seven years of abstinence coming into play. Her two and his five were a combination too heady to fight. The second he pulled Millie to him, and their mouths opened for their second kiss, he was lost. Caught up in a maelstrom of emotion and sensation that consumed him.

By the time they made it to the living room, his clothes were off. He stopped to help her step out of her leggings—her last piece to go—and then completely naked, picked her up and carried her back to his bedroom, kissing her the entire time.

He didn't have to concern himself with going easy on her. Taking it slow. He touched her breasts, caressed her stomach, and when she spread her legs, moved his fingers between them. Planning to stay there a while, move around, turn her on in every way he knew how. But two minutes in, she rolled on him, sat up, straddling him, and lowered herself on his painfully stiff body part. She pulled him in tight, shooting exquisite pleasure through him, and drove him to the point of explosion as she moved on him. He heard her cry out just before he went. Felt her spasms clasping around him. And opened his arms, holding her to him, when she collapsed on top of him.

He couldn't remember a more perfect moment. Couldn't leave their bubble to remember anything at all.

Until he felt her body start to jerk against him. In spasms. And those he recognized. Feeling himself shrink inside her, he knew he had to get to the bathroom and take care of business, but couldn't shove her aside while she was crying.

Lifting her upper body so that she was sitting upright on him, he pushed her hair away from her face, ready to dry her tears. Only to see that the woman was...laughing.

Maybe hysterically so. But with a definite smile on her face, and mirth in her gaze. "Oh...my...god... Dale. I don't know if I should apologize, or thank you. I think probably both, so I'm sorry, and...thank you." The last was said as her breasts came back to his chest and her lips settled on his.

Passionately. And yet, slowly. Not a frenetic hello, nor a goodbye. And he started to grow inside her again.

Millie woke up slowly. Disoriented. Her body sore in places that...

She was naked...

And it all came flooding back. The way she'd come on to Dale. How she'd known what to do was beyond her. Brent had always instigated lovemaking between the two of them.

Then, going at it a second time right away—she'd never done that before, either.

After that...her last memory was lying flat on her back, with Dale doing the same beside her, listening to the escalated breathing of his come down. She'd closed her eyes, reliving it all...

Dale. Turning her head slowly, not wanting to wake him, to start anything up again...or face him, she saw his face relaxed in slumber, the slight shadow of a days' growth darkening his jaw and chin.

What time was it? She'd never seen his bedroom before. Damn sure hadn't looked around when he'd carried her in there.

The clock was on her side of the bed. On a nightstand. 3:04.

She was naked in another man's bed at three o'clock in the morning. Fact slammed into her. Tightening her chest into a knot.

She had to go. Had to go. Had to go.

Sliding off the bed with as little movement as possible, Millie didn't look back as she crept from the room. Praying that Juice, wherever he was, stayed asleep right along with his master. And that Magic didn't make a sound as they left.

What had she done? Brent...oh, god, Brent...

She'd slept with another man.

Had done way more than that. With memories of the things she'd done hours before flooding her, shaming her, confusing her, Millie grabbed desperately for her clothes. She couldn't leave naked. And then, afraid of waking Juice—who'd alert Dale—she slid behind the first closed door she came to in the hallway, just long enough to get into the leggings and crop top she'd put on for practice with the kids the day before.

What had she done?

Who *was* she? She hadn't even known she was capable of such behavior. Making things up that she hadn't even fantasized about before.

She had to get out of there. Get back to Chelsea's cottage and...she didn't know what. She'd figure it out when she got there.

Pants on, twisted, but covering her, she was sliding

into the top when her hand hit something and papers fell to the floor.

Thinking swear words she'd never say, Millie slowed enough to look around her. To notice the L-shaped desk. The two big flat-screen monitors.

Dale's office? He was a gamer? Thoughts tumbled over themselves as she bent to pick up the papers. Moonlight coming in through the window helped her make sure she got them all.

Eyes adjusting to the darkness caused her to see the big bold letterhead on the top of one of the pages.

Mouth open, she put the small stack back on the corner of the desk. And then, as though possessed by the devil himself, glanced back at them. Holding a page up to the moonlight to read the smaller print. Not much of it. But enough.

WG Gunder was granting rights to a major movie studio. The bottom of the page held Dale Wilson's signature.

Putting the page back, as though it had cut her, she smoothed the edges of the stack, praying she had them in order, and hurried to the door. Opening it, closing it softly behind her, she saw Juice and Magic standing there, watching her. Instinctively petting the top of the poodle's head, letting him know she was okay, she grabbed Magic's collar and hurried him to the front door. To her car, and putting it in Neutral, let it slide down the driveway and into the road before she started it up.

Dale Wilson was WG Gunder? Dale Wilson was *WG Gunder*. Brent had raved about the man's first book. He'd been a thriller reader. She most definitely was not.

Brent. WG Gunder. Chills came over her. Followed by

a strange calming warmth. She was human. Alive. With a life she was expected to live in front of her.

And sleeping with Dale? Meant nothing in terms of her and Brent. It wasn't the sex, it was the commitment. And she and Dale didn't have one. By mutual need, and desire, too.

By the time she was pulling into her own garage, she was feeling better. Cheerful, almost. She'd had an incredible, mind-blowing, make-her-forget-every-sad-feeling-she'd-ever-known experience. But it didn't mean anything. Was just a fling.

Hell, the man was so much not becoming one with her that he hadn't even bothered to tell her that he was WG Gunder. Let alone that he'd just been offered a movie deal that would set him up for life.

It hit her then, that Dale was clearly already set. WG Gunder. The man was a #1 *New York Times* Best Seller, at least three times over that she knew. She'd quit paying attention after Brent died.

But the fact was, he wasn't even sharing his real identity with her. Which meant…they were exactly who they'd said they'd be for each other. Like shadows passing in the night, understanding what could and couldn't be, and hopefully, finding their own personal freedom pass into daylight by the time she moved and they never saw each other again.

She wasn't starting a committed relationship with Dale. Wasn't replacing Brent. She'd simply taken another step toward moving to whoever she would eventually be. Finding a way to be alive in spite of losing half of herself.

The thoughts were a little sketchy in some places, but they sufficed. Waiting while Magic relieved herself before letting them both into the cottage, Millie showered, put on her pajamas, set her alarm so she didn't sleep through the next morning's prep details, and climbed into bed.

Stretching. Accepting the soreness as part of the workout life was putting her through. And hoped, as she fell asleep, that Dale would awake with no regrets.

She couldn't be a setback in his life.

And...if she wasn't, and he was okay, maybe they could do the sex thing another time or two before they parted ways.

## *Chapter Fourteen*

Dale heard Millie go. Listened for the click of the front door closing before getting out of bed. He'd been awake from the time she'd turned to look at the clock. He'd watched Juice go after her, knew by the alert hold of the dog's head that he'd been working. And left him to it.

If she was regretting what they'd done, Dale showing up wasn't going to help matters.

If she needed Dale, she knew where to find him. And he'd be there.

He didn't expect her to be, though. After a hot shower, Dale went back to bed. And slept. Waking with the dawn. He prepared for the day as he'd have done if things were good between him and Millie. Showering again, just to have that be a start to the day. Shaved. Put on some nicer shorts, beige, and a long-sleeved, button-down black shirt, with black flip flops.

Whether Millie showed or not, he was going to prepare their feast. Eat the food. And then pack the rest in freezer bags, half for her, half for him.

One thing he'd learned in all the years of his existence was that as long as he drew breath life would go on.

He'd also learned that there were days that brought more pain than others. He made coffee. Sat on the back deck with Juice while he drank it. Telling himself that he was fine.

But he wasn't.

Millie deserved so much more than he had to give. And he wanted her. The encounter they'd had the night before...way beyond sex. Not love. But more than just physical.

Far more.

In some ways, more than he'd had with Lyla. Deeper. More aware of what every moment was worth.

For him, anyway.

And maybe for Millie. While it had been happening. He was guessing, not so much when she woke up. She hadn't even looked his way as she'd slid out of the bed and flitted from the room.

Because of Brent. She'd had sex with another man. Two things there, that Dale could see. One, perhaps she'd felt unfaithful to her deceased husband. Likely she had. Most particularly if he'd been her only lover prior to Dale.

And two, she'd moved on from who she'd always been. Whether she was ready or not, she'd taken an irrevocable step forward. Brent was no longer the only one. And never would be again.

He got it all. Just didn't see where he fit into it—except as the bad guy. Not that she'd blame him for what happened. She'd been as culpable as he had. Had put in her diaphragm before he'd even known that she was ready to take the next step with him, he'd found out later.

He took a brief second to ponder that one, with a hint of interested pleasure, before falling back to reality.

And the fact that, most likely, Millie was blaming herself for being weak around Dale. Giving into momentary temptation. Or, even for wanting more out of life than being a widow. As though that somehow diminished the love she and Brent had shared.

She might see Dale as a bad influence on her.

Or...she might be walking up the beach toward his cottage. In a pair of brown form-fitting pants he hadn't seen before. With a gauzy orange long-sleeved top on over some kind of brown tank.

He didn't stand up to greet her. Didn't want to overplay his welcome. But, damn, it was good to see her.

A boon, WG would say.

Holding up his half-filled cup as Juice wagged his tail and greeted their newcomer at the top of the steps, Dale said, "I brewed a pot, so we didn't have to wait for individual cups. It's still fresh."

When it was just him, he used the single-serving option. She wouldn't have any way of knowing that. Except to assume, since she'd seen his state-of-the-art coffeemaker. Something WG had purchased for his late-night stints.

None of which mattered in the moment except that coffee conversation was innocuous. And above all else, he couldn't risk scaring her away by letting her know how very glad he was to see her. Or to, in any way, put them on any kind of intimate footing that would remind her why she'd run out on him the night before.

She was there.

And that was enough.

Millie had coffee. In the kitchen. No way she could sit when there was so much prep work to be done.

Or sit, unoccupied, with Dale. The second she'd seen

him sitting there on his deck, freshly shaven and dressed up—for him—her body had started buzzing with memory from the night before.

And early morning sex wasn't on the agenda.

Nor did she want it to be.

Letting him know she was going to start the dressing, she put butter on to melt and focused on ingredients. Stopped to lay out all the recipes in a line on the end of the counter, taking the dressing one for herself, and then grabbing a mixing bowl.

By the time she had herself focused, Dale was there, glancing over the recipes. Taking one for himself and getting busy.

They made a great team, as far as chefs went, working around and with each other. Each paying attention to their own creation. She was careful to watch every move she made so there were no accidental bumps or other touches. And when the silence started to get too loud, she'd jabber out loud about whatever memory popped into her mind associated with whatever dish she was working on.

Dale listened. He nodded. Chuckled some. And at one point, when she turned and caught him watching her, he excused himself to the deck to set up the fryer and fill it with oil.

She was thankful for the respite. And starting to worry, too.

Two hours, and there hadn't even been a good morning kiss. Fifteen minutes of pie preparation and there'd been one. And that had been *before* they'd had sex.

Of course, she knew why. It all rested on her. She'd run out on him. And then had shown up as though nothing had happened.

And so, when, a few minutes later, he returned to the kitchen, she continued to slice fruit for the whipped cream salad she was working on, but said, "I'm doing the best I can."

She felt his glance more than caught it out of the corner of her eye but forced herself to turn and meet his gaze directly. It was pointed at the small pieces of grapes and bananas she'd already cut. Not on her, or the slice of apple in her hand. "They look fine to me," he told her. "Small enough to get a piece of everything in one bite."

Whether he knew she wasn't talking about the salad or not, she appreciated his segue from potentially troublesome to harmless. Wanted to just leave it at that. The day was too young to make it any harder. But seeing him standing there, having been run out on, not knowing… "That's not what I was talking about."

He nodded. "I know." And then added. "To both."

She met his gaze at that. Held on. But couldn't put down the apple or move closer. "I'm just glad you're here," he told her.

The honesty in his tone, and also evident from the warmth in his eyes, set her fluttering inside a bit, but also calmed her in the unique way Dale had. "Me, too," she told him, and left it at that.

They'd cooked. They'd eaten. They'd stored leftovers. And they'd cleaned up. All without a single word said about them—the two of them. At his instigation, most of the day had been about Millie's past Thanksgivings. Based on her expressions, the number of times she'd smiled, she seemed to enjoy the topic. Funny thing was, he'd enjoyed it, too. Having never had a close family celebration in his life, he was getting his fill vicariously through the woman who'd invaded his beach, his life, and filled up holes there he hadn't thought possible to fill.

What he also noticed, as the hours went by, was that she rarely mentioned Brent in her stories. Mostly they'd been of her mom and her. In the early days, her grandmother, too. And later, her little sister.

While he'd been a bit surprised to hear that she *had* siblings—he'd somehow surmised that she and Brent had been only children—he'd learned that she'd been four when her little brother was born. And five when her sister came along. Both of them were married, with two children and one child, respectively, and both lived within a couple of miles of their parents.

The more Millie talked, the more he'd realized how the lives they'd all built, the life she'd been planning to move home to, didn't fit the woman she'd become. Didn't mean they didn't all love each other. They'd just grown in different directions.

And...he figured...for the time being, with her wound still so fresh, going home, being with everyone who had what she'd planned for and lost would not only be difficult for her, but would be hard on all of them, too. They'd know that just by being who they were, being around them would cause her pain.

Something he'd never considered before when thinking about family. Could be that WG had idolized some situations. Dale made a mental note to update the guy.

They were sitting out on his deck—her choice, as most of the day had been. He wanted to be a safe place for her, even if that meant never having sex again.

Incredible as it had been.

A few people had walked by, but mostly the space was deserted, as so many congregated down at Sage and Gray's renovated place at the end of the beach. Dale was glad to know they were all together. And didn't feel a need to be there with them.

He was right where he wanted to be.

"We did it," he told her, the first personal conversation between them in hours.

"I know. And it's there. I just wanted to get through the day before we talked about it."

The words were a shock to his system. Sending him into different orbit. But because he didn't want her thinking that he was forcing a sexual conversation he said, "I meant, we did it, as in, we both celebrated a family holiday and lived to tell about it." The deadly silence that was immediately obvious upon his last word prompted him to continue with. "Not only did we make it through, I actually had a really good time."

Surprisingly good. He'd put it right up there with his best Thanksgiving ever, but then, he had very little to compare it to.

"You know, in some ways, I did, too," Millie told him. "It was nice not having the ballgames on in the background, with men cheering or yelling at the screen. While I always thought I liked the cacophony of the holidays, turns out, I like a more intimate meal. One where no one at the table gets lost in the shuffle. You know, when you have so many people there, the voices all talk over each other, or everyone is quiet listening to one story, and you get up from the table and realize some voices you never heard at all."

Dale wondered if Millie's was one of the voices never

heard. The woman had dedicated her life to taking care of others—even in her marriage, it sounded as if she'd followed her husband on the circuit, taking breaks from her career to tend to his —but did anyone stop and take care of her?

Not that she'd ever ask. He got that. He was the same way. And yet she'd... "It was great today," he told her, more intimately open than he'd been with her. "You gave me a real holiday, and I truly enjoyed every minute of it. Thank you."

She nodded. Held his gaze for a moment, but then looked away, as though some other thought had crossed her mind. One not as complimentary.

Knowing that he could be opening them up to the sexual discussion they'd been avoiding since she'd misunderstood him earlier and announced that they should get through the day before they had *the talk*, he asked, "What?"

And was not at all prepared when she said, "I was just wondering if WG Gunder enjoyed the day as much as you did." Shock hit him first. Freezing him in place. And just as quickly, panic struck. How did she know? What did he do? Lie. He had to lie.

Juice's head nudged his hand. Once. Then again, much more insistently, and Dale ran his fingers through the dog's hair. On his head, his neck, and then, reaching down with both hands, pulled Juice's front paws to his thighs and petting the big poodle up and down his sides and back, too.

When he was calmer, he glanced over at Millie. Expecting to see hurt. Accusation. Distance. And saw compassion instead. Her gaze moved between him and the dog, and he got it.

Just as he knew when Juice was working, alerting him to discomfort that Millie might be feeling but not communicating, Millie had learned the signs, too. Not surprising since she was a medical professional trained to notice changes in a patient's demeanor and equilibrium, as well as their vital signs.

Hell, for all he knew, the pulse in his neck was beating hard enough for her to see.

The thoughts brought him a return to at least a semblance of his calm. And he asked, "How long have you known?"

There was no point in denial. She knew. Beyond that, one thing he could not do with Millie was lie to her. Their bond, temporary though it was, was too sacred for that.

She glanced at her watch. "A little over twelve hours."

And he glanced at his. Thought about her looking at the clock on his nightstand, and him seeing it too. Did the math. After she got out of his bed, but before she'd left his house that morning. "How?"

Like it mattered? But it was something he wanted to know. And was buying him time to figure out the rest.

What the fallout was going to be.

"I…didn't want to stand in the living room and get dressed…in case…"

She'd ceased looking at him from the time she'd looked at her watch. Was looking out at the waves that were powerful enough to ease aching souls. He got it.

"…in case I came walking out," he said.

Saw her lower lip jut out as she nodded. Then said, "I

went into the first room I came to, closed the door behind me."

"My office." She'd snooped in his office? He didn't believe it. Just wasn't Millie's style.

"I was...a bit...panicky, couldn't get my arm through my sleeve and it flopped and knocked the pages off the corner of your desk."

The movie contract he'd signed digitally, but had printed out for his files. He'd planned to reread it one more time, from paper copy, to make sure he hadn't missed anything before putting it away.

And now he was on the hook. And off it, too. His secret was out. He'd have to move. And where in the hell was he going to find a home that suited him as perfectly as the cottage on Ocean Breeze did?

"You're secret's safe with me, Dale." He glanced up to see her watching his hands on Juice, who had all fours back on the floor. Dale was leaning forward, rubbing the dog.

He nodded. Wanted to thank her. To apologize for not telling her.

"And I get it," she told him. "You and I, no matter how intense it might get now and then, we're temporary. Two lost souls who understand each other helping the other find their way. That's all. Telling me about your career—that's not part of this. Just like I don't talk much about my nursing stints. I knew you were a writer. You mentioned the article about the turtle because it was pertinent to me. I just...needed you to know I was someplace I shouldn't have been and stumbled on the information. I should never have opened your office door. And I'm so sorry. I've been thinking on and off all day about having to tell you, and…just… I'm sorry."

He'd kept a huge secret from her, one detailing his very identity, and *she* was sorry?

His mind reeled with all she'd revealed during the confession, and went with the one thing he could grasp without risk of losing parts of himself. "You were so worried that you might have to face me in a state of undress when you left my bed, that you dove into my office for safety?"

He asked the question.

Didn't need the answer, though.

The writing was clearly on the wall. He didn't have to be a *New York Times* bestselling author to get that story right.

Yeah, the conversation she'd been dreading was going pretty much as Millie had figured it would. But they had to have it if they were going to move forward. And based on the day they'd just shared, in spite of the elephant on the table, she was pretty sure they both wanted to continue seeing each other.

Whatever business they had together wasn't done yet.

"I…felt…guilty," she told him, knowing that total honesty was the only way. "You were… I had no idea… I did things I didn't even know people did…" She stopped abruptly.

Too much.

Honesty was a must, yes, but she didn't have to bare her soul completely.

Just as he hadn't with his writing. WG Gunder. She still couldn't believe it. Several times that day she'd looked at him and thought of the one book of his she knew the storyline to. A thriller on steroids.

She hadn't had sex with WG Gunder. She'd had sex with Dale Wilson. And hoped to do so again. That's where she had to focus.

"When I woke up, it was like, I didn't know who I was. I needed some space to examine myself, my mind, my feelings, my actions, my reactions. To assimilate what was, with what is, and find some bearings."

"And did you?"

"I'm here, aren't I?" She glanced over then, locked gazes with him, and held on.

Hardly noticing when Juice lumbered over to the deck steps and lay down.

## *Chapter Fifteen*

Though he'd never have believed it, sex the second night with Millie was even more intense than the first. They took it slower. Talked to each other as they touched, played some, and when they came, they did it together, not just with their release, but with joined eyes and holding hands. Those seconds were the most incredible thing he'd ever experienced.

Because they weren't looking for a long-term relationship, neither had any expectations. There was no future together to tend to, which allowed them to just be fully in the moment. Neither had anything more to lose, but individual possibilities to gain.

Not for future relationships—Dale fully understood that Millie was right where he was on that one. They'd had the loves of their lives. That part was over for them. But they could still have experiences on a deeper level. And feel moments of absolute joy. Millie's words, not his. But he adopted them as his own.

They didn't fall right to sleep afterward. Instead, lying propped up on pillows in his bed, he asked, "You want a beer?" Because he did.

With a cockeyed look at him, she half grinned and said, "Yeah. Mint, please," but didn't get up and walk naked with him to the kitchen. He had his robe there. Didn't pull it on. Just walked his tight butt in front of her, admitting to himself that he was strutting his marine-honed muscles for her viewing pleasure, and was just as slow and casual on his return.

He'd already uncapped the bottles and they clicked, and then sipped. Holding her bottle with both hands at her belly, Millie laid her head back against her pillow and then suddenly shot straight up. Put her beer on the nightstand. "I'll be right back," she said, and headed down the hall to the bathroom there.

Frowning, thinking that she'd suddenly been overcome with illness, Dale set his own bottle on the night table that was only there because it was part of the set, pulled on some shorts and sat on the end of the bed, waiting for her.

She was back much sooner than he'd expected, with a wad of Kleenex in her hand. And reality dawned. He'd taken care of his protective situation. Had forgotten all about hers. As, obviously, had she.

Which sent a shiver of dread through him as he looked back to the night before. They'd fallen asleep...until three in the morning.

And reminded himself that he'd used a condom. And everything had been fully contained when he'd removed it. Each time.

The rest...was just for peace of mind.

"Everything okay?" he asked, when he saw her slide the wad of paper into the purse she'd brought in with her when they'd retired, fully clothed, to the bedroom earlier.

"Yeah," she said, not looking at him as she climbed back into bed, pulled the covers up over her breasts and reclaimed her beer, taking a long sip.

He wasn't ready to get comfortable again just yet. "What about last night? We fell asleep."

Her frown confused him. As did her question when she asked, "What about it?"

"I'm assuming by your urgency just now that the device has to come out afterward or anything that might have slipped by could hang around and eventually find a place to land." He knew how it all worked. Had taken health class in high school and college. Just had never been with anyone who used Millie's form of birth control.

And control was of utmost importance. He'd had, and lost, that chance.

"Actually, it's the opposite," she told him, sipping again. Bigger gulps than usual. "You're supposed to leave it in a minimum of six hours afterward."

"But..." He was getting edgier by the second.

"I just felt it slip. And so had to take it out."

He nodded. Then, thinking about the condoms, said, "We're ninety-eight percent protected anyway. And even if we're in that two percent, that little bit of extra would have done the trick." So announcing, he rid himself of his shorts, climbed back into bed and emptied a quarter of his beer in consecutive swallows.

Not because the thought of Millie having his child was abhorrent. But because...

The dead stare she was giving to his bedspread interrupted a train of thought he hadn't wanted to be on, anyway. And he said, "Seriously, Mil, there's nothing to worry about. We can get you a morning-after pill as soon as the stores open."

Mil. He'd never used the shortened version of her name before. Like they were close friends or something. Not just lives on the same short path for a blip in time. But she didn't seem to notice.

She'd nodded. But looked a bit stricken, too, as she turned her head to him and said, "It's not that. I just... one time with Brent and I...the diaphragm slipped." He hadn't needed to hear that, not lying naked with her right after sex. And yet, hearing it didn't bother him as much as it might have, either. Her memory fit with who they were to each other.

"It was the only protection we'd ever used," she said then, as though in a faraway place. One stricken with grief. He wanted to pull her against him. Wasn't sure it was what she needed. So he just sat there, being with her.

Until she said, "I got pregnant."

And the bottom of his world dropped out once again.

Millie couldn't believe what she'd just said. If she didn't have the words ringing over and over in her head, she'd have known she hadn't said them. Dale had heard them.

He was a witness. Was sitting there saying nothing.

"No one knew." She had to get that out to him. "Not my mom, not even Brent."

She'd meant to leave the gaffe right there. Some things didn't get any easier at all. But when she again heard her own words reverberating in the silence that lay heavily in the room, she said, "I'd just taken the test a couple of days before the marathon. Brent was in full training mode." She was there again, looking at the stick she'd peed on.

Elated. Thinking of Christmas at home with their families, giving everyone their news. Wondering if they were starting with a boy or a girl.

"And after he collapsed?" Dale said, drawing the word out slowly in question.

"I lost the baby." That's what she'd wanted him to know. She'd wanted that baby more than life in those weeks after she'd lost Brent. Had clung to it as the only means to stay sane. "Six weeks after his funeral." That baby, keeping her secret, had been the only thing that had gotten her through that godawful day. She hadn't been able to bear the idea of everyone swarming around her, coddling her, if she told them the news. Had needed to get back to San Diego, to the town where she and Brent had been living and had conceived their child. To feel closer to him…

And even then, two years later, after an incredible day and sitting in bed with a man she truly cared about, the fiery pain was excruciating inside her. She'd been trying to drown it in beer. Maybe would have succeeded if Dale hadn't pushed the issue.

He hadn't said a word since her bald announcement. No one knew what to say in such situations. Brent's death had taught her that over and over again. She'd resorted to just letting them know it was okay.

But with Dale…and this one topic…something no one else knew…the air around them was starting to stifle her. So she said, "You have WG, I had a baby…" Trying to put him at ease so he could stop looking for words to comfort her. Or even to draw her attention away from what she was feeling inside. They didn't exist.

"I had one, too."

All previous thought fled as Millie turned to stare at Dale. Had he just said what she'd thought he had?

The tightness of his jaw, his chin, the distance in his

gaze, was her answer. They had this in common, too? Not just their spouses, but the rest?

"Lyla was four months along when she was shot. They said it was a boy."

Two sentences that changed everything yet again.

With tears in her eyes, in her heart, Millie leaned over to Dale, resting her body against his side, and reached up a hand to run it tenderly across the tensed skin on his face. Then lay her head against him and felt his arms come up around her, holding her to him.

"Life isn't over," she whispered.

And felt him kiss the top of her head.

Millie stayed until dawn. Dale was awake, but not moving. He hadn't wanted to disturb her. And wasn't at all sure what the morning would bring.

He felt the change in her when she woke up. Watched her glance at the clock, and as she had the morning before, slide quietly out of the bed. But she didn't run away. Turning, she looked back at him. Caught him watching her.

"You okay?" he asked.

"Yeah, you?"

He nodded. And was done avoiding difficult subjects. They were out there, and he and Millie were handling them. So he asked, "You want to do the decorations together?"

Thanksgiving weekend. If they didn't put out their own decor, someone else would fill the beach in front of that cottage, down far enough to shore to not be intrusive, but still there, filling the entire two-mile stretch for all those who were lifted every year by their water trips to see the beach on Ocean Breeze.

Picking up her clothes, slowly stepping into them, she stopped just as she slid her tank top over those glorious breasts. Brow creased, she looked at him. And then her expression smoothed. "I'd like that," she told him.

He didn't suggest that she stay for breakfast. They weren't a couple. Or starting to become one. They had separate lives to maintain. But the tough stuff they shared due to circumstances fate had brought to them—made good sense to him that they be all in, there.

Which included the sex. They were moving on from the ones they'd thought would be their only sexual partners for the rest of their days.

After ablutions and meals in their separate spaces, they decorated his place first. Instead of jogging. Dale's suggestion since he knew that later in the day, the beach would be buzzing with activity, impromptu gatherings would happen, and he preferred to be on his deck. There, but in the distance.

"On the outside looking in," Millie told him when he said as much to her as they pieced together the Christmas tree with all red, white and blue lights and big plastic ornaments he'd carried out to the sand.

Dressed in black leggings and crop top with an unzipped red hoodie, she'd said the words prosaically, as simple fact. Like, *hey, the waves come and go with the tide*. They hit him as though she'd slapped him. Leaving her in the sand with Juice, he went back to the storage closet in his spare bedroom and hauled out the rest of the boxes of decor. Giving himself a moment to reclaim his peace.

But was still edgy by the time he came back outside. And said, "I do not sit on the deck because I'm still living my life on the outside looking in. I do so for the same reason you buried yourself in work, and also prefer not to join the social gatherings on the beach."

He'd never spoken so strongly to her before. And immediately regretted having done so. Just not his way. Never had been. He was strong. Got the job done. But had always been a man of fewer words, and most of those soft-spoken.

*On the outside looking in.* His words, initially. Given to her when he was describing all the Thanksgivings and Christmases of his life. Nothing to do with being a widower at such a young age. Or having lost his son before the little guy had a chance to take a single breath.

"I've never been one for large gatherings," she said, repeating something she'd told him earlier, when she'd been talking about her big wedding. So why did he feel like she was placating him with them in the current context?

"Nor have I," he told her, thinking back over the thirty-two years of his life. And coming up with the same story. He'd been moved around so much, he'd never really had time to settle into any family enough to feel himself a part of them—or group of friends, either.

And in the Marines...he'd been hell bent on climbing as high as he could as fast as he could. He'd wanted a life there. A lifetime ago.

"You think I'm living life on the outside looking in." He said the words aloud, nearly an hour later as they set up the last of his decorations—a big lit-up snowman with a red-white-and-blue-striped hat, and red and blue lights strung over his big white body.

Millie stood back, looking at the display they'd completed, and said, "Yeah." Again, as though they were speaking about a mundane fact. "I do, too. It's what life has made us."

Him, maybe. Not her. Not until tragedy had struck two years before.

Why the fact mattered to him, bothered him, Dale didn't understand. And that bothered him, too.

Driven by a force he couldn't identify he said, "We weren't on the outside looking in last night." Just not able to let the idea go.

When he was a kid, he'd been unable to control the circumstances of his life—him being on the outside looking in had been out of his control. But he was thirty-two years old. In control of his own destiny in terms of where he lived and what he did with his time. Who he chose to socialize with, or not.

"Nope. And it felt good, huh?" The tone of her voice, the small hint of a grin on her face, went a long way to bring Dale out of his funk.

But for the first time in a long while it hit him that, perhaps, he wasn't as healed as he'd thought he was.

It was possible he'd just gotten good at hiding. Complacent.

Settling for less.

It was possible he'd become...lazy.

And that, he could not accept.

*Sitting on the outside looking in.* Millie had said the words aloud on the beach behind Dale's cottage, but she hadn't been aiming them at him, directly. She'd been having a dawning moment. Seeing herself in the desire to stay on the deck, at a distance, while others in holiday moods decorated their stretches of beach.

And perhaps culminated the two days of decor building with an impromptu gathering on the beach. She'd heard about that last yearly habit from Dale—when he'd first talked to her about the tradition and the hundreds or thousands of sightseers' boats they'd start to see outside their reef starting over the next few days and lasting until the New Year. But she'd heard it from Chelsea, too. As recently as that week, when the woman had called about a maintenance appointment for the air conditioning unit. Chelsea had offered Millie all of what was left of her own supply of decorations. Which, considering the size of the beach, compared to her sister's small yard, was most of it.

But...taking Chelsea up on that offer, as Millie had planned to do...suddenly smelled like outside looking in to her.

On the other hand, if she purchased all her own outdoor decor, what would she do with it when she moved on? So...really...on Ocean Breeze, she *was* on the outside looking in that holiday season. Just as Dale had been most all his life.

Unless she gave a little consideration to Chelsea's repeated suggestion that Millie buy her own cottage on the beach at the end of her lease with Chelsea.

Could she even do that? Put the possibility on the table?

When she'd rented her cottage at the end of the summer, buying a place hadn't even been an option on her radar. How could she set down roots when she didn't have any?

But since then... Ocean Breeze had breathed new life into her. Bits and pieces of it, anyway. She still had no plan for her future. At all. But wasn't living all about looking at opportunities and determining if they were right for you?

For the first time since Brent had died, she felt like she had a home. Each time she turned onto the drive leading down to the beach, typed in the access code to get beyond the gate, there was a sense that she'd arrived where she wanted to be. Rather than just feeling like she'd reached a current destination as she had every time she returned to her apartment over the past two years.

And the dog idea...had grown beyond just a consideration. She was getting a dog. And didn't want it cooped up in an apartment when she went back to work.

There were no plans for that. Other than that she was pretty sure she wasn't going back to the children's hospital. But working with the kids at Young Runners was showing her how much she thrived on contributing to society by helping children grow and be healthy...

What better way to enrich a rescue dog's life than to bring her home to the beach on Ocean Breeze. She'd never feel like she was on the outside looking in there.

Shaking her head, Millie sat on her deck, waiting for Dale, still with no idea what she was going to put on her beach by way of holiday decor.

She and Dale, they'd crossed a lot of lines, spending so much time together, sleeping together, based on the fact that their time together was only temporary. They were helping each other move forward from grief, not embarking on a relationship.

But if she stayed on Ocean Breeze...and there she was, circled back to where she'd started.

She had to talk to Dale.

Before they put up her Christmas decorations. Except

that…he was going to be showing up on her back deck anytime. They'd taken a break for lunch, eaten separately—and for him to take care of some "WG stuff" as he'd put it as Friday was still a business day—and were scheduled to get her stretch of beach done.

Except that she hadn't retrieved Chelsea's outdoor decor from the shed.

A fact that Dale commented on when, ten minutes after Millie had taken the seat on her back deck, he climbed the stairs up to her, with Juice at his heels. "You need help getting the boxes out here?" he asked.

In the long lightweight, but close-fitting beige cotton pants and dark, tight T-shirt he'd had on that morning, the gorgeous six-foot man tempted her to blow off the day's plans and coax him into bed with her.

"Have a seat," she told him, instead, without acknowledging her lack of fulfilled duty.

He sat. Cocked his head slightly as he glanced at her, and said, "What's up?"

She opened her mouth to tell him, but stopped the words before they came out. Petted Magic, who was lying beside her. What if he thought she was trying to make more of them than was there?

"If you've had enough, need to wait until tomorrow, that's fine," he told her. "It's not like I'm going anywhere."

"I'm not sure I want to use Chelsea's decor." She practically spat the words in her haste to get them out there.

Her segue in. And she continued with, "I might want to buy my own."

His nonchalant shrug eased some of the tension in her. So what if she bought the cottage and she and Dale lived on the same beach? It wasn't like they'd be next-door neighbors. And when she went back to work, he'd still have his beach to himself.

"You want me to come with you?" he asked. "Some of the stuff's pretty heavy. We could go now."

Yes. She wanted that. All of it. But, "I have no need for the stuff unless..." She let the sentence trail off. Glanced out to the waves, as she'd seen him do so many times. Hoping he'd just get where she was going and continue with his no big deal responses.

"Unless?"

"I'm going to be here more than just this year." The words rang like a death knell inside her head. And she turned to him as she said, "I'm thinking about taking Chelsea up on her suggestion that I buy a cottage here. I've found this dog...she's a sheltie mix and I thought she'd be scooped right up, but she's still at the shelter. I checked this morning. This girl is so timid of humans because she was mistreated, which is why she hasn't been adopted. And I could bring her home to Ocean Breeze..."

Hearing herself ramble, she stopped. Chanced her first glance at Dale. He was watching her, as though she was a television show that had his attention. One that he kind of liked.

And she said, "It would mean I'm not just a temporary blip on the radar here, Dale."

He nodded. Said nothing. Which wasn't enough. By far.

"So?" she asked him. "Do you have a problem with that?"

The man continued to meet her gaze. "You'd think I would, wouldn't you?"

To which she nodded.

And he said, "Thing is, we've made this work, because we're both in the same small universe. Not Ocean Breeze world, but in our own orbit because of our circumstances. There's no danger in one or the other of us needing more than the other can give because neither of us is capable of that anymore."

Peace settled over her at his words. As it had so many times over the past months. He made it all so simple. And he was right. Nodding again, smiling, she said, "You want to go get some outdoor Christmas decorations with me?"

He stood. "Yep. And then…how about we swing by the rescue center and see about bringing that girl home, too?"

She didn't agree to that one. Not without talking to Chelsea, first.

But she didn't disagree, either.

And in her heart of hearts, she knew what that meant.

## *Chapter Sixteen*

Millie's decorations were in place, with electric run to the outlets that had been installed along the beach the first year that residents had put up the lights. Courtesy of the owner of the property—the limited liability company that had purchased Ocean Breeze and started selling off the dilapidated cottages one at a time.

No one knew who owned the company. But pretty much everyone had a fondness for the entity that made life on Ocean Breeze possible for all of them.

Millie had chosen to portray a skating rink. The ice itself wouldn't be visible to their plethora of boating viewers, but for everyone on the beach, it was a sight to behold. Dale had suggested lining the outer edges of the twenty-by-twenty piece of shiny rollable rubber with white lights and had grinned when he'd heard Millie's gasp that first night when they'd plugged everything in.

She'd chosen half a dozen skaters, who all stood in skating positions within the iced area, with their bodies and skates outlined in colored lights. There were benches, also outlined in solid lights—one red, one green—and a lamppost with colored lights climbing up it and a lantern hanging from the top.

Millie had adopted the dog, too. Briel, an already

house-trained two-year-old, hadn't been able to come home with them that weekend as she was being spayed that Monday, but Millie had brought her home that Monday night as soon as she'd been released from recovery—and Magic, just for the time being, had moved in with Juice and Dale.

Briel was a sweet pup. What Dale saw of her over the next little bit. Generally, when human beings were around, the girl hid behind furniture. Juice or Magic generally joined her, at least part of the time, and were slowly coaxing the girl to trust Dale, too.

Millie had won over the girl by day two. She'd told Dale that she'd spent Briel's first night on the floor with her. As close as Briel would let her get. And parts of every night after that, too, until the dog had slowly started crawling on her belly toward Millie.

Dale wouldn't have believed it if he hadn't seen it happen one night. He, Juice and Magic had been spending quite a bit of time at Millie's place, because of Briel, and in the middle of an old rerun, Millie had seen the girl looking at her from around the corner of a chair. She'd dropped down to the floor immediately, flat on her belly, and the dog had come out.

Crooning to the small Sheltie mix, Millie had slowly walked her over to Dale, who'd finally had a chance to pet her. And for a second there, he'd felt like they were a family. Their version of one at any rate. He and Juice with his friend, Magic, her and Briel. Single parents—who had sex with each other most nights—with canine kids was as close as they were going to get to capturing even a hint of the plans that had been stolen from both of them.

And maybe it was enough.

The five of them were outside on her deck, facing Millie's lit-up ice rink on another Monday evening, the second week in December, when Millie's phone rang. "Harper," she said, putting down a bottle of the peppermint beer they'd put on to brew before Thanksgiving to answer the call.

Dale wasn't eavesdropping. He was watching the stream of boat lights bobbing off in the distance, but couldn't help but hear the concerned gasp, and then the couple of "of courses" and "sures" that followed. She was standing as she hung up the phone.

"That was Harper." A woman who lived on the other side of Scott and Iris. A ballerina who also taught conditioning and was a friend of Chelsea's. She's going to be in LA over the holidays. She's the choreographer of a huge Nutcracker performance in LA this year and has to be on site during the show, too. She said she has some news and is on her way down."

He stood, too. Ready to call Juice and head home. Millie didn't need him there to visit with a neighbor.

And he didn't think either of them needed to host another resident in either of their homes. Not together. Didn't fit who they were. Even with all of the neighbors out walking the festive beach at night, he and Millie had managed to stay separate from the revelry when together. It had become like unwritten code with them. They weren't a couple and didn't interact with others as one.

"I'll head out," he said, already moving toward the stairs, when Millie stopped him.

"She said she wanted to speak to both of us," she told him. "She's next door, at Scott and Iris's, and the Bartholomews are there right now, too. She's just leaving to head over."

He still had time to make an escape. Might have done if a phrase that had been revisiting him regularly lately hadn't popped into his mind.

*On the outside looking in.*

If that was him, what he wanted, then it was.

Except it wasn't.

But he had to ask, "You okay with this? Being around others when we're together?"

Her shrug didn't tell him much. "We're friends, Dale. And I've made an offer on a cottage here. Unless you have plans to quit hanging out, then it's bound to happen eventually. Harper sounded...odd... Dale. Like something major was happening." Her worried tone had already reached out to him when her face froze and then took on a definite look of worry. "You don't think something's wrong with her, do you? Or that they've all decided I don't fit on Ocean Breeze?"

The alarm in her tone settled Dale some. Buying a home on Ocean Breeze wasn't just a jerk reaction to the holidays. The great Thanksgiving Day they'd shared. The place really meant something to her.

Why that fact should have any bearing on him, he didn't ask. Didn't want to know.

And didn't have time to beat himself up about it, either, or answer her, as Harper appeared around the edge of Scott's bright, white light–lined Santa sleigh, and headed up toward Millie's deck.

Magic was down the stairs in the very next second, with Juice following right behind. Briel, who'd been lying close to the two much bigger dogs, crawled behind Millie's chair and laid her head on her front paws, facing the steps.

Dale and Millie remained standing right where they were. As though they were both Briel's caregivers, not just Millie. He'd known she wouldn't leave the dog alone outside. He'd simply not considered leaving her side.

"I'm sorry for the drama," Harper started in as soon as the three of them were sitting. "Something's come up and I have a favor to ask of you, Millie, specifically."

He needn't have been there then. Why had Millie thought differently? *Outside looking in.* And that was fine. "And another one of you, Dale," the woman finished, turning her gaze on him, before immediately turning back to Millie again.

He'd known Harper for at least a couple of years. Had had half a dozen conversations specifically with her in all that time. Most of which had taken place the previous winter when Scott had hurt himself surfing and the two of them had helped Iris care for him.

And a favor could be asked from LA, over the phone.

"I have a friend who's just moved in to stay at my place for a couple of months. She's having a baby," the slender ballerina said then. "Due in January.

"For a couple of other friends of mine who can't have one."

And Dale's jaw dropped.

Overcome by a shocking flood of envy, it took Millie a second to put Harper's words together. The woman was sitting there saying a baby was going to be born on Ocean Breeze in two months?

Harper looked between them both and said, "These

friends of mine...they've wanted a baby for so long. And I knew this woman who desperately needed money because she and her older sister were on the verge of losing their farm. They're single, trying to keep their home, and I...kind of put them all together. Along with a woman in my conditioning class who runs a fertility clinic, The Parent Portal."

So what favor did Harper need from Millie? She'd help if she could. In spite of the emotions tumbling inside her. With force. For the woman who couldn't birth her own child. For Millie's own loss. And Dale's. "What can I do?" she asked, leaning forward, hearing the thickness in her voice.

The soft smile on Harper's face, as she looked Millie right in the eye, struck Millie. Until she realized, through Harper's response, the difference in herself in her interactions with others. Her time with Dale had not only opened her up with him, but, apparently had freed some of her former ability to relate on a deeper level with others, too.

Scary as the thought was, she was taking it on. "Tell me," she said to Harper.

"Our surrogate, Tamara, had a scare last night."

Millie gasped and some of her fright must have shown on her face as Harper quickly said, "It's fine. She's fine. But she lives in the middle of the state, on a farm, fifty miles from the nearest hospital. The arrangement was that she'd come stay with me here after the holidays, until the baby's birth. And while her doctor says that arrangement is still fine, that there's no worry, I'm..."

"...worried," Millie finished for her. "You need me to go there? To stay at the farm and be there in case the baby starts to come early?" She'd go. In a heartbeat. What was one more Christmas spent tending to others if she was helping what she hoped was a new friend? And neighbor. And perhaps saving a baby's life?

Briel and Magic. Dale could watch them. Harper's favor of him? If Millie was busy with Tamara.

"No!" Harper smiled, then said, "Actually, what I had to ask is so much less I don't feel quite as guilty...she came here to stay at my place, starting today. I just hoped that, for the next couple of weeks, while I finish out the show in LA, with you being a nurse, you'd check in on her. And that... I could give her your number just in case she needs something."

Smiling, Millie said, "Absolutely. Of course." Anything to help bring a healthy baby into the world. There were parts of her that weren't ever going to change. Needing to tend to others' physical well-being was one of them.

"And Dale..." Harper's voice broke into Millie's thoughts.

Millie glanced in his direction...the first time since the conversation had started. And felt an ache she didn't understand. But that lingered even as she followed the conversation between the man she was sleeping with and the woman who'd just asked the first favor of her on Ocean Breeze.

"In the event...anything happens...we're hoping you'll take care of Aggie for me...and now Magic and Briel, too, if Millie's busy with Tamara?"

Dale's slight nod seemed fine, as he said, "As always." The words were normal, too. So why did Millie feel that there was something off about him?

Or was it just her that was...floundering. Flooding with senses on overload. Sex. Holidays. Couple's visit. Babies.

What did she do with it all? Where did she put it? How did she live it?

Ready to jump up and excuse herself to the restroom, just to have a moment alone to calm herself, Millie was flooded with relief as Harper stood, and said she had to get back to Tamara and make sure she was settled before she headed back to LA yet that night.

At the surrogate's request, they were leaving Aggie at Harper's place for the time being. Harper stopped before leaving the deck, looking around, and Millie wondered if she was pleased, or displeased by what she'd done with the space in Chelsea's absence. But Harper hadn't been studying the decor.

"There you are, sweet girl," the woman said, bending down to Briel. "I've heard about you and can't wait until we see you running the beach with the rest of the kids."

The words were soft. Spoken in baby talk.

And when Briel, still behind Millie's chair with her head on her paws, wagged her tail, Millie found her peace again.

Dale left Millie's shortly after Harper on Monday night. Ran away, was more like it. So much was happening. Too much.

Sensations were running through him as though he was a pubescent teenager. The constant awareness of being on the outside looking in.

And Millie...was she in or out?

A question that made no sense to him. They weren't a couple. He was done with that. Not a choice, a circumstance.

So what was he needing Millie in or out *of*?

He was home, on his own deck, with a fresh bottle of his darker ale, brewed before Millie came along, when his phone buzzed a text. You okay?

More weirdness. They didn't check up on each other. As soon as he had the thought he remembered a night when he'd walked down the beach just for the purpose of making sure she was okay. He'd turned around and gone home without her knowing, but still...

But still...they didn't openly check up on each other.

What did that say about them? What they were becoming? He had to let the text go.

So he did. For the minute or two it ate at him. And something stronger than his sense of unease prompted him to text back, Fine.

And then, a minute or so later, You?

He received a thumbs-up in response. And, taking his beer with him, went into his office and let WG have the reins for the rest of the night.

The guy might not know any better than Dale where he was going, but Dale could always rely on WG to get there. With a hugely successful end result.

Things were changing. She was changing. Too much. Too fast. And yet, when Millie considered what parts of her new world she'd change, she came up blank.

Her offer to buy the cottage down the beach had been accepted. The mortgage papers had come through a digital signing service, and she'd signed. There were still closing signatures that needed to happen, and Millie couldn't wait to get it all done.

By Wednesday of that week, Briel was coming out during the day when Millie was home alone. Starting to follow her around. From a distance that was growing smaller and smaller. And when she spoke to the sweet girl, as she did often, Briel would pick her head up off her paws and look at her.

She'd seen Dale on Tuesday night. Had walked down to his place just to hang out for a bit after dinner. They'd sat on his deck, talked about the boats whose lights they could see bobbing in the water, about the training she'd done that day. They'd sipped peppermint beer.

And, for the first time ever, he'd mentioned his work in progress. A psychological thriller involving a woman trying to escape a cult leader who kept everyone in line by making them doubt their own minds through constant gaslighting.

The whole thing was so unlike Dale's calm, soft spoken, kind demeanor that she'd spent the rest of their time together asking him about the career no one else knew about. About where he got his ideas. His writing process.

And while, because she'd had to get back to Briel, she hadn't stayed long enough for sex to hop up onto the table, she'd been feeling much more in sync with her new normal as she made her way back home along the brightly lit and decorated sand from his place to hers. She had no idea what about Dale did that to her, settled her, but she was glad to have him in her life.

A reality made more obvious when she felt an impromptu flood of happiness when the man showed up on her deck on Wednesday with a bucket of fresh crab. She'd been in her kitchen, cleaning paint brushes, had seen him coming up the beach, and had gone out specifically to meet him. "You up for a crab boil for dinner?" he asked, coming up her steps with Juice beside him.

"Of course. Always." The response was natural. "I have no idea how to go about producing one, but—" she glanced at the pot with claws hanging out over the edges "—I'm assuming you do…"

"I do," he told her, slinging a soft-sided cooler off his back to the deck floor. "Everything we need is in there."

Inside, Juice went straight to Briel, who'd dodged into the living room and behind a chair at the sound of Dale's voice. But by the time Dale—and Millie, with his tutelage—had corn on the cob cut into pieces, chopped onions, potatoes, and a plethora of spices boiling in the big pot on her stove, Briel had made it to the entryway into the kitchen, where she stood with Juice and Magic, watching.

Fresh crab legs and shrimp went in the pot for the last fifteen minutes, and then, producing a couple bottles of beer from his cooled stash, Dale took his plate out to the back deck.

Smiling, Millie followed right behind him. And felt as though the grin hadn't left her face since he'd shown up on her back porch by the time she'd finished the meal. "I *was* having grilled chicken salad tonight," she told Dale, taking a sip from her beer as she watched him tackle his second plateful. "This was much better."

He nodded. "I actually learned this one from Scott. He's the beach crab aficionado. Has a place where he goes once a week to get crab fresh caught that day."

There was a slight breeze coming off the ocean, but with her fire going and a long-sleeved shirt on, Millie was completely content with the mild temperature.

So much so that after cleanup was complete, she wandered back out to the deck with a fresh bottle of beer, intending to sit out whether Dale stayed or not.

But was glad when he reclaimed his seat.

Two minutes later, when Juice and Magic came out, with Briel at their sides, and the three animals—two so large, one so small—lay down together by the deck steps, something happened that used to be a not uncommon occurrence with her.

She teared up.

Overflowing with a heart filled with gratitude.

Spilling happy tears.

Something that hadn't happened since Brent died.

## *Chapter Seventeen*

Darkness fell and the beach lit up with joy and merriment. Same old, same old. He'd been watching it happen every night for weeks, every one of the past five holiday seasons. He didn't mind it all. Some nights he even kind of enjoyed it.

Sitting there with Millie and the three dogs, Dale wasn't ready to call it a night. "You feel like a walk?" he asked her. Feeling not a single twinge of regret, even after he heard the words leave his mouth.

There were others out strolling, among the displays. Some residents walked along the displays every night. Some occasionally. There was always someone out.

He'd never been among them. A fact he'd shared during their building of their own light shows Thanksgiving weekend. Most of what the boaters saw along the two-mile stretch every night, he'd heard about, but had never seen.

"Really?" Millie's eyes were wide as she looked over at him. "You want to?"

He was pretty sure he heard anticipation more than a lack of such in her tone, and so, "I do," he told her. To please her. To prolong the evening. And to rid himself of a growing physical tension in his nether regions than anything else.

Since Harper's announcement on Monday, Millie hadn't seemed open to sexual activity between them. Of course, there'd only been the one night in between. Seemed like weeks to the parts of him that had grown used to visiting the parts of her most every night.

Odd thing was, he missed holding her. And being held.

Other than their sexual encounters, he and Millie didn't touch at all. They weren't together. Weren't a couple.

"I've been on this beach for five years, watching all those boats come and go every November and December, and figure maybe it's time I knew what the fuss was all about," he added, by way of justification. He just wasn't sure whom he felt he had to convince. Her, or himself.

Millie was already putting on running shoes and moving toward Briel, to coax the dog into the house, with Magic standing just inside the door. And something else just popped out of Dale's mouth. "Juice, go," he said, pointing to Millie's door. And then, when the dog complied, said, "Stay."

Juice cocked his head, looking expectantly at Dale, and he pointed to Briel and gave a command he'd never before given the dog. But Lyla had. "Work."

Juice moved instantly, nudged the sheltie's neck and walked the dog further into Millie's cottage.

Millie looked at Dale, brows raised, and smiled.

And Dale smiled back at her.

Every once in a while, life worked perfectly.

Millie loved looking at all the light displays. She and Dale walked the entire two-mile stretch of beach, starting to the right of her place, down the shorter distance to that end, and then back by her place to head down toward Sage and Gray's place at the other end of the beach, their turnaround every time they jogged.

Her face hurt from grinning so much, as they passed display after display, each one telling a story of its own. From Santa's workshop to a giant Christmas cookie, everything was brought to life by millions of lights. Many of the scenes had moving parts, and passing by a Santa train that ran along the whole stretch of that cottage's beach, Millie turned to Dale and said, "Maybe we can do that next year with the skating rink." And then stopped.

*We?* He'd helped her set up her original scene, as she had his, by way of helping each other over the hump of facing the first. Not as a couple building a fun holiday display.

Not as though they had any ownership of anything, together.

Dale didn't comment.

But she knew he'd heard her. Nothing had changed in their environment between that statement and every other one she'd uttered along the way. All of which he'd come back with at least a one- or two-word comment.

And just like that, Millie was back on earth, in her real life. Not the one she'd seemed to be slipping into which she was subconsciously thinking could somehow be as good as what she'd lost.

The lights were still beautiful to her. But they were just lights. Not some hint of a magic yet to unfold. Or an anticipation of what more might be waiting for her.

She'd had her chance. Just as Harper's friends were getting theirs. She'd checked on Tamara both Tuesday and Wednesday, stopping to chat with the young woman who'd told her as Harper had that Tamra and her widowed older sister were on the verge of losing the farm that had been in their family for generations. The money Harper's friends were paying her was going to bring their mortgage up to date. And from there, the two sisters had plans to rent out the farmland at a price that would keep them out of debt. For extra money they were going to open a fresh honey, egg and home-grown vegetables stand. They'd also had an offer from the state to rent out part of their land for windmills. A new opportunity on the horizon which they were researching.

Tamara loved her life on the farm. She understood that it might appear odd to others, just her and her sister in the home in which they'd grown up, but she was truly happy there. And was excited to be giving a couple such a wonderful gift by way of being able to save her own future.

None of which Millie shared with Dale. But as they reached the halfway point of their way back—walking closer to the water than anyone else, by unspoken consent, to avoid having to make conversation neither of them felt up to making—she said, "I always thought, no matter what else I became, or did in life, I'd be a mother." She was a nurturer of children.

Always had been. Always would be. No matter what vagaries fate dropped off her way.

"I never much thought about myself as a father," Dale said, his hands in his pockets, his voice loud enough to be heard over the waves, but gentle, just the same. "Never had much of a father figure to look up to and just didn't think about being one."

Her mind flew immediately to the little boy Lyla had

been carrying. And she asked, "How did you feel when you knew you were going to be one?" Some people didn't want children. Some weren't elated when they found out a baby was on the way. Some were scared to death. All normal, acceptable reactions to what would be a drastic, forever life change.

"I'd have thought I'd be a bit panicky at first. I don't know the first thing about being a father, but it felt...right. I started to think about things I'd never spent time on before. Like maybe being a sports coach someday. Being thrown up on. Ways to make money stretch further so the baby would have everything. Hearing him call me Dad..."

His voice broke off on that one. Millie let the silence, the waves, take his grief, walking side by side with him, step by step as they did so.

Several seconds later, Dale cleared his throat, and said, "Not that I knew the baby was a boy then." And finished with, "I got my orders to deploy a few weeks after we found out. Then it was all about finding a psychological service dog who could help Lyla with her anxiety while I was away..."

He'd lost his son. And gained Juice. Nowhere near an equal tradeoff. There would never be anything that would equal that pain. But still, she was glad that Juice had been there for Dale when he got home.

Another minute passed in silence. Millie wasn't looking at the lights anymore. She was watching the sand at their feet. The splashes of water that reached their running shoes every now and then. And thought back over the things Dale had listed when he'd found out he was going to be father. Wanting to just walk forever, listening to more of them.

They'd almost reached her house when he said, "There's no reason you can't still be a mother."

The words cut into her. All the way to her core. How could he...he knew...

"You don't have to be married to have a baby," the next words came softly. "Especially in today's world of advanced sciences. Look at Tamara and the couple she's helping. They found a way. There are banks where you can go to get what you need..."

A sperm bank.

She'd have thought she'd be choking on the very idea of such a thing, and there she was, walking beside him, actually listening to him. Considering what he was telling her.

Because he was Dale. Her kindred soul. The one who'd been able to see inside her, because so much of the same was inside himself.

And maybe, somewhere down the road, she *could* have a child of her own. She'd never even thought about the possibility. Could come up with many roadblocks and hardships she'd probably face without even trying. Like her child wanting to know who their father was, needing family history, not just medically but emotionally, too. Long years of going it alone. But Dale was right. Opportunity was out there. Giving her hope. There were choices even in such an intimate part of life.

And not just for her.

"You could have a child, too," she told him. "More easily than I could. You'd just have to hire someone to carry it for you, like Harper's friends did. With lawyers, of course, so you're protected. But you're financially set, for that and raising a child." He hadn't said so. Didn't live in any way that gave indication to any wealth at all. But, even aside from book royalties, WG had just signed a movie deal that would be enough to keep some families for years. "You work from home," she added, "so you'd be there, even if you hire a nanny while you write, and you're the most intuitive, gentle man I've ever known. A child would be blessed to have you raising it."

She hadn't meant to sound so impassioned, but she wanted more for him than sitting alone on his deck year after year. She'd made so many strides during her months on Ocean Breeze, but Dale was doing much of the same as he'd done before she'd arrived. Other than hanging out with her, of course, but that was only temporary. Until she took back up with her life.

He didn't say a word to her entreaty, which made her sad, but she let the subject go. Hoping that maybe she'd said enough to get him thinking, at least. If she'd even just cracked a door open for him, she'd feel better. They were talking pipe dreams at the moment.

Spurred on by their walk through fantasy land.

She knew that. But she thought about what Dale had said all the rest of the way home. She could still be a mother someday. Maybe, after the first of the year, she'd ask Harper for an introduction to the woman who ran The Parent Portal. Just in case she wanted to do some research so she'd know how much money she'd have to save if she were ever going to seriously consider having a baby on her own.

No. She could do her own research if the occasion ever arose.

In that moment, that time, she wasn't done birthing her new self. Nor was she done with Dale. For his sake as well as her own.

So thinking, she reached out and took his hand as they approached her back steps. She didn't know why, didn't stop to think about the parameters that bound them together—and the things that could blow them apart. She'd just felt. And moved.

The next second awful feelings returned full force. Her heart lurched and dread filled her when his hand lay limply in hers. Not wrapping around it. Before she could think of something to say, or even have the idea to pull her hand gently back, they'd reached her steps.

And Dale, lifting his hand with hers in it, clasped his other one over it and, facing her, said, "Why don't we?"

Confused, close to tears, riding a downward spiral on the roller coaster of emotion she'd been on over the past weeks, she actually had a second's thought that maybe she'd be better off to close the heart that was opening up wider and wider every day. To go back to being the calm, helpful being she'd become after Brent's death. Albeit with fewer working hours.

Which would leave nothing but emptiness...

Looking up at Dale, she heard his words again, realizing he hadn't finished them. "Why don't we what?" she asked him.

"Why don't we do it together? My sperm, your egg. You carry the baby. I pay for everything. We raise it, between the two cottages, right here on Ocean Breeze?"

Waves of emotion washed over her. Hope. Fear. Lots of fear. Want. A need to laugh. To cry. Drowning her in sensations she couldn't sort through.

Shaking her head, feeling almost woozy, Millie frowned up at him. Was she hallucinating? Hearing things?

The serious, yet expectant look in Dale's intent gaze aiming straight into her eyes told her otherwise.

All she could think of to say was, "I—I have to go in."

And, with a nod, he let her hand go.

He shouldn't have said anything. At least not like he had. When he had.

He'd put a big-ass wrench in the gears. But Dale most definitely had a lightness in his heart he hadn't known, maybe ever, as he walked with Juice back up the beach to their place.

Millie hadn't said no.

His idea was a good one. Had merit. Given their circumstance, it made all kinds of sense. They both already knew, with one hundred percent clarity, what they would never have again in life. Had gotten stuck in the not having. In the loss.

But they'd also shown each other over the past months that there was life left ahead. Things they didn't yet know about that could bring them joy. Like going to a movie theater and seeing his story portrayed there.

He'd talked to her about WG. And it had felt...nice. Sharing a part of himself that he'd expected to take to his grave without ever revealing his persona to anyone in his private or public life. Only an agent and editor, both of whom he'd never even met, had known WG's true identity. Might not seem like much to anyone else, but to Dale, the revelation, and Millie's reception of it, had been huge. She'd been interested. Shocked, maybe. But it hadn't changed how she looked at him. Talked to him. Treated him.

Hell, he'd celebrated his first holiday ever. And had actually enjoyed the damned thing.

He'd told her about his son and the world hadn't exploded. Juice hadn't even come to the rescue on that one. He and Millie were good together. In spite of their limitations. They shared the little things that made life less lonely. Brewing beer. Cooking. Purchasing and putting out Christmas decor. They'd made the sexual part work without putting chains or stress on either one of them.

No reason they couldn't do the parent thing, too. Two one-parent homes seemed to be as much the norm as one two-parent home anymore. And with Millie buying a cottage, and the two of them living on the same beach…his proposal fit. As concisely as the rest of their coming together had done.

Most importantly, while he'd never had the chance to know her at her best, he'd seen her at close to her worst and had been impressed with her ability to face her challenges and come out on top. He knew the person she was. And couldn't think of anyone more suited to be a mother. To his or any other child.

But if it *could* be his…how great would that be?

In a perfect world, that was.

Maybe he wouldn't be a good dad. Maybe he was being selfish even considering the idea of becoming one. And yet, as Millie had said, with his financial future secure and working from home, he might be a great parent. There was so much he could teach a child. How to laugh, being one of them. He'd never done a lot of that. Needed to get better at it.

He'd have to get out more. Attend school functions.

Maybe even watch ballet classes. None of it struck fear inside him.

Once again, he and Millie had opened a door he'd thought nailed shut. He'd been thinking wholly of her, when he'd first come up with the fact that she could still be a parent. And she'd brought the idea of a chance for him, too. He had to believe that there'd been no mistake about that. His and Millie's subconsciouses had been speaking to each other from the beginning. Drawing truths and realizations out of each other that they hadn't been able to access on their own.

Just as, over the past five years, WG had been showing him a creative side he hadn't known he'd had. WG had taught him how to get out of his own way, shut up his doubter, his critic, and just type as it came to him. He didn't have to have all the answers starting out. Often, he didn't have any of them. He'd start with an idea and WG would present the rest. He didn't get it, logically. Couldn't explain how it worked. Which was part of the reason he'd kept the guy to himself. Part of him thought he was a fraud. And yet, every day, or night, he presented himself to the page, went into deep thought with his characters, and WG did the rest. It was all about trust.

Trust. Millie.

With the force of a tsunami, truth hit Dale. The reason he and Millie were able to pull each other out of grief and into life. It was all about trust.

He trusted Millie Monroe.

Stopped in his tracks in the sand, Dale let the knowledge settle for a beat, and then continued up to his cottage with the thought ringing loudly through him. He didn't just know Millie, share like circumstances with her, spend time with her, have sex with her...he trusted her. With his deepest truths.

In his cottage, with Juice staring up at him, Dale hummed with energy. He didn't want to sit alone watching boat lights bobbing, or people strolling on the beach. Reruns weren't calling to him, not without Millie. He'd never been much of regular television type of guy. Wandering into his office, he dropped into his chair. Stared at the large monitor directly in front of him. Called up the work in progress and put his hands on the keyboard.

His main character was struggling so hard to maintain mental autonomy from the fiend who had her mother and sister under his control, and was gaining on her. In a moment of self-doubt, filled with anxiety and wondering if she'd imagined the gaslighting, if she was alienating the one man who could keep her safe from the evils taking over the world, she met the gaze of another woman in the complex. Saw a light in her eyes that resonated with her. Just before she was summoned for the very first time to the master's quarters.

WG stopped there. Chapter End. He was done for the night.

Dale had no idea what was coming next. Not any kind of physical abuse. Too obvious. Not the leader's way. And while he wrote thrillers, they never involved sexual abuse. Just not a place he wanted to go.

Where he wanted to go was down to Millie's. To see if she was out.

Grabbing a beer, he sat on his own deck instead, but didn't stay long. Looking at the beach, he kept reliving his last conversation with Millie.

Had he really suggested that they have a child together?

Was the idea so ludicrous?

Being a parent was what they both wanted—probably more than anything else. They'd never replace the babies who'd never been born, but they were young and healthy. There was no reason either of them couldn't try again to bring a child into the world.

Beer only half consumed, he went in to shower. To shake off the day. Climbed naked into bed, and sat there, sipping from what was quickly becoming warm beer.

And looked at the empty space in the bed next to him. He'd thought it would always be such, when he went to sleep for the night. That was a given. But Millie had done a great job of filling what she could of the emptiness inside him. Because he trusted her. He'd let her in.

She hadn't just happened. He'd opened himself up to her presence in his life. Five years, all the people he'd met, and Millie had changed him within weeks of his having seen her for the first time.

Pieces were falling into place, as they did for WG at the computer. He sat there, letting them.

And then, without thought to how late it had grown, he picked up the phone.

## *Chapter Eighteen*

Sitting on her deck, watching the now silent, but still lit beach, Millie grabbed for her phone on the first ring. That late at night, alarm speared her, thinking of her family. Her Mom and Dad.

Her first glance at the screen, calmed those fears, but alighted another one. Dale. He'd never called before. They either texted or stopped by each other's decks.

He was breaking up with her. She'd tried to hold his hand. Something couples did.

Her first instinct was to end the call so the ringing would stop. But she was done running. Burying herself in the sand so she didn't have to face any more pain.

Hurting was a part of living. But she'd learned over the past months that it didn't have to become the only part. No matter how deep the grief, how encompassing the hurt.

New days still dawned. And just like the waves in the ocean flowed, life would continue.

Potting Briel, who'd let Millie pick her up to lay in her lap, she looked into the girl's big brown questioning eyes and, sliding her thumb across the green icon on her screen said, "Hello?"

"Lyla, Brent…they weren't meant to be."

Millie's mouth dropped open, her stomach knotted.

She pulled her screen back from her face, looking at the end call button. And felt Magic sit up beside her.

She couldn't not hear whatever Dale had to tell her. The next breath would come. And then the next. A day would pass, and then another.

Each one providing her the opportunity to choose how she spent it.

She'd realized one thing for sure. She wasn't going to spend her time on earth on the outside looking in. She'd already lost two years. Dale was at the beginning of six. She didn't want that to happen to her.

"I don't know if it's fate. Or some other stronger power, but I had no say in what happened to Lyla. No chance to save her. Nor did you with Brent. You, with your medical training, were right there and it didn't make a difference."

If he was trying to turn a knife in her, he was succeeding. And still she held on. It was Dale. She had to hear him out.

"I had no idea there was a you out there. Someone who, like me, has put limitations on their heart. And yet one day there you were. Not just on the beach, I'm used to people arriving, some staying some not. All part of the flow of my world. But you…you interrupted my sacred time."

"I'm sorry." The words came of their own accord. She hadn't ever meant to hurt him. To make his way worse.

"Don't be, I'm not. That's the whole point of this. Don't you see, Mil? Fate, for want of a better description, took from us. Because, for whatever reason, the choices we'd made thinking they were for the rest of our lives, weren't meant to be."

He'd already said that. The words didn't twist as tightly inside her the second time through. "But fate didn't just leave us high and dry. It directed me here. And when the timing was right, it directed you here, too. It can't be just a fluke that we both are driven to jog regularly, or that we picked the exact same time in the day to do so because we're also both driven by a need for solitude out there."

Millie relaxed back into her seat, looking out at the ocean, soaking in Dale's words. They were hitting the deep chord in her that he'd been touching since those first jogs he was describing.

Instilling the truth he was conveying. Magic lay her big head next to Briel on Millie's lap.

"Look at all the changes, all the positive growth in both of us—two souls who'd been stagnant since we lost the lives we'd expected to have—since we met. Miracles don't fall out of the sky randomly, Mil."

Tears filled her eyes. She nodded, but knew he couldn't see. It was the best she could do. If only she'd met Dale... when? First grade? That's the only chance he'd have had to own her heart before Brent had.

"We've both had the traditional dream. Started that life. Had what we were going to get of it. It's done. We can't change that. But maybe we're being shown that life can still be full, that we can still have a lot of things we sought in that traditional life. Just have them differently."

She tried to swallow. Tears were clogging her throat.

"We've had the loves of our lives, Mil, but maybe we can still have the rest."

Shaking, Millie glanced down to see Briel and Magic both staring up at her, and quickly smiled at the girls. Petting them gently. Softly. Where Juice absorbed tension, Briel had been tortured by it. And Magic just trusted.

"That wasn't meant to be—maybe this is," Dale said then.

And Millie felt words fighting for release. But couldn't get them out.

Instead, she hung up.

Dale couldn't believe it at first when he realized Millie had disconnected their call. He'd figured it all out. They were meant to find each other.

She was the one who'd suggested he could have a child, too. He'd seen it for her, but hadn't even considered the possibility for himself.

Staring at the screen that said call ended. And then eventually went black, he had no idea what to do next.

It wasn't like he could sit down at the computer and have WG flow things into place for him.

He was naked. In bed. Sipping warm beer. Staring at his phone. Sleep wasn't going to happen. He'd already showered. WG had given what he had to give.

He'd screwed things up with Millie.

Which meant she was hurting. Because of him.

Out of bed so quickly Juice jumped up in work mode, Dale quickly calmed the dog, pulled on a pair of sweats and a hoodie, slid into running shoes, and headed out, Juice right beside him.

The jog down the beach to Millie's didn't take long. And felt like years.

Expecting to see her cottage in darkness, he had no idea what he was going to do when he got there. Throw a rock at her bedroom window?

If she was awake, she'd look out, see him and then choose whether or not she wanted to talk. If she didn't come out, she'd at least know that he was around, available if she needed him, and he could head back to his place and get some sleep.

Or...he was going to look like some damned stalker who perhaps badly needed a head adjustment.

The last didn't ring true to him. For the first time in five years, he felt as though he had real clarity.

He stared hard as the cottage first came into view. In darkness, as he'd envisioned. But he continued forward, waves whooshing in, receding out, his footsteps soundless in the sand.

He didn't see Millie, at first. The chimney of her fireplace hid part of her deck from view from the beach. But Juice must have known she was there, as the dog suddenly sped up, leaving Dale's side to head up to Millie's deck as though it was home.

By the time Dale drew close enough to see that the nurse was sitting not in her usual seat, but his, with Briel on her lap and Magic right beside her, he'd already been well discovered.

Four sets of eyes watched him climb the steps.

He didn't say anything. Didn't explain his presence. Wasn't sure how he could do so. Nor did he ask how she was doing. The streaks of tears on her face—made more pronounced by the small flames coming from her fire—spoke for her.

The way she was looking at him, watching him, more with pain than rejection, did the rest. Taking her seat, he leaned back, spread his legs in front of him, and just... sat there.

Minutes passed. Fifteen. Maybe more. Briel had jumped down to lie curled up between Juice and Magic. All three dogs were asleep.

As he and Millie should have been.

Life shouldn't be so hard. And yet...he'd had easy. Easy was sitting alone, night after night, watching life pass by on the beach. Easy was being on the outside looking in.

"I'm afraid." Millie's words pierced the night.

And he said, "Yeah." He was, too.

She turned to look at him then, and he held her gaze. They had each other's backs. And had been the source of so many of each other's answers.

Then, turning her gaze back to the fire, not the beach, she said, "I scared myself tonight, reaching for your hand. It's what I would have done with Brent. And while I knew you weren't him, and was in no way thinking of him in that moment, or wishing you were him, why did I do that? We aren't a couple."

Relief flooded Dale. He had that answer. "Not in the traditional sense," he told her. "Neither of us wants that or has it to give. Which is why we don't have to fear it."

She nodded. "Then why did I grab your hand?"

"Because you were having a good moment, one filled with a new hope, new possibility, and you reached out. Human contact is a way to communicate when there are no words. Not just for lovers, but for total strangers sometimes. And certainly for friends."

"Is that what you'd call us? Friends? Because I've been sitting here trying to figure it all out."

"I think we're friends, definitely. But it's more than that."

"Yeah, more. What's the more?" She was looking at him again and Dale held her gaze without difficulty.

Shrugging he said, "I don't have a name for it." But

then, WG-like, words popped into his head. "Soul mates, maybe."

"Soul mates." She said the words, more emphasis on the first than the second, as though they weren't new to her. More like, she was landing on something that she could consider.

And then, turning to him, she asked, "So why didn't you hold my hand back?"

And Dale just stared.

Millie recognized the deer-in-the-headlights look on Dale's face. Not from sight, but from the sense of helplessness emanating from it.

Some things you just couldn't wrap your mind around. Couldn't act, or even react. That look on his face shed new light on the lack of *action* or *reaction*, when she'd grabbed his hand in hers.

Holding hands wasn't them. But her need for human contact in that moment had broken their code. The big question was, "What happens when it happens again?"

She saw him frown, and added, "When one of us breaks our code, like I inadvertently did when I grabbed your hand?"

The hand-holding was a nominal event. A blip. But other things that could come up, might not be. "Like what if I fall asleep after sex and end up staying all night? What if, when that happens, one or the other of us cuddles up to the other and we wake up in each other's arms with the sun shining in the window?"

His expression cleared and he said, "Then we have sex again."

Okay, bad example. And he got the point. She could tell

that by the brooding look on his face. She wasn't wrong to question. To foresee danger in her path.

Unless doing so kept her on the outside looking in, as he'd been doing for the past five years. And, by his own admission, for most of his life.

And perhaps, in her own way, she had been, too. Keeping herself on the outside. She just hadn't been looking in.

Was she really going to blow the chance for an odd, but happy family, because of the fact that doing so presented potential dangers?

She'd married Brent and the absolute worst had happened. She hadn't even seen it coming. And had she seen it, would she have turned down his proposal of marriage? Walked away from him?

Or would she have chosen, knowing that he had a heart defect, to live every moment she could with him? To make memories, to make certain that she did all she could to give him as many glorious moments as his young life would be able to take before his heart gave out?

The answer to that one was a hands-down given. She'd have married him, of course.

And would she have rather known about the defect ahead of time, thus curtailing activities that made Brent happiest, in an effort to possibly prolong his life by a year or two?

Her answer there presented just as immediately. No. She and Brent had been truly happy until the moment he died. Even that moment, he'd gone out on a moment of total glory. Had they known what was coming, they'd have lived with the shadow of death a constant companion inside them.

Dale's earlier words on the phone, the ones that she

hadn't been able to process, came back to her then. *That wasn't meant to be—maybe this is.*

He'd been talking about them giving each other the chance to be a parent. Giving each other a child. In spite of the fact that they couldn't give each other the love of their lives.

"Maybe this is," she said softly.

Then looked over at him, met his gaze and held on.

Dale didn't end up in Millie's bed that night. Or the next couple of them, either. They jogged, he'd walked down with beer one night, she had another, but they never got any further than each other's decks.

She talked about her kids, the progress they were making. Told him a little bit about her daily visits with Tamara. The surrogate was doing well. Didn't need a nurse. But Millie didn't think it was healthy or kind to leave the woman all alone in a strange place—even one as lovely as Ocean Breeze—without regular human contact.

On Saturday night of that week, he talked about the book. About the woman who'd shown up on the page, connecting with his heroine, unexpectedly. She wanted to know where he was heading with the new character. He had no idea. She didn't pass judgment on that.

Or on him, telling him that she wanted to be the first to know when it all made it out of him.

As though there was no doubt it would. Which struck him so oddly, his expression must have shown surprise because she immediately said, "What?"

Nothing. The word didn't make it past his thoughts. "You're just so sure it's going to happen," he told her.

Frowning, she asked, "You aren't?"

Raising his brows, he shook his head. "It's not something I can force. It's either there or it isn't." More of life that was out of his control. And maybe part of the reason Dale never let WG have his day in the sun.

"Seriously?" Millie took a sip of the last bottle of mint beer. Held it up and said, "We need to get another batch of this going," and then, without pause, continued with, "You're a creator, Dale. You've got a valuable talent. Something you're born with, not something you can learn or force. It's not meant to be controlled, but to be given the freedom to flow. To express without judgment. Five years on the *NYT* Best Sellers list and you still don't trust that, at least?"

Reeling back a bit, Dale studied her. Ready to tell her that she didn't understand, couldn't possibly since she wasn't inside him. But was too distracted by her words playing themselves again in his mind. He liked them.

Wanted to hang on to the possibility that they could be true.

And then lost all train of thought when she said, "I threw my diaphragm away."

Millie had been trying since Wednesday to broach the child subject with Dale. Other than when she'd been specifically focused on someone else, like Tamara, it was all she'd been able to think about. While she painted on carved wood in her craft room, lay on the floor, teaching Briel to play or jogged on the beach, the topic was right there. Pushing at her.

At no point, had she even thought to introduce the topic as she had. And quickly inserted, "I'm not saying I want to get pregnant. Just that, I think condoms are enough protection."

His grin caught her off guard. "Are you, perhaps, telling me that you miss my body and want to go have sex?"

Shocked at the instantaneous flooding of desire that shot through her, Millie spurt out an awkward laugh, and almost accepted his backward invitation.

But something held her back. Driving her to say, "I'm telling you that I'm open to conversation about the two of us giving each other a child. If you still have interest in the prospect."

Sitting up straight, he leaned toward her, his gaze intent. "Then let's have it. The conversation," he said.

Unexpected warmth flooded her, with a hint of sexy, but so much more. His eagerness...she wanted that. A father for her child who wanted him or her that badly.

"I've always been one who analyzed things before jumping into them, and while, yes, life has taught me that you can't foresee all the dangers that might be in your path, I think we'd be irresponsible if we didn't consider some of the more obvious ones."

He shrugged. Nodded. "Shoot," he said. Then added, "Bring them on."

Figuring he might be sorry what he'd asked for, Millie spit out the most obvious, and bothersome to her. "What happens if either one of us meets someone and decides we want to have a partner? Not a love of your life kind, just a partner. Someone to live with, share life with, vacation and shop with, share bills and household chores with."

Dale's eyes narrowed. "You want those things?"

Smiling, she shook her head. "No, but you might someday."

And then what happened to her? And more importantly to their child? It was an eventuality they had to face. "Four months ago, you'd have bet money you'd never in a million years consider having a child," she challenged him. And when his only response was pursed lips, she said, "So how do you know, now that you've opened yourself back up to life, that you won't someday want more?"

Eyes like pinpoints on her he said, "How do you know you won't?"

She didn't, she supposed. Then said, "So, if either one of us does, what then?"

Brows raised, Dale didn't even hesitate before saying, "Before it would ever get to that point, I'd already know that she accepted you as part of the deal, and that she'd be a great bonus mom who would love the child as one of her own."

Millie sat back. Stunned. Days of fretting and she'd never seen that one coming. Could it really be that simple?

Lifting his bottle to his mouth, Dale asked, "What else have you got?" Seemingly without any concerns as to what she'd throw at him.

Which made it easier to start tossing.

"Finances," she said. "You said something about you'd pay for it, and while the gesture is nice, no, thank you. I'd need to share expenses."

"Expenses aren't just calculated in dollars," he told her. "You're the one who's going to be doing all the heavy lifting, at least for the first bit. Nine months of carrying the child. And then, I'm assuming you'd breast feed, so up to another year beyond the birth. Tamara's getting a hefty sum for her efforts, mother's milk not included."

So he was going to pay her to have her own baby?

But his, too. Something he'd pay anyone else to do if he went the egg bank and surrogate route.

As odd as it seemed, she liked his rationalization. Kept things on the soul mate, not lover, plane. "Okay," she said. "After the first year, we regroup on finances." By then she'd be working again. Somewhere. Not that, financially, she had to do so for a few years, at least, but for her own sense of self-worth...

"Next," Dale said, bringing her attention back to him. And his readiness to take on whatever she shot his way. Almost like they were involved in some weird game of table running. She'd serve the ball, he'd whack it back, score, and she'd watch the thing whiz by.

"Decisions," she said. "Education, public, private or home-schooled. Vacations, how long, with whom, going where. Daycare or no..."

"Just like anything else," he told her, his gaze open as he held hers. "We discuss each situation as it presents until we reach a unanimous decision, which will often include compromise on one or both sides, but not always only on one person's side. All of this stuff is important, Mil, but to me, it comes back to one thing."

She stiffened. Was it something she could sign on for? Or was he about to deliver the deal breaker? "What's that?" she asked because she had to, not because she wanted to do so. And braced herself.

"Trust," he told her. "I trust you. Do you trust me?"

Peace settled over her like an ocean breeze. Of course. Dale had a way of finding his way through her sometimes murky waters and showing her that everything in life was manageable. Showing her her missing pieces.

He was watching her expectantly, waiting for her answer and Millie was absolutely completely certain as she looked him in the eye and said, "Yes, I do."

## *Chapter Nineteen*

They hadn't said they were going to do it. They'd just paved the way to leave the option on the table.

Over the next week, Dale thought of little else. He wanted to be a father. To actually have a family of his own. To give someone the life he didn't have growing up. To give the world a human being who would contribute to its well-being in whatever way that human chose.

To have someone to leave WG to, because, while Gunder would retire at some point, his work would live on, with potential to keep on giving indefinitely.

He pictured himself at ballet classes, sporting events, musical concerts, swimming lessons. At amusement parks, on airplanes, in doctors' offices, principals' offices, and walking through the grocery store with little arms grabbing at things from the seat of the cart.

He could see himself sitting on the floor with a slightly older version of those little arms building a town out of LEGO blocks.

And everywhere he looked, he saw Millie, too, in the background, having her turn. Teaching the child all of the family things that Dale hadn't had and didn't know. He pictured her on the beach, playing ball and laughing.

He'd only ever heard her laugh a couple of times in all the months he'd known her, all the times they'd shared.

For that matter, he couldn't remember the last time he'd laughed out loud.

Over the next week, they saw each other every day, even had sex with a condom once, one evening at his place, but she left right afterward—had to get home to Magic, who was with Briel, who still wasn't spending any more time on the beach than necessary to visit her potty spot.

They made another batch of mint beer—non-alcoholic. Talked about the kids she was coaching—they had a meet coming up over the holiday break—and about an actor being talked about for Dale's movie deal. About Tamara, and the fact that Harper wasn't due back until after her last show the night before Christmas Eve. He told her that WG was on hiatus over the holidays, but that Dale was writing an article about homemade brew for a nationally syndicated cooking blog.

They took another walk along the holiday lights on Thursday of the third week in December, one week and one day before Christmas. Darkness had fallen, but just and more people were out. In sweats and jackets, with Juice walking between them, they stayed down closer to the water, for their privacy.

And Dale thought about the five Christmases he'd spent on Ocean Breeze. On his deck. Enjoying the peace with Juice. Reading. Writing. Eating junk food all day because he rarely allowed himself to indulge. And chatting with various neighbors who'd been out and stopped by. Scott, always. Others, as it happened. Or not. He'd had invitations to join gatherings for holiday meals. Just hadn't wanted to do so. He'd been content with his own plans. Not unhappy.

And that year, the thought of spending the day alone sounded...like grief. For Millie who would also be alone, as much as for himself. "We're going to do Christmas like we did Thanksgiving, right?" he asked Millie as the end of the beach came into sight in the distance. She'd left her long dark hair down, and it was blowing softly around her shoulders as the breeze kicked up. He held himself back from smoothing the strands. He just wanted to touch them.

And it wasn't him and Millie. They didn't randomly touch any part of the other. But holiday dinner...he was waiting on her answer.

"I could bake a ham," she said slowly. "And au gratin potatoes. And my mother's pea salad. It has a lettuce base, green onions, dressing. And bacon and parmesan cheese..."

She was starting on a ramble. And he said, "We don't have to if you'd rather not." No expectations. No pressure. They were soul mates, not partners.

"Oh, I want to." She turned to look at him. "I wasn't sure you would. But... I was thinking about something else, too, that we could, maybe do, before dinner..."

Make a baby? The thought popped in his head. The most perfect Christmas gift ever. The thought coming from a man who'd never hoped for anything specific for himself giftwise. He'd received gifts for his birthdays and at Christmas, but, other than the birthdays he'd celebrated with Lyla, the gifts had all been from people who didn't know him well. Looking back, he started to think that maybe that had been more his fault than anyone's.

Millie hadn't finished her sentence. "What would you like to do first?" he asked her, his tone encouraging. Whatever it was, if she wanted his involvement, she'd have it. Just because, unlike him, she was speaking up about it.

"I'd like us to take Juice to the hospital to visit the kids," she told him.

And Dale felt more than just peaceful.

He felt as though he was a part of something good.

Sadness begat sadness. And happiness begat happiness. Words from somewhere in her past hit Millie as she and Dale and Juice drew closer to the end of the beach. She'd been riddled with guilt on and off all week. For wanting more with Brent gone.

For reaching out for her own piece of real happiness, when others were suffering. For wanting her own suffering to be done.

For moving on from the life she'd promised her heart to forever.

She wanted a child of her own, even if it wasn't Brent's. More specifically, she wanted to have Dale's child. To share parenting with him.

The thought made her happier than she could ever remember feeling. Because her happiness in the past had been shadowed with tragedy?

Or just because...what?

And did it matter? She could cling to what had been for the rest of her life. Remain encased in sadness. Or she could dare to reach for happiness. Within her limitations, of course. She'd had the love of her life, romantically. But being with Dale...

Dogs barking interrupted her train of thought, and before she realized what was happening, Angel and Morgan were dancing around Juice's feet. "Morgan, no no," a childish voice said then, as five-year-old Leigh Bartholomew came running up to them, her pudgy little legs encased in leggings and running shoes.

"Hi, Mr. Dale, and I'm sorry they bothered you. I was s'posed to put them inside 'cause Uncle Scott saw you coming, but then I got 'istracted by Miss Iris's cookies and didn't mind quick enough...and, oh no, now I'm in trouble and Daddy—he's my new Daddy, you know—is going to tell Mommy that it's okay, but Mommy says I always have to mind..." Shaking her head, the little girl gave a big dramatic sigh.

And Millie's heart burst open. Kneeling down, she said, "Hi, Leigh, I'm Millie, and your Mommy's right, you know, you do have to mind. You know why?"

Leigh nodded and said, "'Cuz she says so."

Biting back a smile, aware of Dale standing there watching them while the three dogs played on the beach, she said, "Well, yes, that, but do you know why she says so?"

Leigh's face scrunched, leaving shadows and lines cast from the bright lights of the Bartholomew beach display. "Because she loves me." The little girl answered after obvious thought.

"And because she's already been a little girl, and she learned the things that can hurt you, or make you happier, and guess what she's always wanting for you?"

"To make me happy," Leigh said, then slid her tiny hand into Millie's. "You want to come up and see my baby? Mommy just finished feeding him. She has to wear a funny bra, you know."

Alarm sliced through Millie as she glanced up at Dale. Not as much for herself, as for him. And them as friends. Not the couple that others on the beach had to assume they were.

Allowing herself to be pulled by the little hand dragging at her, Millie's gaze implored Dale to do what he needed to do. Join them. Go. Join them. Please.

And she had to stop herself from reaching out to grab his hand with her free one, when he fell into step beside her.

They didn't stay long. Sage had taken the baby inside to put him in his crib, and as soon as Leigh heard that they'd left without her, she ran inside after them.

As Scott came up to him, Dale heard Iris say to Millie, "Leigh has to sing him to sleep every night."

And added a good night song to his list of things he'd do on the nights he had his son or daughter. When he had one. If he had one.

Scott offered him a beer. As badly as Dale felt like he could use one, he declined. He didn't want to obligate them to stay that long. Gray joined them shortly afterward, and as Iris turned to grab a beer, Millie moved a little closer to Dale. He liked having her there.

And needed the two men to quit looking between the two of them. The last thing he and Millie needed was pressure.

Then Gray asked Millie about Briel, saying he'd seen her outside once when he'd been at Scott's, and Dale relaxed as the veterinarian praised Millie's handling of the abused girl, and gave her a few other tips to help ease Briel into life with people who wouldn't hurt her.

It was all about building trust.

That last note hit loudly within Dale as he heard Millie say, "Speaking of Briel, I need to get back to her and Magic. Chelsea's poor big girl has had to sacrifice a lot of beach time to sit with my lost one." She needed to get her and Dale back into their own world.

Or at least, got them alone again. As soon as he heard her first words to him when they were out of earshot, he knew she'd brought some of his friends' world with her. "Did you see the way they were looking at us?" she asked him.

He nodded. Then said, "We knew it would happen," as if that somehow made things okay. But he was rethinking the whole child thing, as he viewed the situation through the eyes of the people he'd adopted as his extended family over the years. From a distance. On the outside looking in. But still…family.

"And if we have a child together?" She put the glaring issue right out there. "What then?"

He'd move. The answer came to him as clearly as needing to eat when he got up in the morning. A given. He wasn't going to let the opinions of others rob them both of the chance to get what they wanted and needed out life. He'd move if he had to, he amended silently. And then, as though WG had gone back to work, the words came to him. "We tell them ahead of time what we're doing and why," he told her. "Just as we should probably do now for us. Get out in front of it, to put an end to the natural curiosity. We're a widow and widower," he said, as they walked, with Juice once again between them. Putting his hands in his pockets, he let the words keep coming to him. "That's nothing to be ashamed about. And I think we're both at the point where others' pity, if it comes our way, can be accepted with the compassion with which it's offered without making either of us feel…less."

He was speaking for himself. Coming from three more years of grieving than she'd had. But hoped she'd reached the same point anyway. He might have sooner, too, if she'd come along before she had.

Millie hadn't said anything, but was walking steadily. Calmly. As was Juice. The standard poodle wasn't working. Taking note, Dale said, "Same thing if we decide to have a child. We tell our neighbors if it comes to be, rather than have them watch you growing a baby and speculate, let them know we aren't a couple, aren't getting married, we're just good friends who want to have a child. They can judge. Talk behind our backs. But I don't think they would. The people here…"

"…I know," Millie interrupted when he took a breath. "They're great about caring, but not butting in," she said. "It's one of the reasons I decided to buy a cottage here. I love this place."

She loved Ocean Breeze. And would love their child.

But not him. Never him.

Dale accepted the truth with a melancholy that would probably always be a part of who he was.

Millie had spent two years dead alive. And a lifetime before that planning her future years in advance, targeting every potential pitfall, tending to them all. Thinking she could prevent tragedy by being diligent and aware.

She was a nurse. Who better to have seen a sign during all the years that she'd spent with Brent, lived with him, trained with him, slept with him that her husband's heart was defective?

And fate had had a different goal. Preempting all her years of objective choices.

Leaving her on earth lost and alone. Maybe trying to tell her that she had to live each day to the fullest, rather than spending so many of them waiting for the right moments for things to happen?

Little Leigh...she'd come right up to Millie. A total stranger—though one the little girl would have known had been vetted by the adults in her world—and the girl had taken her hand with total openness. And trust.

Because Millie had a way with kids. She'd always had. And was meant to have one.

Dale didn't drop off with Juice when they reached his stretch of beach. She'd have said something to him if he had. But when they reached her place, and he hung back rather than turning to head up with her, she said, "You want to come in?"

There was only one reason for him to do so that time of night. They'd eaten. She didn't stock beer. Had no reruns for them to watch because he hadn't brought any down with him. And she had nothing new to show him.

His instant turn made her smile inside as he said, "Of course."

The man had one hell of a healthy sexual appetite. She'd give him that. And actually, fed off it, too. Sex with Dale was far beyond anything she'd known in the past. Because they were older than she and Brent had been. And Dale was more experienced. She'd eventually reasoned that one out to the point where she could get by the guilt and throw herself into the activity one hundred percent.

And a small part of her quietly acknowledged that in some ways she and Dale were closer, in a deeper way, than she and Brent had been. Simply because they'd both suffered so intensely. She was a different person than she'd been when she and Brent were married.

He waited outside while she let Briel and Magic out, and when they stood there, supervising while the dogs did their business, he grabbed her around the neck, pulling her up against him and opening his mouth over hers. Right there on the beach.

Though he let her go almost as quickly, Millie had already flooded with desire. Needing his hands, his touch. His muscled marine form on her, under her, in her, beside her.

Juice led the way inside, with Briel following dutifully behind the dog she'd seemed to have adopted as her parent. Magic brought up the rear. As though she knew she was a guest in her own home.

Following them, Millie turned to Dale as he came inside, and said, "Condom optional. Your choice."

And, back straight, walked slowly toward her bedroom.

Dale had his pants off before he'd hit the hallway. Stripping off his jacket and shirt, he walked into her room, fully up, ready and proud.

He was going to make a child. To build greatness out of ashes.

He was going to have sex with the most beautiful woman in the world. The thought slowed his step. Lowered another part of him some. But didn't stop him.

Truth was, in the few months he'd spent with Millie,

he knew her better, understood her more deeply, than he ever had Lyla. He was older. More mature.

He'd learned the full value of what he'd had. What he'd lost.

And wasn't going to waste the chance to make the most of what he had left. To be happy. And to nurture and raise a happy person.

Millie had stripped off everything but her panties and lay on her sheet, her eyes smoldering as she watched him slowly approach. Making her enjoyment of his body quite obvious by the way her gaze seemed to linger on every part of him. Making him instantly, achingly hard again.

She was there, fully alive, wanting him. His hunger for her had reached new heights. And he wasn't going to waste a second of the happy moments that were waiting for them. He had as much right to happiness as Millie and everyone else on earth did.

And spent the next hour soaking it up. Soaking it in. He touched Millie from her toes to the hair on the top of her head. Kissed her. Tasted her. When she reached to turn off the light, he reached after her and turned it back on to its lowest setting. Just enough that he could look at her.

"I want you to know I see you," he said softly. "That you are *consuming* me." The words were just there.

But when she said, "You are *so* consuming me, too," with such heated tenderness, he realized how badly he'd needed to know that.

He entered her then. Slowly. With passion. But tenderness and purpose, too. With nothing between his penis and her welcome. Whether they were creating a baby in those minutes or not, the coming together was momentous. Forever memorable. Perfection. It was him to her. No walls.

## *Chapter Twenty*

Getting into the box of Christmas decorations in Millie's garage—leftovers starting from when she and Brent had secretly lived together during college—and putting up the tree was all Dale's idea. She'd prevaricated the first time he'd mentioned the idea.

Hadn't responded the second time.

The third time, he'd said, "A child should have a Christmas tree," and peace settled over her once again. He wasn't convincing her to do something against her grain. He was reading her. Showing her the things she wouldn't allow herself to see. Helping her move past grief and into the future.

While encouraging her to bring Brent with her, too.

He'd been doing so ever since she'd moved to Ocean Breeze.

As it turned out, that Sunday, five days before Christmas, they had to trash the cheap tree that had been boxed in the heat for too long. And went out and bought a lovely bigger one. With a stand and colorful tree skirt that would light up a kid's eyes every year when it came out of storage.

And bought a few ornaments, too, to at least be able to cover most of the branches.

Millie stood back at one point, in the store, watching Dale as he went over all the options available, picking things up, flipping switches where there was one, moving on to the very next. He didn't pass over a single aisle, or choice. And it hit her, their future child wasn't the only one who needed a Christmas tree.

From that moment on, she was as involved as he was, discussing light choices, deciding more was better than less. Going with a menagerie of ornament styles, rather than choosing a theme. Figuring that they could be added to in the future...

And a realization hit. Too late. But still there. "We need to get a tree for you, too," she said. And when he shook his head, she insisted with, "If you're going to be a father, Dale, you have to have Christmas in your home."

Because the child would be both places. Going back and forth. And...her heart slowed, her heart getting heavier as she looked clearly at an aspect of the future they hadn't discussed. The holiday moments each of them would spend alone when the other had the child.

Dale, not seeming to notice said, "I was thinking we'd do Thanksgiving at my house, and Christmas at yours." He spoke as though there was nothing at all odd about the arrangement. And maybe there wasn't. Two people in separate homes parenting a child had to make choices that fit the child.

Dale had stopped. Was looking at her. "Unless you don't want to do that," he said. Clearly concerned. And thinking of her, not just the child. Or himself, either. Because that was Dale. From everything she'd observed and heard, it had always been Dale. And always would be, too. Even having had his own future stripped away, he'd still been tending to everyone on the beach as needed.

And had been a surrogate dad to every dog that lived there, too.

He'd been a "father" even when he hadn't believed he'd ever have the chance again.

With a smile, she looked him in the eye and said, "I *do* want that. But I want to switch off, each year. Thanksgiving at your house one year, mine the next. Same for Christmas. So these things—" she waved toward their two full baskets "—belong to both houses."

Belonged to the child they were in the process of trying to create.

The one that, maybe, they had already created.

The reminder—one that had been popping up in her mind, sending excited shockwaves through her system, over and over in the two days since they'd first had unprotected sex—put an added pep to her movements as she followed Dale to the cashier.

Looking around her, she felt as though she was a solid part of her fellow shoppers that day. Not just the shadow-of-a-life that she'd been for so long.

Dale enjoyed putting up the tree and hanging the lights and decorations. Both the ones they'd purchased, and the ones Millie had had. Family wasn't just about the moment, but the past that had brought them to the moment, made them who they were.

And about the future, the humans who would join.

For a few moments there, he felt like a kid himself. He wasn't helping to decorate someone else's tree. He was decorating his own. He was half owner of that tree for life.

WG butted in then. The woman in the compound... at the end of the book, she was going to have her own Christmas. Alone or with someone, he didn't know. At the compound or in the hospital, a house or jail, he didn't know that, either. But she was going to have a tree that belonged to her.

Dale nodded silently, taking mental note.

Then, as Millie excused herself to make a couple of chai lattes for them, he dropped to the floor in the middle of the room, staring up at the tree.

As a kid would do. To drink his hot chocolate before bed on Christmas Eve. The memory came to him. Just a flash. He couldn't place it. Wasn't even sure it had happened to him, or if he'd just seen it in a movie, but he held on to it for the future. Because he had one.

He felt the nudge at his elbow. Reached over automatically to let Juice know he was okay and met air. Turning, he looked to see Briel, on her stomach, head on her paws, right there, almost touching his thigh, looking up at him.

Shocked, and more moved than he'd known he could be, Dale sat still. Didn't want to scare the girl off. Gaining the trust of a canine was not to be taken lightly. One that had been mistreated... Briel lived through instinct. She'd come to him.

"Hey, girlie," he said softly, looking down at her without moving a muscle. "Such a pretty girl, and so sweet," he continued, speaking from the heart because she'd know if he wasn't. "I want to be your friend," he told her. The glow of the Christmas tree prompted more. "Your family," he said. "You can trust me to never ever hurt you, to protect you from anyone who tries and to always have treats. Just ask Juice."

Juice. Where was Juice? Glancing up, Dale looked around him on the floor, then toward the archway leading into the kitchen around the corner.

And froze.

Juice was standing there with Magic, one on each side of Millie, who was standing with two cups of hot tea in her hands. And tears in her eyes.

She cared about him. Of course she did. They were soul mates. Who had sex and were trying to create a child together.

Over the next couple of days, Millie worked her mind around the huge influx of emotion that had hit her as she'd come around the corner from the kitchen with Juice, to see Dale sitting on the floor with Briel. She heard the words he'd said to the little sheltie mix again and again.

Telling herself that they were her sign that she'd made the right choice to choose Dale to be the father of her child, rather than a sperm bank. First, her child would have two parents, which gave him or her double the chance for love and protection. And second, the baby, if there became one, was going to be so incredibly lucky to have Dale Wilson in his or her life.

Both facts were a given to her.

She just wasn't sure if she believed the reason why that moment seeing him alone with Briel continued to haunt her. Fate giving her a thumbs-up on a choice.

But it was all she had and so she went with it. About her day. Jogging. Seeing her kids and ending the practice with a little holiday party complete with homemade cookies. To bed with Dale. The emotional high gear where he was concerned, was fate telling her that she'd made the right choice regarding the conception of her child.

And it was that validation that had her texting him 911 Harper's on Thursday morning, Christmas Eve Day, and dropping her phone the second she'd hit Send. She'd already called for an ambulance. The door was unlocked.

Pulling the edges of the sheets and covers up off the end of the double bed in Harper's guest bedroom, she scooted herself onto the bare mattress, then reached over the bundle to gently touch Tamara's naked thigh. "Help is on the way," she said. "Until then, we're going to be just fine. I'm just going to check you again for dilation," she said.

Breathing heavily, squinting in pain, Tamara nodded.

The woman hadn't said a word since her water broke. Except to scream once and say, "It hurts," about thirty seconds later. Getting Tamara to her recently vacated, unmade bed, Millie had done a quick check to see that the expectant mother was only three centimeters. They still had time. Likely several hours. She'd told Tamara she'd take her to the hospital.

That was when the first contraction had hit so hard the woman had gone into fetal position. And started moaning.

Less than three minutes before she'd texted Dale.

And she might not have time even for him to get there. "I feel her head," she said, completely calm then. "She's coming now. When you feel the need to push, don't fight it. Just give it all you've got. I'm right here, and you're going to be just fine."

She didn't like the amount of blood she was seeing. There should only be a pint or so beginning to end. Keeping that information to herself, she kept up a tirade of calm talking. Encouraging Tamara, rubbing her inner thigh gently. Reminding her of breathing rhythm. Even breathing with her.

She could see the baby's head by the time she heard the door open and Dale was there. One glance and he was at Tamara's head. "Hey, there, I'm Dale," he said. "I've never done this before, but I was going to be a father once, and read up on it all. You okay with me being here?"

He was distracting Tamara, Millie got that. Sent him a look of supreme gratitude, and a smile, too. For Tamara's sake. She could use some warm cloths. And sanitary gloves. Both of which she had at home.

There was barely time to even have the thought as Tamara tensed, moaned, and Dale slid an arm around the woman's shoulders, lifting her slightly and said, "Look at you, all strong and ready. I've got your back, you push all you want." His tone was soft. Full of praise.

And calm, too. Dale had a gift for it. And was generous in gifting it to others.

Millie soaked it up right along with Tamara. In professional mode, she had no doubt about her ability to birth the baby that was coming. She just wasn't sure what lay ahead. And didn't have the necessary supplies to do her best with any of it.

There was already some tearing. She had no sutures.

And nothing she could give Tamara for the pain.

But she kept an anticipatory smile on her face as she watched the baby start to emerge from the woman's body. Aware every second that Tamara was watching her.

She'd glanced up to see the younger woman focusing on Dale, too. And found herself drawing faith that all would be well from the warmth emanating from those brown eyes.

"Is she coming?" Tamara half screamed, with another major push.

"She is!" Millie smiled for real as saw the full head emerge, with no blue coloring at all. The baby was still getting oxygen. Everything else could be attended to by those who'd soon be arriving with medical supplies.

"Her head is out," she said, maintaining her professionalism, but smiling, too. At both Tamara and Dale.

"See, I told you you've got this," he said, an arm still bracing Tamara's shoulders and upper body, with his other hand holding one of hers. "First time out and you're a pro."

Two more pushes and the baby girl's body slid into Millie's waiting hands. Grabbing some of the sheet from the unused side of the bed, she quickly wrapped the baby, umbilical cord still attached, clearing airwaves, and sent a smile up to both faces peering at her with wide, concerned eyes, as the brand-new little girl let out a wail. It was weak.

But there.

Dale's only experience with birth was from what he'd read when Lyla told him she was pregnant. Videos he'd watched of birthing classes while overseas, to help himself, and Lyla, feel as though he was more a part of the process.

The only actual birth he'd ever been a part of had been on television. With him sitting on the couch in his home staring at a screen.

He put in a call to Harper the second he heard the baby wail. The couple, whose child had just been born, had been notified Tamara was in early labor and were almost at Ocean Breeze.

With his phone to his ear, he followed Millie's staccato instructions at Mach speed, gathering clean baby blankets, wash cloths and a syringe, and raced back into the bedroom, handing all the supplies in hand to Millie. And nearly felt weak at the knees at the warmth in the smile she gave him. He had no idea what the hell he was doing.

But he was there. Doing it. With Millie. Helping a new life into the world.

But didn't stop to give even a glance to the new baby as he heard a hard knock at the door, and ran to let in the paramedics.

Millie exchanged some conversation with them. Medical terms.

And then, with a glance at Dale, moved up to place pillows behind Tamara's back and head as the team of two went to work preparing mother and baby for their trip to the hospital.

Dale had no idea why he felt he had to approach the bed, as well. But he did so. Standing beside Millie, to smile at the young woman. "You did it," he told her. "You just gave a wonderful loving couple the baby they couldn't have on their own."

Tamara smiled with sweat still on her brow. Looking exhausted. But not unhappy. "I just got something, too," she said, "You two."

Dale glanced at Millie, looking for a sign that childbirth caused women to say things that made no sense. Her gaze was on him, briefly, but then, she reached a hand to smooth the damp hair back from Tamara's head and said, "I'm a nurse. I just did what I'm trained to do."

Tamara shook her head then, sharing a glance between the two of them. "No, you two. I haven't had a great example of marriage. My parents were a disaster. My sister married too young and they weren't happy even before he got sick. There's this guy back home who's been asking me out, but I kept saying no. But seeing you two… the love radiates between you. I could feel it. That's what I clung to when I thought I was going to die. And look… the baby's fine, and I'm okay, too… I'm never going to forget how I felt seeing you two look at each other…"

Her words were interrupted as the new parents rushed into the room. And a third paramedic arrived with a stretcher.

Dale backed up to the wall as everything happened at once. Millie gave a report while Harper's friends welcomed their daughter into the world, cutting the umbilical cord. Tamara was lifted onto the stretcher. The baby placed in a small plastic crib gurney, with Millie saying she'd ride along in case the doctor needed anything more from her and they were gone.

All of them. Out the door in a bundle of rush.

Leaving Dale standing there, staring behind them.

On the outside. Looking in.

A lot of women said things during and immediately after birth that they wouldn't ordinarily have ever uttered. Most of it filled with an overload of emotion. Not that they lied. Just that…things had to be taken in context. What might have seemed to have overwhelming significance in the moment of intense fear and pain, would have fading importance as the woman's life returned to normal.

Millie knew the facts. Had been present for and had assisted in many births during her schooling and a rotation in the birthing center of the first hospital she'd worked at, too. She'd heard a couple of doozies, too. A woman who'd announced to the room as her baby was coming, that she felt as she did when her husband was inside her.

That had been one for the books.

And still, she couldn't get Tamara's avowal out of her head as she rode home in a ride-share that afternoon. Thinking about the new parents who'd be staying at the hospital that night, rooming in with Starlight Gold. Star, for short. They'd given Millie updates she already had, thanked her again and again for bringing their daughter safely into the world. Asked questions they'd already asked about the birth itself.

And still, she heard Tamara's words pounding in her brain.

The younger woman had told everyone to whom Millie had been introduced, from the doctor attending her to orderlies, about her revelation regarding the couple who'd birthed the baby. Describing in detail the looks on their faces. The way they seemed to speak without words. And had worked perfectly together to give Tamara the kindest, most spiritual birth of all time. Because of the love that emanated between Dale and Millie. If you believed the woman.

Tamara had just given birth in a potentially alarming way. The baby wasn't hers. She'd never even held it. Millie and Dale had become her birth story.

And while Millie had smiled, having the utmost respect and compassion for the younger woman, she'd wanted to tell her to stop. To explain to everyone within earshot that Tamara had it all wrong.

After cleaning up the mess in Tamara's bedroom, she collected the other woman's things, packed them as she'd already agreed to do, and gave the suitcase to Harper to drop off to Tamara at the hospital. The woman's sister had already arrived and would be taking Tamara back to their farm once she was released.

And then, leaving ruined sheets and bedding in a sealed trash bag in their garbage can, she headed back to her place via the road. Not the beach. Passing Dale's place, but not stopping.

He'd likely be out on the deck.

And that was likely one of the reasons she'd taken the road home. That, and she badly needed a shower and the road was faster.

Standing under the spray in her master bathroom, Millie thought back over the day, hardly comprehending all that had happened before dinnertime. She'd birthed a healthy baby girl.

In the throes of immediate danger, she'd contacted Dale.

He'd come running.

And had been a miracle worker with Millie's panicked patient while Millie handled medical issues with no supplies.

She and Dale were soul mates. Meant they conversed on a level deeper than everyday consciousness.

Not that they were in love. They were not. She was not. And he couldn't be. It would ruin everything.

She punctuated the thought by turning off the water, and, dried and dressed in sweats and a T-shirt, walked barefoot out to see about getting something to eat. Too late for lunch. An early dinner.

Of apple slices, cucumber slices, crackers and grape jelly. With some slices of Havarti. Because she was having some kind of weird craving? Even if she had a fertilized egg inside her, the embryo wouldn't have implanted yet. No, she wanted healthy and cucumbers and apples were all the fresh fruit and vegetables she had in the house. The crackers and jelly and cheese were there for comfort. Just as Dale had taught her. Something he'd gleaned from Lyla.

Millie ate, trying to decide if she was going to hurry up and get to the grocery store before it closed to pick up what she needed for Christmas dinner the next day. She'd been planning to go that morning, after her visit with Tamara.

Because she'd been putting off doing so ever since the Christmas tree went up in her house. More specifically, since after that, when she'd seen Dale on the floor in front of it, had seen Briel lying with her nose right up to his arm. And heard him talking to her.

Could she be in love with Dale?

She couldn't do Christmas with him. Not with her struggling like she was. It wouldn't be fair to either one of them.

If she'd broken the cardinal rule, she'd ruin things between them.

And was two days too late in her realizations if she was pregnant.

But really, anytime would be too late as far as she was concerned. Her soul had never had a mate like him. And she wasn't done helping him discover all the possibilities he'd been missing. Or blossoming into the post-Brent person she was meant to be.

Carrying her little plate of weird food into the living room, she stood there chewing, looking at the tree, as though it would tell her how to get through the next twenty-four hours without alienating or hurting Dale. And...there was a present under the tree.

Way under it. As though someone had purposely pushed it so far in that it was barely visible. Had she been walking through the room on her normal route to the kitchen, or sitting in her normal seat on the couch, she wouldn't have seen it. Standing along the wall, leaning her shoulder against it, she saw the plain green wrapping paper. Around something that was not boxed, based on the wrapping. And was only an inch or so thick.

Dale had to have left it there. No one else had been in the place, and only Chelsea had a key. Clearly the woman hadn't been in Millie's cottage during the past couple of days.

He'd bought her a gift.

She didn't have anything for him. Hadn't even thought to get something. They weren't a couple.

But...soul mates probably bought gifts for each other. If something occurred from that place that seemed to tell them about each other. To speak to their minds.

She hadn't received any such message.

She had a couple of hours yet before the stores closed. Throwing on running shoes, Millie pulled her hair back into a ponytail, grabbed her keys, apologized to Briel and Magic for leaving again so soon and headed out the door. To buy groceries.

She couldn't cancel Christmas on a man who'd put a present under his first Christmas tree.

Even an ex–soul mate, who'd gone and fallen in love so would no longer be able to tune into the loop would get that much.

## *Chapter Twenty-One*

Sitting out on his deck just after dark, Dale sipped from the bottle of non-alcoholic beer—the only kind he had left—he'd opened to usher in the holiday. And then had added a shot to it.

To drown out the silence in his life—depending on which time he sipped.

He'd been waiting to hear from Millie all day. Even after realizing that he was expecting something that wasn't a part of who they were to each other. Other than the few extraneous situations where they'd planned to be together, they just happened upon one another.

They didn't call, or check in.

Unless there was an emergency. Which clearly there wasn't.

It was on him that he'd expected her to let him know how things went at the hospital. To give him an idea of when she'd be back. She'd never, ever given him any indication that she'd do such.

Once their child was born, they'd have to set up regular communication schedules. As parents of the same child. That wasn't yet.

They had said they were spending Christmas together.

And the holiday started with Christmas Eve. By his definition. Didn't mean it was hers.

Sitting there with the beach alit with the holiday light displays, Dale watched the lights of layers of boats bobbing out on the water. Thought about the friends and families aboard them. Thousands of people would likely view their beach that night. Getting as close as they could to the wonderland.

And there he was, a very wealthy bestselling author with a movie deal, in a front row seat. Not envying them. But...maybe.

He and Juice had walked down the beach at dusk. Just in case Millie was out. Had worried about Briel and Magic inside, needing to go out. Figured as soon as Millie got back, he'd suggest she leave him with a key in the event of future unplanned absences.

But for all he knew, she could have been there. Inside. He didn't knock. It wasn't their way.

He could leave his seed inside her to create a baby. But he couldn't ring her doorbell. Something not quite right about that.

But...he sat forward, squinting against the glare of thousands of colorful lights on the beach to see the lone figure walking among them, with...was that Magic and... Briel? He watched the advance without moving. Just took it in.

"Hey," Millie climbed the steps to his deck, with Briel and then Magic right beside her. The little dog went straight up to Juice who'd stood to welcome them.

Without a word, Dale reached into the small cooler he'd brought out, pulled out a bottle, and handed it to her without adding the shot. No questions asked. No explanations needed.

The holidays were hard.

Millie sipped. Staring straight ahead. And eventually said, "I can't be in love with you."

He nodded. "I know."

Then, minutes later, "You can't be in love with me, either."

"I know." He took a sip of his beer. A long one.

"You're sure?"

The tone of her voice, half fear, half demand, pulled his gaze toward her. Her eyes were glistening with the twinkling red, white and blue colors in front of them, pinning him in place.

Was she asking if he was sure she couldn't be in love with him? Or that he was sure he couldn't be in love with her? Either way, "I'm sure," he told her without a blink.

Some things just were. Had to be.

"The baby's parents send their thanks," she said then. "They're rooming in with Starlight tonight."

"Starlight?" he asked, brows raised.

"Starlight Gold," she told him, with a bit of a grin. "They first met Harper, a huge ballet star, under stage lights, when they were in the nosebleed section several years ago."

He nodded. But said, "I'm fine if our kid is Billy, or Sally, or…"

"Brenda Sue?" she asked, naming the heroine of a series he'd just recently bought for them to stream.

"I could go for Lyla or Brent. Good people who died far too young and deserve to be remembered." He looked at her as he said the words.

Her eyes glistened, and then she said, "I think that's too much weight to put on a little one. Maybe we find another way to make sure they're remembered."

They didn't need a way. He got that as she said the words. Neither of them were ever going to forget what was in their hearts.

"Such as?"

"We don't let the joy we used to know die through their deaths."

He liked her idea. A lot. And wasn't at all surprised that, in a single sentence, Millie managed to eradicate the moroseness that had been threatening to overtake him that evening.

Life wasn't easy. Or perfect. But it had its moments. And as long as he remembered that, stayed open to them, they'd continue to appear. Because joy didn't die.

"You brought Briel. Does that mean you can stay awhile?"

"I brought both of them because they've been alone all day."

It wasn't a no. He heard that one loud and clear. "You want to go have sex?" he asked then, glancing over at her.

And got hard even before she said, "Yes, please."

Millie didn't spend the night. She fell asleep in Dale's arms, but woke just before midnight, and slid from his bed.

"You don't have to go," he murmured in the darkness.

Sliding into her sweats, she said, "I know." But she had things to do.

A breakfast casserole to put together so it could chill

overnight. And a present to wrap. Addressed to Juice. It was the best she could do.

Had seemed absolutely right to her when she'd had the idea in the store.

"What time do you want me in the morning?"

"As soon as you want to be there."

She'd bake the casserole when she got up. It could be reheated whenever he arrived. That was the beauty of them. No expectations. No one who'd be disappointed if they ate the casserole at one and the ham the next day, even.

The walk down the private, secure beach was nice. And she wasn't alone. Not only were Magic and Briel right by her side, but there were still boat lights shining from out beyond their reef. People enjoying their Christmas Eve. Hopefully gaining holiday spirit from them.

Peace and joy. That was the best life had to offer, and it turned out that she could still give and receive both.

She hadn't expected to sleep but was out as soon as she relaxed under her sheets just before two. And was still up by six, filled with an eagerness she hadn't known since Brent's death. She had things to do. Casserole to bake. And cinnamon rolls. She'd bought the ingredients the day before. Thinking she'd make them for herself to fill her time on Christmas Eve but had chosen to have sex with Dale instead.

A circumstance she regretted not at all. Remembering the night before with a smile on her face, she was still in her robe, naked underneath, with only her teeth brushed, when she heard Juice's bark at her back door.

Instantly filling with fear, she hurried to the door, afraid the dog had come down to warn her of an emergency with his master, and saw Dale, showered, shaved and smiling, standing on her deck. In black jeans and a green button-down shirt.

Before seven in the morning.

Like the kid it sounded as though he'd never been.

Grinning, she pulled open the door, gave him instructions for pulling the casserole out of the oven, and putting the rolls in, and headed off to shower. No way she was sitting down to Christmas breakfast with the man, looking like last night's leftovers.

She might not be able to let him love her. Or give him the love she felt. Ever.

But she most definitely wanted him to want her.

The look in his eyes when she reentered the room dressed in black leggings and a thigh-length, figure-hugging red sweater with her newly purchased Santa earrings hanging from her lobes, told her how undeniable his desire for her had grown.

"Well, Mrs. Claus, you want to skip breakfast and come sit on Santa's lap?" he drawled, his entire demeanor filled with very sexy good cheer.

"Only if you want to explain to these three why they don't get a bite of the breakfast Magic and Juice have been sniffing on the counter," she told him.

With a shrug, he reached into the refrigerator and handed her a tall flute. "I made mimosas," he told her. With non-alcoholic champagne, just in case.

Surprising her, just as she had him with casserole and cinnamon rolls. He'd already eaten one of the treats, she noticed as she lifted her glass to his in a toast.

"Merry Christmas, Millie." His eyes grew serious with the words as he held her gaze.

"Merry Christmas, Dale," she said back, filled with warmth, with calm.

And something more that maybe only appeared on Christmas Day. A bit of magic that made even broken hearts feel whole again.

Christmas was about gifting others in ways that made them happy. And Millie figured she and Dale had just succeeded in making that happen.

He'd eaten way too much. Breakfast had been a huge surprise. The cinnamon rolls icing on the cake. He and Millie and taken the dogs for a walk on the beach and had come home with two plates of cookies and various other goodies. They'd taken both to the hospital, giving them to Tamara, visiting with her sister and a man, Tom, who'd driven her sister to see Tamara. Judging by the glances the man continued to give the woman who'd given another couple a chance to have a biological family of their own, Dale figured he was the guy Tamara had talked about the day before shortly after giving birth.

Turned out he was a fireman. And a farmer. And, Dale summed up, an all-around nice guy. If a little too into football for Dale's taste. While he'd followed teams over the years, he had no desire to fill Christmas Day with the sport. At least, not that one.

The new parents were so happy Dale had a little trouble being in the same room with them. It was like they were contagious. Giving him whatever had inflicted them with a ridiculously giddy joy. Laughing at the smallest move of a little finger. Talking baby talk as though there were no other adults in the room.

"You think we'll be like that?" Millie asked, sounding... happy...as they walked back out to his vehicle.

Biting back his "I hope not," Dale considered her words for a second longer. Tried to imagine how it would feel to be holding his own child. And said, "I have no idea."

"That is, if we even get pregnant."

It was the first time all day there'd been even a hint of melancholy about her, and suddenly more aware of more than just the day they were celebrating, he asked, "Do you know for certain we aren't?"

She hadn't shared personal details with him. He hadn't asked.

"No," she told him. "But that doesn't mean anything. I'm not due for another week."

Which meant...given the math lesson he'd had from Lyla, they'd been copulating at the exact right time to have a real possibility.

He didn't say anything else as they drove home. Wasn't sure what she needed. Or if he even had it to give.

He was no closer to figuring her out when they arrived home and she busied herself in the kitchen, getting things on for dinner. He offered to help, but heard that it was all done, just had to bake, and took the dogs outside, instead.

She joined him on the deck fifteen minutes later, two non-alcoholic mint beers in hand, and sat. "It's been a good day, huh?" she asked him after they toasted.

"So far," he told her, a bit unnerved with not knowing what had brought her down. Except, he did, right? He wasn't Brent.

And never would be.

Just as she'd never be Lyla. Except that, thoughts of the wife he'd lost hadn't brought grief in their wake that day. They'd been more like…a comfort. As though Lyla approved of Dale's awakening.

Millie apparently wasn't there, yet. Unfair of him to think she could be. He was three years ahead of her.

Millie had been the one who'd filled his day with a pleasure that he'd never imagined. It was his job to give her what joy he could. And feel good about that.

"I didn't get you a present." Her words fell between them like a death knell.

"Okay," he told her, as relief flooded him.

He'd seen a gift under the tree. Had been hoping it wasn't for him. Buying gifts for each other hadn't been discussed. And wasn't them.

They weren't a couple.

"You got me one," she said then. "I saw it, tucked behind the tree." Her gaze was troubled when she looked at him. And he almost laughed out loud when she said, "Ever since we headed home, I've been worried about ruining such a great day. I just didn't…"

"The present isn't for you," he interrupted. She'd been worried about a gift? When she'd given him the grandest holiday ever? "It's for Briel."

Mouth open, she stared at him. "Seriously?" she asked, and when he nodded, she jumped up and went inside.

Dale waited, smiling as he watched the waves coming and going. Wondering if he'd ever learn to trust life as much as he trusted the movement of that water.

He took a sip of beer and watched when Millie came back outside with the two gifts. Giving one to him, said, "It's for Juice," and took the other, coaxing Briel over to her.

Both dogs sniffed at their gifts. Juice bit into hers.

Then lay down in front of Dale and watched him. As though she might need to go to work.

Briel just shied away from the sound, but hung close to Millie. Magic stepped up then.

She opened the package with one rip. And Millie sat there, mouth open. "It's for when you're unexpectedly gone all day, you can just let Briel in before you go," he said, drawing on the day before to explain a gift he'd left for the girl two days before. "And for anytime she needs or wants a second place to be. Like, if you're ever gone overnight, or..."

He'd been pulling at the paper in his own hands as he spoke. More as a way to escape how ridiculous he suddenly felt, and then he stopped and stared. He'd bought Briel a home away from home collar—with his house key attached. She'd purchased Juice a patch for his service vest that said my second home is also where my heart is, and had pinned a key to it.

Neither of them said a word. He looked from the patch over to her, leaned over, and kissed her. Long and hard.

He and Millie had just exchanged house keys.

Millie stood in front of the packages of home pregnancy tests, wondering why she was even there. With her contacts in the medical field, she could make a quick stop and have an answer within minutes.

And then someone she knew would know. Either that she was. Or that she'd thought she was.

She wasn't open to that. To the burst of joy from those who were glad she'd healed and moved on. For the questions to which she'd have no satisfying answers.

She'd called home on Christmas—no way she could

not do that—just before she and Dale ate dinner. He'd been carving the ham. Within earshot. But hadn't said anything more than, "Everyone okay?" Which she took to mean her too, and she'd given him a resounding "Yep," and moved on.

Because...where did they fit? Her parents, her brother and sister, weren't going to understand her new life.

And the harder she tried to find a way to explain it to them, the further away the words seemed to be.

Starting to get anxious, she grabbed a box for its color—purple—and went to the self-checkout. Scanning as quickly as possible and shoving the package into a bag. Where no one would see it.

And look at her. Wondering if congratulations were in order.

She took the long way home. Stopping at a public beach where she used to have lunch sometimes while on break from work, sitting on a bench facing the water. And all she wanted was to go home to Ocean Breeze.

She didn't owe any explanations to anyone. Except herself.

And maybe that was the problem. The things she kept telling herself, that she'd had her chance. Had had the love of her life. That there were things she didn't have anymore so couldn't give them to anyone else, still rang true.

And yet, they didn't. Not really. She'd never again have what she'd shared with Brent. First love. A younger love. The forever she'd thought was meant for her. The forever to which she'd committed herself.

But not because of anything she'd done. The choice, the chance, had been taken from her. Along with the child she and Brent had created together. The baby he hadn't even known about. The one he'd been going to find out about that night during their victory celebration.

As she sat there, Millie felt so out of touch with it all. So much had happened since then. It had been so long ago.

A different lifetime.

Not the one she was currently living. In love with a man and knowing that that love would ruin things between them. Standing, with her hand still on her lower belly, whether it was shielding a uterus with a newly embedded embryo or not, she walked with purpose to her car. Before she took that test she'd planned to take, in total privacy, as soon as she got home, she had to talk to Dale.

Passing her own driveway on Ocean Breeze, she parked at his place. Grabbed the bag on the seat beside her and shoved it down into her purse. Then grabbing the straps of a bag she'd never taken to Dale's before, she walked around the side of his cottage to see if he was out.

He was not. But she heard the door open to the back deck as she turned to head back. "Millie? I saw you pass by my office window. What's up?" He looked at her face and asked, "What's wrong?"

He was down the steps before she could assure him that everything was fine. That she hadn't meant to alarm him.

But maybe she had. Because what she had to tell him was alarming as hell.

"Did you start?" he asked her. And then, before she could respond he said, "Is it worse than that? Tell me, Mil. Whatever it is, we'll deal with it together."

There. Right there. Together.

Staring at him, she couldn't stop the tears that filled her eyes, as she said, "I want more, Dale."

With an arm around her he led her up onto his deck,

into a chair, and then went down on his haunches in front of her. "Whatever it is, it's yours," he told her. "You know that. You want it, you reach for it."

Shaking her head, she sniffed, and kept crying. "I want something that's not mine to take. Only mine to give. And so, as you say, I have to do as I have to do." The words came to her. Just out of the blue. Along with a certain knowledge of her next moves. And a flooding of the peace she'd first found on Ocean Breeze.

Pulling the bag out of her purse, she unpacked the box she'd rolled inside it, holding it up. "You got a couple of minutes?" she asked. And when, brows raised extra high, he nodded and stood, she did too as she said, "Back in a few," and let herself into the home for which she owned a key and into the guest bathroom.

Her strength, her certainty, only went so far. Not all the way to the master bathroom.

She peed. She waited. When time was up, she didn't look at the result. Instead, she carried the device out to find Dale.

And ran into him outside the bathroom door.

Literally. She smacked right into him, almost dropping the answer she held.

"And?" he asked, holding her gently by the sides, as he peered into her eyes. As though he could read all he needed to know there.

Thing was, he probably could, if he knew what it was he had to know.

"I didn't look yet," she told him. "There's something I have to tell you first."

Frowning, he didn't step back or loosen his hold on her. "What?" As though, whatever it was, didn't concern him.

"I'm in love with you."

She almost wept again at the relief of final understanding. Of giving up the fight. "I haven't been lying to you," she quickly assured him as he stood there staring at her. "I've been lying to myself, which I only just realized on Christmas Eve, and then had to face when I was standing in the store, considering taking a pregnancy test for the second time in my life. I thought about the first time, how it had been, how I felt...and it all just came flooding at me. I loved Brent, as much as my young inexperienced heart had ever loved anyone. And now, if it's possible, I love you even more. And differently. Deeper. Because I'm not the same person I was then. I know more about what's at risk. And I think that's why I was fighting so hard not to see. When I think about losing you...losing a baby..." Her eyes flooded and she closed them. She shut her mouth, too.

Whatever the apparatus in her hand told her, she'd come to Dale's for one purpose only.

And she was done.

He couldn't move. Couldn't take his hands from Millie's sides. She was grounding him as his world spun out of control.

He heard her last words. Heard her fall silent. And stood there, staring at her.

Until her eyes closed against a fresh spate of tears and she didn't open them again.

She was lost to him in that second, and the world went bleak again. With a background of black. He felt the nudge against his hand. Couldn't let go of Millie to avail himself of the help being offered.

The nudge came again. Harder. And Millie opened her eyes.

"It's okay," she said. "I know I broke the rules. I just couldn't take this next step without you knowing. You gave me your trust, Dale. I'd be breaking that precious bond if I didn't tell you as soon as I figured it out."

Trust. He nodded. "I do trust you," he told her, as though the news was brand-new to him.

It wasn't. So why did it feel that way?

"I'd do anything for you," he said then. Remembering how he'd felt such a short time before when she'd come to him in obvious—to him—distress.

She nodded. "I know. And it's not fair to put this on you, I get that, but…"

Dale lifted a hand from her waist without thought. Set it gently against her lips. "We do still have it to give," he said, peering at her as though she was a puzzle he was solving. "As usual, you have to point out the obvious to me, but…it's been right here for a while, hasn't it?"

Millie's knees went weak. She almost fell with relief. Against him. He held her upright. Looking her in the eyes. "We called it fate. Soul mates. It was love growing, wasn't it? It was." He answered his own question before she had a chance to nod.

Melting from the intensity glowing from his eyes as he opened his whole heart to her, she recognized her own awakening in his gaze. And knew what would come. "I can't bear the thought of losing you," she said to him.

"There are bound to be some tough times. We are who we are," he told her. "And I've spent five years learning how to be a pretty damned good recluse. But that key I gave Briel? It's for you, too. The spare key to my heart. When I fall back, I'm counting on you to use it."

She nodded. Hoping she'd do so. But what if she was in a bad spot the same time he was. Or...God forbid...what if she jumped in again, and fate took him from her, too?

Dale was searching her face as the fears flitted through her. She didn't want him to know that as much as she knew she loved him, she also had severe doubts. Prompted by hard-learned life lessons. Not just nebulous trouble borrowing.

"Would you rather walk away?" He held on to her as he asked the question.

"Of course not."

He nodded once. Continued to study her expression, as she did his. Where were the answers? They'd had them for each other from the beginning.

"Do you want to?" she asked back. She had to know. And would understand, either way.

"Absolutely not."

She liked that. A lot. Warmth spread through her and she said, "There's good and bad in every life, right? You focus on the good and take the bad when it comes." Great, she'd fallen to spouting clichés.

"Trusting that when the time comes for either or both of us to leave this earth, we'll be held up by the power that's stronger than both of us." Dale's voice grew in strength. In purpose. Reaching through her fears to her soul. Something the bad could never take from her. "Don't you see, Millie?" he continued. "That power outwitted us. It had two of the most proficient fighters of further pain on earth. And look where it brought us. Right back to love. And not just casual love. But something deeper and more consuming than we've ever known. It got us from the inside looking out."

His hands on her sides were sweating. Trembling.

And she asked, "You want to look at the results?"

"I want to ask you to marry me first."

She stared up at him. Silent. Not at all prepared. She was still trying to deal with the fact that she was in love with him.

"Millie Monroe, will you marry me?"

But when the words were spoken her answer was there. "Of course," she told him. In the end it was just that simple. Two words. As soon as they were out, she kissed him. For a while. Neither of them stopped.

Until she dropped the device she held and Dale dove to rescue it from Juice's curiosity.

He glanced down. So did she.

And, as fate would have it, they *were*.

A baby was on the way.

\* \* \* \* \*

# Get up to 4 Free Books!

**We'll send you 2 free books from each series you try PLUS a free Mystery Gift.**

**FREE Value Over $25**

Both the **Harlequin® Special Edition** and **Harlequin® Heartwarming™** series feature compelling novels filled with stories of love and strength where the bonds of friendship, family and community unite.

---

**YES!** Please send me 2 FREE novels from the Harlequin Special Edition or Harlequin Heartwarming series and my FREE Gift (gift is worth about $10 retail). After receiving them, if I don't wish to receive any more books, I can return the shipping statement marked "cancel." If I don't cancel, I will receive 6 brand-new Harlequin Special Edition books every month and be billed just $6.39 each in the U.S. or $7.19 each in Canada, or 4 brand-new Harlequin Heartwarming Larger-Print books every month and be billed just $7.19 each in the U.S. or $7.99 each in Canada, a savings of 20% off the cover price. It's quite a bargain! Shipping and handling is just 50¢ per book in the U.S. and $1.25 per book in Canada.* I understand that accepting the 2 free books and gift places me under no obligation to buy anything. I can always return a shipment and cancel at any time by calling the number below. The free books and gift are mine to keep no matter what I decide.

Choose one:
- ☐ **Harlequin Special Edition** (235/335 BPA G36Y)
- ☐ **Harlequin Heartwarming Larger-Print** (161/361 BPA G36Y)
- ☐ **Or Try Both!** (235/335 & 161/361 BPA G36Z)

Name (please print)

Address                                                                 Apt. #

City                              State/Province                        Zip/Postal Code

**Email:** Please check this box ☐ if you would like to receive newsletters and promotional emails from Harlequin Enterprises ULC and its affiliates. You can unsubscribe anytime.

**Mail to the Harlequin Reader Service:**
**IN U.S.A.:** P.O. Box 1341, Buffalo, NY 14240-8531
**IN CANADA:** P.O. Box 603, Fort Erie, Ontario L2A 5X3

Want to explore our other series or interested in ebooks? Visit **www.ReaderService.com** or call **1-800-873-8635**.

*Terms and prices subject to change without notice. Prices do not include sales taxes, which will be charged (if applicable) based on your state or country of residence. Canadian residents will be charged applicable taxes. Offer not valid in Quebec. This offer is limited to one order per household. Books received may not be as shown. Not valid for current subscribers to the Harlequin Special Edition or Harlequin Heartwarming series. All orders subject to approval. Credit or debit balances in a customer's account(s) may be offset by any other outstanding balance owed by or to the customer. Please allow 4 to 6 weeks for delivery. Offer available while quantities last.

**Your Privacy**—Your information is being collected by Harlequin Enterprises ULC, operating as Harlequin Reader Service. For a complete summary of the information we collect, how we use this information and to whom it is disclosed, please visit our privacy notice located at https://corporate.harlequin.com/privacy-notice. Notice to California Residents – Under California law, you have specific rights to control and access your data. For more information on these rights and how to exercise them, visit https://corporate.harlequin.com/california-privacy. For additional information for residents of other U.S. states that provide their residents with certain rights with respect to personal data, visit https://corporate.harlequin.com/other-state-residents-privacy-rights/.

HSEHW25